# ROOM FOR
*Two*

# ROOM FOR
## *Two*

ABEL KEOGH

**CFI**
**Springville, Utah**

The views expressed within this work are the sole responsibility of the author and do not necessarily reflect the position of Cedar Fort, Inc., or any other entity.

ISBN 13: 978-1-59955-062-6

Published by CFI, an imprint of Cedar Fort, Inc., 2373 W. 700 S., Springville, UT, 84663
Distributed by Cedar Fort, Inc. www.cedarfort.com

LIBRARY OF CONGRESS CATALOGING-IN-PUBLICATION DATA

Keogh, Abel, 1975–
  Room for two / Abel Keogh.
    p. cm.
  ISBN 978-1-59955-062-6 (acid-free paper)
  1. Widowers  2. Pregnant women  3. Suicide victims—Family relationships  4. Fetal death
  5. Grief  6. Resilience (Personality trait)  I. Title.

  PS3611.E69R66 2007
  813'.6—dc22

                    2007013390


Cover design by Nicole Williams
Cover design © 2007 by Lyle Mortimer
Edited and typeset by Kimiko M. Hammari


Printed in the United States of America

10  9  8  7  6  5  4  3  2  1

Printed on acid-free paper

# AUTHOR'S NOTE

Out of respect for their privacy, I have changed the names of some of the people who appear in these pages.

For Brent

# CHAPTER
## *One*

I don't remember the last thing I said to Krista that Saturday afternoon, but I know it was not "I love you." Even when I think long and hard about our final conversation, our last words to each other elude me, which is probably for the best.

The last time we spoke was on the phone. There was shouting. A lot of shouting. In hindsight it seems like it was all on my end. I don't remember Krista sounding angry or frustrated. Our conversation ended when I threw the phone down in disgust. When I arrived at our apartment twenty minutes later, I was furious. I slammed the door to the car, feeling the muscles in my arm clench.

In the pale light of the November afternoon, the fourplex had a dreary, mournful look. Brown leaves, having long lost their cheery autumn reds and yellows, were scattered over the matted grass. I looked up at the apartment window, hoping to see some sign of Krista. The blinds were closed and the lights were off. The place looked deserted. My anger began to morph into fear.

I took the concrete steps two at a time to our apartment. I paused and took several deep breaths in an attempt to calm down before opening the door. I didn't want to go into the apartment yelling. Maybe the whole day had been some kind of misunderstanding.

I inserted the key into the lock and opened the door. The apartment was in the same condition as I had left it. A pile of cardboard boxes lay flattened and stacked neatly in one corner of the living room. Other boxes, half-full of computer games and books, were stacked against the far wall. Yesterday's newspaper was scattered on the floor; a color photograph of a police standoff was displayed prominently on the front page. The apartment itself was ghostly quiet, as if no one had lived there for years.

"Sweetie, I'm home." I tried to put as much kindness into my voice as possible. I didn't want to have another argument—at least not right away.

Silence.

"Sweetheart?"

A gunshot echoed from our bedroom, followed by the sound of a bullet casing skipping along a wall.

Everything slowed down.

I screamed Krista's name and started toward our bedroom. My legs felt heavy, like I was running through waist-deep water. As I entered the room, the acrid smell of gun smoke filled my nostrils. Krista lay slumped against unpacked boxes of clothing along the far wall.

I screamed and moved to Krista's side. This couldn't be real, could it?

Krista's blue eyes stared straight ahead. Her body trembled as if she was suffering from a mild seizure. My Ruger nine millimeter handgun lay next to her body on the corner of a white packing box. A wisp of blue smoke floated from the barrel.

I grabbed the cordless phone from the nightstand and dialed 911.

Krista's body shuddered violently. Blood began flowing from the back of her head, down the boxes, to the floor. The sound of the blood hitting the boxes reminded me of water coming out of a squirt gun.

"Krista!"

I kept expecting to hear a ringing sound on the other end of the phone, but there was only silence. I pulled the receiver away from my ear. Had I dialed 911? What was taking them so long to answer?

I was about to hang up and dial again when a faint female voice broke through the silence. "911. What is your emergency?"

"Send help!" I screamed into the phone. "My wife just shot herself!" My voice shook as the words tumbled out of my mouth. I pressed my hand against Krista's seven-month pregnant belly, hoping for some indication that our unborn daughter was still alive. I couldn't feel any movement.

"What is your address?" the operator said.

I opened my mouth, but no words came out. We had moved into the apartment a week earlier, and I hadn't memorized our address. Then, amid all the chaos, there was a moment of clarity. I remembered the landlord had written our address on the back of his business card when I signed the lease. I pulled the card out of my wallet and relayed the information to the operator, my voice sounding calm, as if I were giving her directions to a party. Then the moment was gone and panic returned.

"She's pregnant," I sobbed into the phone. "She's pregnant."

The 911 operator asked if I knew CPR. I did. I knew what to do—breathe into the mouth, push on the chest—but instead I did nothing. I just sat there horrified.

Krista's eyes now had a dull look to them, as if the blue had suddenly turned gray. Then her body stopped shaking. The pool of blood continued to grow. The operator's words faded into white noise. I knelt at Krista's side for what felt like hours, waiting, hoping to feel the baby move.

At some point I became vaguely aware of the distant wail of a police siren. It grew louder until it sounded like it was right outside the door. Then everything was quiet. I stood, frantic that the police had driven past. I took several steps toward the living room when I heard a quick knock followed by the sound of someone opening the front door. A moment later a police officer entered the bedroom. His eyes went from me to Krista to the gun lying near Krista's head. He stood in the middle of the room, as if he wasn't sure what to do.

"Help her!" I screamed.

The officer moved to Krista's side and put his fingertips on her neck to check her pulse. I took a step toward him, wanting to help. His eyes darted to the gun.

"Get out of the room," he said firmly. He said something into the radio that was attached to his shoulder and then brought his ear to Krista's mouth to see if she was breathing. He pulled her legs, as if moving a piece of delicate china, so she was lying flat on the floor. The box where Krista's head had rested was soaked with blood.

"Get out," he repeated. This time he looked right at me and pointed to the door. I took one step back.

"Go!" he said.

I took another step back. It was like I was in a dream, running toward a cliff. Even though jumping off was the last thing I wanted to do, my legs kept moving until I toppled over the edge.

I took a third step when I heard a noise just outside the bedroom door. I turned and nearly bumped into another police officer. He rushed past me as if I didn't exist. The two officers talked quickly, quietly. I could not understand what they said. All I could hear was that one gunshot over and over. Its echo blasted the walls inside my head.

The first officer started chest compressions while the second breathed into Krista's mouth. I stepped back into the living room. A third officer brushed past me on his way to the bedroom. He returned a moment later and told me to sit on the couch.

I sat down. The third police officer stood between me and the bedroom. He was young with blond hair. Most of his attention was focused on whatever was happening in the other room. Occasionally he glanced back at me.

It was then that I realized I was still holding the phone to my ear. The 911 operator was asking me questions. Her voice was still calm and collected. It pulled me away from the chaos inside the apartment.

"Are the police there?" she asked.

"Yes."

"Are they performing CPR?"

"I don't know. They told me to leave the room."

"Has an ambulance arrived?"

The living room window was located directly behind the couch. I turned and peeked through the blinds. Three police cars were in the middle of the street, their red and blue lights still flashing. A dozen people had gathered on the far side of the street and were pointing to the apartment, shrugging their shoulders. I could hear other sirens growing louder in the distance.

"I don't see an ambulance," I said.

"I'm going to stay on the phone with you until it comes," the operator said.

The blond police officer took a step toward the bedroom. He spoke with the other officers and then said something into his radio. I heard the words *ambulance* and *quickly*. The rest of his words were drowned out by the approaching sirens.

More police arrived. Soon the apartment was filled with blue uniforms and silver badges. The air was a cacophony of wailing sirens. One of the officers said something about getting the crowd to remain on the other side of the street, and immediately two officers headed outside.

Another siren, this one different from the others, grew loud and then abruptly ended. I pulled the nearest corner of the blinds aside just as the ambulance stopped in front of the apartment. Without another word to the 911 operator, I hung up the phone.

Two paramedics, black bags in hand, ran to the apartment. An officer directed them to the bedroom. A minute later one of them quickly exited. Through the blinds I watched him retrieve a stretcher out of the back of the ambulance. The sight of the stretcher gave me hope that Krista was still alive.

"Is she going to be all right?" I asked the officer who was still standing watch. His attention wasn't on me when I spoke. His head snapped back at the sound of my voice.

"What did you say?" He seemed surprised that I had spoken.

"My wife. Is she going to be all right?"

The officer squatted in front of me so we were at eye level. His pale blue eyes told me everything before he spoke. "I'm sorry," he said. "She died a few minutes ago. We did everything we could to save her. But there's a chance the baby is still alive. We're going to transport your wife's body to the hospital."

I took a deep breath and looked at the floor. I told myself that at any moment I would wake up screaming. I waited for everything around me—the apartment, the police, and the voices in the bedroom—to fade into blackness. But the noise and color and the smell of gun smoke remained.

I looked up at the officer, hoping he'd tell me it was all a joke, but he wasn't looking at me anymore. His attention was focused on the couch. I followed his gaze. Next to me lay a gun case and a plastic bag filled with nine millimeter bullets. The lock to the gun case lay between them. The bullet casings sparkled like gold coins.

"Why don't you sit over here?" the officer said. He pointed to a glider rocker next to the couch. I sat in the chair, the one Krista and I had bought so we could rock our new baby, but I wasn't able to take my eyes off the gun lock and the bullets. In my mind, I pictured Krista kneeling clumsily next to the couch, her protruding belly in the way, unlocking the case, and then methodically loading the clip with bullets before walking back to the bedroom.

The phone rang. The sound was piercing. Someone had set the ring on high. The police ignored it. I waited for the answering machine to pick up. It didn't. I waited for the person on the other end to hang up. The phone continued to ring. A police officer came back from the bedroom and said something to the blond officer. The ringing drowned out their conversation. I stood up, half expecting to be ordered back to the chair, but the officer's attention was on whatever was happening in the bedroom. I walked to the phone, picked up the receiver in mid-ring, and hung up.

The next thing I knew, the blond officer was standing by my side. I thought he was going to say something about the phone. "I need you to move to the kitchen," he said. "They're going to move your wife's body to the ambulance. You don't want to see this."

I didn't want to go to the kitchen. I wanted to ride with Krista to the hospital. I wanted to see my baby daughter brought into the world alive and healthy. I tried to remember how many minutes an unborn baby could survive in the womb without oxygen from its mother.

"Sir," the officer said. He motioned with his head in the direction of the refrigerator. My body obeyed the command and walked to the kitchen.

The small kitchen was in the far corner of the apartment and set up in such a way that I was shielded from the living room. I leaned against the electric stove and stared at the floor.

Grunts emanated from the living room as the stretcher made the tight corner to the front door. There was a metal clang as the stretcher bumped against the wall.

"Careful," someone said.

*Yes, be careful,* I thought. *You can save the baby. Maybe, by some miracle, you can save Krista too. Modern medical science can perform miracles.*

The stove was beginning to dig into my back, but I didn't move. The officer looked into the living room and then back at me. The sounds of the people carrying the stretcher faded away, and then the front door closed. Silence filled the apartment. A minute later, the ambulance siren roared to life, then quickly faded into the distance.

I returned to the glider rocker. I tried not to stare at the objects on the couch when I walked past and instead focused on the conversations of the police. One of them said, "What are we going to do with him?" and motioned toward me. The other officer shrugged.

The remaining police milled about the apartment. No one spoke to me. It seemed like I sat in the rocker for hours until one of the officers said, "I need you to come with me." I looked up. There were only two officers in the apartment now. The officer who spoke to me was thin and had curly brown hair. His eyes were hidden behind a dark pair of sunglasses. I thought it odd that he was wearing sunglasses indoors. The other officer held a large roll of yellow crime scene tape in his hands.

"Where are we going?" I said.

"The hospital."

I followed the officer outside. I half expected to be greeted by the crowd and flashing red and blue lights. Instead, there were only two police cars parked parallel to the curb; the lights on the top of the cruisers weren't flashing. The crowd I saw earlier had returned to the surrounding apartment buildings. I wondered if I'd seen any people at all. Maybe my mind had been playing tricks on me. With the exception of the police cars, the street looked just like it had when I arrived. The officer opened the passenger side door of his vehicle. I looked back at the apartment and watched as the other officer taped off the door with crime scene tape.

# CHAPTER
## *Two*

I expected the maternity wing of the hospital to be bustling with proud, bleary-eyed fathers and grandparents carrying stuffed animals for the newborns and flowers for the mothers. But when the elevator doors opened, the hallway was empty. As I followed the police officer down the hall, every room we passed was dark and vacant.

There were six nurses clustered in a tight circle at the nurses' station. Their conversation abruptly stopped as we approached. All six turned and looked at me. Their faces showed something between sadness and rage. It was then I realized they had been talking about me or, at the very least, about Krista and the baby. The police officer said something to a nurse in purple scrubs. The nurse opened the door of a postpartum room and motioned for me to enter. I could feel the gazes of the rest of the nurses as I walked past.

The room contained a bed, a couch, and a few plastic chairs. A television was mounted on the wall opposite the bed. Three framed photographs hung on the walls. One showed a green field with bright yellow flowers. The others were of snowcapped mountains and a river winding slowly through a valley.

I sat on the couch where I could see into the hallway. The police officer was talking to a woman in jeans and a white blouse. She wore small-framed glasses and in one hand carried a spiral-bound notebook. They spoke for several minutes, and both would occasionally glance in my direction. Then the woman said a final word to the police officer and walked into my room.

"Are you Abel?" she asked.

I nodded.

The woman introduced herself as a social worker at the hospital. She asked if she could sit next to me. I moved over to make room for her on the couch.

"I hear you've been through a horrible experience this afternoon," she said. Her voice had a loving quality to it. It was reassuring to be with someone who sounded like she cared.

"Are you cold?" she said.

"No," I said, a little confused by the question.

"Do you know why your body's shaking?"

I looked at my hands and then at my torso and legs. My body was trembling—something I hadn't noticed until she pointed it out. I didn't feel cold.

"I don't know why I'm shaking," I said.

"Would you like a blanket?"

"Yes."

The social worker walked to the door and said something to someone I couldn't see. A moment later the nurse in purple scrubs handed her a blanket. The social worker returned to the couch and draped the blanket over my shoulders and legs. It was one of those hospital blankets they keep heated, and I pulled it tight around me, wishing it could shield me from the horror of the day. The social worker took my hand in hers. Her hand was warm and smooth. We sat in silence for several minutes. Slowly the shaking subsided.

"Do you know if your family's been contacted?" she said.

"I don't think so."

"Is there a family member close by we can call?"

My mom lived fifteen minutes up I-15 in Ogden. My father, however, was in Casper, Wyoming—over four hundred miles away. My parents had been living like this since August. My mom had moved to Ogden to take care of her mother while my father taught photography at a community college. He'd come down during school breaks. The separation was supposed to be temporary, but it would drag on for years.

I didn't want my mom to come to the hospital alone. Knowing how she handled bad news, I worried she would cause an accident on the drive over. My dad should be the first to know. He could arrange everything else. I tried to think of his phone number, but for some reason I couldn't remember it. I couldn't even remember the area code for Wyoming. I tried to think of the phone numbers of Krista's grand-mother, friends, or neighbors—someone who could drive my mom to the hospital. My mind was blank.

I looked at my black and blue sneakers and said, "I can't think of anyone to call."

There was a knock on the door, and a middle-aged man in green scrubs entered. He introduced himself as the doctor who delivered my daughter. He offered me his hand. I didn't shake it. I waited for him to tell me that my baby was dead.

"Your daughter is in critical condition," he said.

"Is she going to die?" I asked.

The doctor looked at the floor for a moment as if he was trying to come up with the best way to break bad news to me. "I don't know," he finally said. He quoted some statistics about the chances of survival for premature babies her age. I tried to listen to what he was saying, but he was talking fast, and the numbers he was throwing out only confused me. When he was done speaking, he asked if I had any further questions.

"Can I see her now?" I said.

"She'll be ready soon. A nurse will come by shortly and take you to see her." He paused and then said, "I'm sorry. I wish I could tell you more."

He left without shutting the door. In the hall I watched the police officer chat with one of the nurses.

"Why is he still here?" I asked.

"Who?" the social worker said.

"The police officer. Why is he still here?"

"I don't know." But there was something in the social worker's voice that indicated she wasn't telling the truth. I wanted to ask her another question, but I couldn't concentrate long enough to form one. My thoughts shifted rapidly from Krista, to my baby who was some-where in the hospital, to my family. Out of the rapid succession of thoughts, the name of a family friend popped into my head. I gave his name to the social worker and said his phone number should be listed in the phone book. He would contact my mom and bring her to the hospital. The social worker wrote down his name and handed it to the police officer. Someone I couldn't see handed the social worker a Styrofoam cup with a straw.

The social worker returned to the room. "Here's some water," she said.

The cup was heavy. There was a lot of ice in it. I took a sip of the water and then set the cup on the floor next to my feet. I wasn't thirsty.

The social worker asked me more questions about what happened. I tried to answer them the best I could, but my mind was still having difficulty focusing. I wanted to take my hands and reach into my brain to find the words, the ability to speak that I'd apparently lost, but I wasn't sure how to use my hands either. We sat on the couch in silence.

A nurse entered the room. She was older and had gray streaks in her hair. She reminded me of someone's happy grandmother who always had a treat to give her grandchildren. "Would you like to see your daughter?" she asked.

I followed her past the nurses' station. The other nurses made a point not to make eye contact with me.

We came to two large wooden doors. The nurse swiped her badge, and with a metallic click the doors opened. She led me to a stainless steel sink.

"You need to wash your hands before you can see her," she said. I lathered my hands and arms with antibacterial soap and rinsed them in warm water. Then I followed the nurse to the far corner of the room where my daughter lay. My heart broke as soon as I saw her. The only premature babies I'd ever seen were on TV. I didn't realize how tiny and helpless they really looked.

IVs and electrodes were attached to every part of her body. A respirator pushed air in and out of her lungs. There was a tiny pink bow on her head of thick chocolate-colored hair. The amount of hair on her head surprised me. I counted her fingers and toes—ten of each.

"How much does she weigh?" I asked.

The nurse looked at a chart. "Two pounds, six ounces."

"She's so small."

"She's about the right size for her age."

I put my hand out to touch my daughter but then yanked it back. I worried that touching her would add to her trauma.

As if reading my thoughts, the nurse said, "Go ahead. You can touch her."

I stroked her arm with my index finger. Her skin was warm and soft. I touched the bottom of her foot and put my face close to hers.

I kissed the top of her head. She smelled like new baby. Her hair was soft on my lips.

"Her skin is very pink," I said.

"Pink is good," the nurse said.

"She's beautiful."

"Do you have a name for her?"

A name. Krista and I had yet to agree on one. I tried to think of all the names I liked but couldn't remember them. The only name that ran though my mind was the one Krista liked the most: Hope.

"You don't have to name her now," the nurse said. "You can think about it for awhile."

"She has a name," I said. "Hope. Hope Krista."

I wanted to stay, but the nurse told me Hope was scheduled to be flown to Primary Children's Hospital in Salt Lake City and they had to prepare her for the flight. She led me back to the waiting room. As we passed the nurses' station, I noticed the police officer was still chatting with one of the nurses. He said something that made the nurse laugh, and I remembered that some people were still happy that day.

The social worker was sitting on the couch, waiting for me. I sat next to her.

"We've contacted your family," she said. "They should be here soon."

There was a knock on the door. I looked up, expecting to see my mom. Instead, a middle-aged man dressed in a light blue shirt, dark slacks, and a sports jacket entered the room. He carried a yellow legal pad under one arm.

"Are you Abel?" he asked.

"Yes," I said. I was confused. I could tell he wasn't a doctor. Who else would want to see me?

"I'm Detective Smith with the Layton Police Department," he said. "I'm investigating your wife's death." He showed me his identification, a silver badge that flickered under the fluorescent lights.

I didn't understand. My wife had shot herself. What could there be to investigate? The detective took one of the plastic chairs on the other side of the room and placed it directly across from me. Opening the legal pad to a blank page, he took a pen out of his shirt pocket and then looked me right in the eye.

"I'm going to be very open with you, Abel," he said. "There's a dead body. Because of that, I have to treat this case as a homicide unless it's proven otherwise. Do you understand?"

Suddenly, I realized why the police officer had been stationed outside the door, why I had been watched all afternoon: I was the main suspect in my wife's death. I nodded to the detective so that he knew I understood.

"I'm going to ask you some questions," he continued. "Some of them will be very personal in nature. These questions are part of my job, and I have to ask them. Do you understand?"

I nodded again. A queasy feeling arose in my stomach. My only exposure to police interrogations was what I had seen on TV or in the movies. So far this was nothing like them. The detective looked at his watch and then wrote something on the notepad. He asked for mine and Krista's social security numbers and birth dates.

Then the questioning began.

"Tell me what happened this afternoon."

I told the detective about unlocking the door to the apartment, calling for Krista, and hearing the gunshot. I wasn't sure how much detail he wanted, so I kept my remarks brief.

"When you found your wife's body, did you touch or move it in any way?"

"No."

"Why not?"

The question left a dark feeling inside me. I had panicked instead of trying to help. I was unable to follow the 911 operator's instructions. Perhaps Krista might have lived if I had only remained calm.

"I didn't know what I could do to help her," I said.

"How often did you fight with your wife?"

The question seemed out of left field. "I don't know. A couple times a week," I said. On average, this was probably true. But lately the number of disagreements had grown to one or more a day, and our arguments had become more serious and drawn out. I couldn't remember the last time we went a day without a harsh word to each other.

"Did you have a fight with her today?"

"We had an argument," I said, emphasizing the word *argument*. To me a fight was something physical with punches and shoving. An argument was verbal. I wanted the detective to know that nothing physical had taken place that morning—or any other day.

"What was the argument about?"

I paused. I was having a hard time remembering anything that had happened before I arrived at the apartment.

"We spent the night at her grandmother's house—"

"Why did you spend the night there?" the detective said. His question had interrupted my train of thought. It took me a few moments to think of the answer.

"Krista wanted to spend the night there. She wanted to spend most of today there too."

"So you spent the night at her grandmother's house?"

"Yes."

"When was the last time you saw Krista?"

"Early this morning. I needed to run some errands. When I left, Krista was still in bed. I came back later and she was gone."

That memory of Krista was etched strongly in my mind. The covers were pulled tightly around her. For some reason, the way the sheets were wrapped around her belly made it seem bigger than usual. Her eyes were closed, and she had a peaceful look on her face as if she was having a pleasant dream. Suddenly I realized that was the last time I had seen her alive.

"How long did it take you to run errands?" the detective said.

"I don't know."

"You don't know how long you ran errands?" The tone of the detective's voice was incredulous.

I thought over the errands that morning: a trip to the grocery store, Jiffy Lube, and Home Depot. "It was about two hours," I said. "There was a long wait at Jiffy Lube."

The detective continued to take notes after I finished. I pictured him writing the word MURDER in big, bold letters on the legal pad. The detective turned to a clean page and then paused as if he were thinking of the next question.

"So when you returned to her grandmother's house, Krista was gone."

I nodded.

"Why did Krista go to your apartment?"

"I don't know."

"Did she tell you she was going to the apartment?"

"No."

"Were you concerned when you realized she had returned to the apartment alone?"

"Not really."

"Why not?"

"Because I didn't think she was suicidal." The words came out loud and angry. The detective stopped writing. He looked me in the eye for a long moment before he resumed questioning.

"What did you do when you realized Krista was not at her grand-mother's?"

"I called the apartment. Krista answered on the first ring. I asked her what she was doing at the apartment, and she told me she was unpacking. She said she'd be back soon." Her voice had sounded far away, distant. It was as if I was speaking to someone who was hypno-tized or daydreaming, as if she wasn't listening to me.

"And that was all you talked about."

"Yes."

"Did she come back to her grandmother's?"

I shook my head.

"Were you concerned when she didn't return?"

"Yes, a little. I called the apartment again, and she told me she was still unpacking but would be done soon."

"What time was this?"

I had to stop and think. "I don't know. Eleven o'clock. Maybe eleven fifteen."

"What time did you arrive at the apartment?"

"About ten minutes to two."

"What did you do between eleven and the time you returned to the apartment?"

"I talked to Krista once every thirty or forty minutes. Each time she told me she was on her way back to her grandmother's house." I remembered being frustrated with Krista's behavior as I paced the TV room downstairs, waiting. She said she had wanted to spend the entire day with me, only to leave and spend the morning alone at our apart-ment. On the TV, a movie, *Broken Arrow*, played. I remembered this because I was so frustrated and worried about Krista's behavior that I was criticizing the cheesy dialogue and John Travolta's acting as a way to calm down.

"What made you decide to return to the apartment?"

"I called and she didn't answer."

"Did you think she was on her way?"

"Yes, but when she didn't show up, I called again. When she didn't answer this time, I started to worry and drove out to the apartment."

"What time did you leave?"

"About one thirty."

The detective paused, and I could see him calculating the time it would take to drive from Ogden to the apartment.

"Have you ever hit your wife?"

I told myself the detective was just doing his job. "No. Never."

Detective Smith flipped back a few pages and read some notes before asking the next question.

"We recovered a gun at the crime scene. Who is it registered to?"

"Me. It's my gun."

"How long have you owned it?"

"About two years."

"Did Krista know how to use the gun?"

"Yes."

"When was the last time she used it?"

"A few months ago. We went target shooting." My mind flashed back to that day. Krista, her brother, and I spent an entire Saturday in the mountains, shooting at pop cans and gallon milk jugs filled with water. From thirty yards away, Krista was able to hit whatever target we set up for her. She'd always been a good shot.

"Where did you keep the gun?"

"In my top dresser drawer."

"Did she know where you kept it?"

"Yes."

"Did you keep the gun loaded?"

"I kept bullets in one of the gun clips."

"So you kept a loaded gun in your home within easy access of anyone?"

"I kept the gun in a case. It was always locked."

"Who had keys to the case?"

"Just myself."

"How many keys are there?"

"Three."

"Where are they now?"

"I keep one on my key chain. I don't know where the other two are. I packed them when we were moving."

"Do you have a key with you?"

I took my keychain out of my pocket and removed the small, silver key. I handed it to the detective. He peered at it intently and then wrote some more notes on his legal pad.

"Do you mind if I keep this?" he asked.

"You can have it," I said.

"Can you please hold out your hands?"

I held out my hands for the detective to examine. He looked at my palms and touched them with the back of his pen. He asked me to turn them over, and when I did, he examined the back of them.

"They asked me to wash my hands when I saw my daughter," I said.

The detective nodded and made another series of notes.

"Did Krista have a life insurance policy?"

"Yes."

"How much was it worth?"

"I don't know. It was a basic policy through work. Maybe ten thousand dollars. I don't even know if it covers suicide."

"When you found your wife's body, did you notice the gun?"

"Yes."

"Where was it?"

I realized the gun had fallen in an odd place. "It was on the corner of a white box next to her head."

"Did you touch or move the gun?"

"No."

Then the detective asked me again about the events of the day. By the time he finished questioning me, I'd related the story of that morning and afternoon three times.

"I need to go back to your apartment and look at the crime scene," the detective said. "To make this easy for everyone, I'd like you to write a note allowing me to take any evidence related to this event from your apartment." He turned to a clean page on the legal pad and handed it to me along with his pen. The silver pen was heavy. I wrote the following note:

> I give my permission to the police to search the apartment
> and take whatever evidence they need.

I hoped it was good enough. My mind still wasn't working, and I was having a difficult time writing a basic sentence. I hesitantly handed him the note and watched his eyes as he read it over. He seemed to read it several times, as if making sure it said exactly what he needed it to.

"This is good," he said. "Please sign and date it at the bottom."

I scribbled my name under the note. I had to ask him what the date was.

"November tenth," he said, checking his watch.

I dated the note and handed the legal pad back to the detective.

"Thank you," he said. "These are all the questions I have for now. I'll most likely have some follow-up questions later."

The detective closed the legal pad and returned the chair to the far wall. The social worker told me she'd be right back and followed the detective out of the room. She closed the door behind her. For the first time since the police officer walked into my apartment, I was alone. The room was quiet and sterile. It seemed like hours since I was told my family had been contacted. I wondered where they were.

I held my head in my hands and told myself that everything was going to be all right. I told myself this over and over again until I heard the door open. I glanced up, expecting to see the social worker. It was my mom. Her gray eyes were calm, as if she was relieved to see me.

"Abel, what's going on?" she said.

Didn't she know? I thought someone, the police, the social worker, or a nurse would have told her.

"Krista's dead," I said. And as the truth sunk in, I started to cry.

# CHAPTER
## *Three*

I didn't sleep much that night. In the morning I told my family it was because the living room couch was uncomfortable. But the real reason was this: When I closed my eyes, I relived opening the door to the apartment, hearing the gunshot, and running back to find Krista's body. The only way to stop the images was to keep my eyes open and think of Hope. I thought about the last time I saw her before she was taken to the waiting helicopter. The nurses had brought her out in a transportation unit where, if possible, she looked even smaller and more helpless. She was attached to a large machine that would keep her on life support during the short flight. I pressed my hands against the plastic shell that encased her. I wanted to hold her in my arms and whisper into her tiny pink ear, "Everything's going to be all right. I'll see you soon."

At some point sleep must have overpowered me for a few moments because at two thirty in the morning I awoke suddenly. I walked to the kitchen and stared out the window at the street, which was dark and quiet. I noticed my dad's truck in the driveway and wondered when he had arrived and why he hadn't come and talked to me.

After a few minutes, I saw a car drive down the street in the direction of the house. My heart leapt as I envisioned the car pulling into the driveway and Krista emerging. I saw her run toward me, the two of us laughing and crying as we embraced. Instead the car stopped and made a U-turn.

I paced back and forth for a few minutes and then returned to the window, hoping to see another car or some sign of Krista. This went on for almost an hour in the dark, cold kitchen. I returned to the couch only when my legs were too cramped and tired to stand.

I stared at the ceiling until dawn.

The next morning my dad drove me to Primary Children's Hospital. The floor of the pickup was littered with fast food wrappers and soda cans—signs of his seven-hour drive to Ogden. I could see bags under his bloodshot eyes. Considering how exhausted he looked, I was surprised that he volunteered to drive me to the hospital.

We made the drive in silence. I expected him to ask questions about the previous day, but he didn't. Maybe my mom had answered all his questions after he arrived. Or perhaps he was still in shock and couldn't think of anything to say. Personally, I was glad for the silence. I was tired, and my mind was still having a hard time accepting the events of the previous day as being real.

My dad drove the speed limit the entire way to Salt Lake City, despite the fact it was Sunday morning and traffic on I-15 was nonexistent. I kept glancing over at the orange speedometer that continually hovered right above or below sixty-five miles per hour. I wanted to ask my dad to drive faster but kept telling myself that the truck was old and slow and my dad was tired.

It took an hour to reach the hospital, which was nestled in the foothills above downtown Salt Lake. Once inside, we followed the signs to the neonatal intensive care on the fourth floor. A sign on the door informed us that all visitors needed to call the nurses' station to be admitted. I picked up the receiver of a white phone on the wall next to the door.

"Yes?" The voice on the other end of the phone seemed weary, as if she had been working all night.

"I'm here to see my baby," I said. I hoped that would be enough to get inside.

There was a loud click as the wooden doors unlocked. A heavyset woman sat behind a desk at the end of the hall. She waved us forward when we entered. We walked past a waiting room where a father and two children were spread out on the couch and chairs. They looked worn-out and sad.

"Can I help you?" the woman said. It was the same tired voice I heard on the other end of the phone.

"My daughter was flown here last night. I'd like to see her," I said.

The woman asked my name, my daughter's name, and then for some identification. I handed her my driver's license.

"You're the baby's father?" she asked.

"I am."

"Just a moment," she said. She copied some information from the driver's license and then handed it back to me. She paged someone and then returned her attention to a pile of paperwork in front of her. She didn't look back up.

Next to the nurses' station was a whiteboard with the first name and last initial of all the babies in the ICU. I scanned the list until I came to the last name on the board. Baby Keogh. Next to her name was yesterday's date and a room number.

"Are you Baby Keogh's father?" A nurse approached. Her blonde hair was pulled back into a ponytail. Her eyes were the color of the sky. She was smiling. She reminded me of Krista. "I'm Peggy—one of the nurses who are caring for your baby. Let's get you scrubbed up and I'll take you to her."

Peggy turned on the light to an oversized janitor's closet next to the whiteboard. The far wall of the closet was filled with large bottles of antibacterial soap, boxes of plastic gloves, face masks, and other medical supplies. A large stainless steel sink was bolted next to the door. "Wash your arms up to your elbows," she said.

We scrubbed our hands and arms and followed Peggy to a large room at the end of the hall that was decorated in muted pastel blues, pinks, yellows, and greens. I figured those colors were to brighten the sterile-looking room, but I wondered how cheerful any of the parents ever were. There were four babies in the room, three in incubators. The fourth, alone on the far side of the room by a window, was bathed in a bright light from a lamp directly above her. I knew right away the baby under the light was my daughter.

Hope was hooked up to even more IVs and monitors than she had been the previous night. She lay on several soft blankets and had round cotton patches over her eyes to protect them from the light. The patches made her look like she was wearing thick baby-sized glasses. The pink bow was still in her hair.

"She sure is cute," my dad said.

I looked around at the rest of the babies. "How come Hope's not in an incubator?"

"She's hooked up to too many machines to fit comfortably in one," Peggy said. There was a touch of sadness in her voice.

I gently touched Hope's hand. I kissed her head and whispered, "How's my little girl?"

Then I did something I hadn't done the night before. I studied her face. Looking at Hope was like looking at a smaller version of Krista, only with my brown hair. Hope had Krista's chin and narrow face. I could almost visualize my little girl all grown up, looking like her mother's twin. I heard footsteps approaching. I turned, half expecting to see Krista. Instead a thin, middle-aged man with glasses approached. He was wearing a blue shirt and canary yellow tie underneath a white lab coat. His shirt and tie reminded me more of a businessman than a doctor. He carried a clipboard with an inch-thick stack of papers attached. He introduced himself as Dr. Green—Hope's doctor.

"Your little girl's quite a fighter," he said. "Her body has gone through a lot of trauma in the last twenty-four hours." He flipped through the papers on his clipboard.

"Is she going to make it?" I said. I dreaded the answer that was coming. I was not optimistic.

Dr. Green pushed the glasses up the bridge of his nose. "It's hard to give her a long-term prognosis at this time. She's responded well to the various tests we gave her last night. However, there's a good chance that if she survives, she'll have some long-term brain damage." His voice was calm and professional, but from the look on his face I could tell he was worried.

"Long-term brain damage?" As I repeated the doctor's words, a dark, ominous fear grew inside me.

"We're not sure how long your daughter was deprived of oxygen before she . . ." Dr. Green paused as if he was searching for the right words, ". . . came into this world. Do you know if lifesaving measures were performed on your wife?"

"I don't know. I wasn't in the room."

"If your daughter went without oxygen for an extended period of time, there's a good possibility she could have difficulty learning to walk or talk. It may mean she has a harder time intellectually when she becomes older. Of course, she may be perfectly healthy. Right now, we don't have enough information to determine anything. We need to run more tests."

"How long until you know more?" I said. It felt like my voice was being stretched in my throat, as if I didn't know how to ask the right questions.

"A few days. I'll work with some specialists to come up with a more accurate diagnosis." The doctor stroked Hope's arm with his finger. "Do you have any questions for me at this time?"

I shook my head. I was still numb. I watched Hope's chest rise and fall with the sound of the respirator. I wanted some time alone to think.

"My office is down the hall. If I'm not around, please have a nurse page me."

I watched Dr. Green walk toward the door, his soft-soled shoes padding away soundlessly. My dad pulled out his camera and started taking pictures of Hope. After a few flashes filled the room, he asked me to stand next to her so he could get a picture of the two of us. I didn't want my picture taken but agreed to it anyway. I reasoned that taking pictures would help Dad feel useful. Taking pictures, after all, was what he did for a living.

"Smile, Abel," he said. I didn't know if my face remembered how to smile, but I tried to raise the corners of my mouth into something more than a grimace. Later I would look at these pictures and see a deep sadness to my face that no smile could hide.

After another series of flashes, the camera made a whirling sound as the film rewound. My dad searched his pockets for some film. "I must have left the rest of the film at home," he said dejectedly.

"We can take more pictures tomorrow," I said. I hoped that I wouldn't be involved in any more photographs.

"I'm going to call Mom and see when she's coming down," Dad said.

"Thanks," I said. I was grateful to have some time to myself.

On the way out of the room, my dad stooped and looked at the other babies. From where I was standing, I could tell they were all larger and healthier-looking than Hope. The baby nearest Hope yawned and opened its eyes for several seconds before going back to sleep.

I placed my index finger in Hope's hand. One of the things I liked about babies was that they instinctively grabbed your finger. I waited for Hope to grab mine. She didn't move. Gently I curled her hand around my finger. Her hand was so small that it couldn't fit all the way

23

around. I thought about taking Hope home from the hospital, healthy as ever, and tucking her safely in her crib. I thought about her learning to crawl, walk, and talk, and taking her to her first day of school. I thought these things because it was what I wanted to do even though I didn't think they would ever happen.

A tinkling noise like that of a small bell chimed from the computer next to Hope. I looked up at the screen. A small light was flashing. I looked frantically around for a nurse. Peggy was cooing and talking with the baby closest to the door.

"Something's wrong with Hope," I said.

Peggy stopped what she was doing and walked over. She smiled and pushed a mute button on the machine. The ringing stopped.

"What's wrong?" I said. I didn't like Peggy's calm demeanor. I wanted her to be as worried and anxious as I was.

"The bell's a reminder to change one of her IV bags." She pointed to an empty bag hanging near the lamp. She unhooked the bag from the IV stand and walked out of sight. She returned a moment later with a full one.

"What's in the bag?" I asked.

"Breakfast."

Peggy readied the new IV bag. In less than a minute the clear liquid was once again heading to Hope's arm, one drop at a time.

"Would you like to hold her?" Peggy asked.

"Can I?" I asked. It looked impossible, considering how many IVs and machines she was hooked up to.

"It'll be a little tricky, but we can do it."

I pulled a high-legged stool from the wall and placed it next to Hope's bed. Peggy moved the respirator close to my chair and removed the cotton patches from Hope's eyes.

"Let me double check these wires and tubes," Peggy said. "We don't want them popping off." She inspected the length of each one carefully. Another nurse walked over to help and slowly lifted Hope from the bed. Peggy placed a blanket under Hope's body and then carefully wrapped her in it. Together the two of them placed her in my arms.

I was amazed how little Hope weighed. It was like holding a large doll instead of a baby. Hope's head rested against my chest. The warmth from her head slowly worked its way through my shirt.

"You won't be able to move much," Peggy said. "Some of those wires are pretty tight."

I sat up straighter and adjusted Hope's position in my arms. Peggy was right. I couldn't move or adjust Hope without putting further tension on the tubes and wires.

"Are you comfortable?" Peggy said.

I nodded, and Peggy left to attend to the other babies.

I looked at Hope and wished she would open her eyes or provide some indication she was aware of me and of the world she was in. But Hope didn't move. Her eyes remained closed.

I held her until my arms and back screamed for relief.

Tuesday morning Detective Smith called and asked if we could meet. He said he had some follow-up questions. I told him I would be at the hospital all day, and he agreed to meet me there. I wasn't worried about the interview. There had been two articles in the paper about Krista's death. The second one, which had appeared Monday morning, contained a statement from the police stating that Krista's death had been officially ruled a suicide.

When the detective arrived at the hospital later that afternoon, I was sitting in the waiting room with my dad. The room was full of parents talking in hushed tones and bored-looking kids playing with toys or watching cartoons on the television that was bolted to the wall.

"Is there a place we can talk privately?" Detective Smith said.

The neonatal intensive care unit had two private family rooms. I did not know what those rooms were used for, but I had seen a couple come out of one crying. I asked a nurse if one was available. She knocked quietly on one door and slowly opened it. "You can use this one," she said.

With the exception of the television mounted on the wall, the room could have passed for someone's living room with its thick carpet, a La-Z-Boy in one corner, and a well cushioned couch. I sat on the couch. The detective turned the La-Z-Boy so it was facing me and sat on the edge of the chair. He leafed through the pages of his legal pad and took a few moments to read his notes before he started the questions.

"After we last spoke," the detective said, "I returned to your apartment. Near your bed we found a photograph that was torn into small pieces. Do you know why Krista would do that?"

"Who was the picture of?" I asked.

"I don't know."

I couldn't think of any photograph Krista would destroy.

"Without seeing the photograph, I can't help you."

The detective nodded and wrote something on the pad. I wondered if the detective knew the identity of the person in the photo and wasn't telling me.

"We found a second key to your gun case in the apartment. Have you located the last one?"

"No. I haven't been back to the apartment." I thought of the last time I saw our bedroom: the packing boxes soaked with blood and a large bloodstain near Krista's body. I shuddered.

The detective cleared his throat before the next question. "The last time you spoke to your wife, did she say anything to indicate she was going to kill herself?"

"No. I mean, she didn't seem completely with it, but I never thought she was suicidal."

"What do you mean she didn't seem with it?"

"She seemed preoccupied. Like she wasn't listening to anything I said."

While the detective was writing, a question passed through my mind, and I thought now was the time to ask it. "Did you find a note?"

The detective looked up from his notes. "No. "

"Don't people usually leave some type of note when they kill themselves?"

"It depends. Those who plan to kill themselves generally leave a note."

"And those who don't?"

There were several moments of silence. The detective took a deep breath before answering. "Those people are usually out of their mind." The detective closed the legal pad. "That's all the questions I have," he said. "How's the baby?"

"She's alive, but no one here seems to know if she'll make it."

"If for some reason she doesn't survive, will you let me know? I'd like to make a note in the file."

The detective's comment struck me as cold and heartless. I told myself that it wasn't his job to become emotionally involved in cases.

"Okay," I said. "I'll let you know."

On the way home from the hospital that evening, I asked my dad to stop by the apartment. Now that the police investigation was finished, I wanted to retrieve some clothes. For the last three days I had been wearing borrowed clothes from a cousin, and I was eager to wear something more comfortable and familiar.

It was dusk when we arrived. The street was quiet. The apartment building itself was dark. Not a light shone from the other three units. It was as if everyone had decided to move away from a building where people killed themselves. There was no longer yellow crime scene tape across the door.

"The clothes I need are in the bedroom closet and the top drawer of the dresser," I said. "They should be anyway. I don't know if the police moved anything." I handed my dad the key to the door and a list of clothing I needed. "I'm sorry, but I don't know what kind of condition the room is in," I said. Images of blood-soaked boxes and carpet were seared in my mind. I told him this so he would be prepared for any mess that remained. It was also my way of telling him I had no desire to go inside.

My dad walked slowly up the stairs to the apartment as if he was dreading what he would discover. He opened the door and disappeared into the darkness. A moment later the living room light went on, and I watched his shadow move across the blinds as he walked back to the bedroom.

It seemed like my dad was gone for a long time. While I waited, I wondered if all my clothes had been moved or if the mess had been too much for my dad to handle. Finally my dad emerged with a cardboard box full of clothes—a few shirt sleeves hung over the side.

My dad set the box next to the truck, and I rummaged through it to make sure there were enough clothes for the next few days and a suit and tie for Krista's funeral. In the twilight I was unable to tell if any of the clothes had blood on them. I would have to check for that later.

"I'm sorry that took so long," my dad said as I looked through the box. "It took me a minute to get Krista's message off the answering machine."

I froze. "There was a message from Krista?"

"You don't know about the message?" My dad seemed genuinely surprised that I didn't know of its existence.

"What did she say?" A dark feeling began to grow in the pit of my stomach. I braced myself for the worst.

"She said, 'No matter what I do, the consequences are the same.'"

I sat down on the curb and repeated the words again in my mind. Consequences? What consequences?

"Does the message mean anything to you?" my dad asked.

"No, nothing."

But I wasn't thinking about the message anymore; my thoughts were on the answering machine. I remembered before I left to pick Krista up that I called the apartment only to have the phone ring over and over. Later, while the police worked to resuscitate her, someone had called and I had to take the phone off the hook. Both times the answering machine did not pick up.

The question was, how did Krista leave a message on the machine? We didn't have cell phones. Unless she called from her grandmother's place or a pay phone before she arrived at the apartment, she could not have left a message. I put my head in my hands and rocked slowly back and forth. I thought back to when I dialed 911. The phone had been next to the answering machine. As hard as I tried, I could not remember the message light flashing.

"Was there a green light flashing on the answering machine?" I said, looking at my dad.

My dad stroked his beard with his left hand the way he did when he was thinking. "I don't believe so."

"What made you check the answering machine?"

"I don't know." He paused again, thinking. "I felt I should check it. To be honest, I don't know how your answering machine works. I started pushing buttons and I heard her voice."

Suddenly everything clicked. Krista hadn't called our phone and left a message. She had erased our old greeting and made a new one. However, after she had created the new message, she forgot to turn the answering machine on. That was the message she wanted me to hear when I called her before driving over. I explained the theory to my dad.

"To me it confirms that Krista wasn't in her right mind," Dad said after thinking about it for a minute. "Why else would she leave such a cryptic message?"

"I don't know," I said. "I don't know."

✦ ✦ ✦

When Dr. Green invited my dad and me into his office, I knew the news wasn't going to be good. All of our previous conversations about Hope had taken place next to her bedside. I assumed he wanted to use his office because it was a place where we could have some privacy.

Dr. Green's office was small, barely large enough for a filing cabinet, a desk, a bookshelf, and a couple of chairs. It had thick blue carpet. Diplomas and certificates hung on the far wall. Hope's medical file lay open on his desk. The doctor pulled his chair around to the front of the desk so he was directly in front of me. We were sitting so close our knees almost touched.

"Several specialists have conducted a series of tests on Hope in order to get a clearer picture of her long-term health. We've done some brain scans and tested her nervous system." He picked up the scan of Hope's head from the file. The scan was taken from the top of her head. I could see the two hemispheres of her brain. There were several large dark spots on the scan.

"These dark spots," Dr. Green explained, "are where there's blood on her brain. This is usually a sign of severe brain damage. As far as the specialists and I can determine, she has little or no brain activity." He said the last sentence slowly and looked me directly in the eyes as he spoke, as if to make sure there was no misunderstanding.

Even though the results weren't a complete surprise, my heart lurched at the news. The doctor, my dad, and the blue carpet blurred together. I closed my eyes to stop the tears from falling.

"Is there any chance that she might recover from her injuries?" my dad's voice broke through the darkness. It sounded like he was choking back tears too.

"There's an outside chance her condition could improve a little," Dr. Green said. "However, even a slight improvement would still mean Hope would depend on life support as long as she lived. Babies in Hope's condition who are left on life support typically don't live past their second birthday. They live their life pretty much as Hope is right now. They are rarely aware of their surroundings or of those who might be caring for them."

One tear fell to the blue carpet, then another. I heard the doctor pick up a box of tissues from his desk. I blindly grabbed for the box but was unable to find it. I opened my eyes and grabbed a few tissues. The tissue box was bright green and had pictures of daisies. The box struck me as strangely beautiful.

My dad placed his hand on my shoulder. I handed him some tissues.

"Since Hope can't speak for herself," the doctor continued, "you're the one that needs to speak for her. You need to let us know what sort of lifesaving measures, if any, you would like us to take if her condition worsens. You don't have to make that decision today. Take some time and think about it. But we'll need to know soon. Hope's condition could change very rapidly."

I nodded and reached for another tissue.

"Do you have any questions?" Dr. Green asked.

I shook my head and then held my head in my hands. My daughter had been part of my life for only four days, yet the knowledge that her odds for survival were slim to none brought me to the lowest point in my life. Until that moment I had never truly understood the love a parent has for a child. Knowing that Hope would not make it was like learning I was going to lose my arms or legs. Just as one might have seen no way to live without them, I saw no purpose in my life without her.

"Thanks, Doctor," my dad said. "We appreciate everything you've been doing."

"I'm always available if you have any questions," Dr. Green said. "Please stay here as long as you need."

The doctor moved his chair behind the desk. I stared at the medical books on his shelf until I heard the doctor shuffle past and the door close. I grabbed another handful of tissues, wiped my eyes, and blew my nose. I looked at my dad, whose eyes were red, though no tears had fallen. He stroked his beard and was looking past the desk at the far wall. I could tell he was searching for the right combination of comforting and encouraging words. Finally he cleared his throat and asked, "What are you going to do?" From the sound of his voice, I could tell he already knew the answer.

"I want to be alone with Hope," I said and walked out of the room.

I sat by Hope's side and cried until my head throbbed. When I was done weeping, I looked out the window next to her bed. From it I could see a panoramic view of the Salt Lake Valley—from the skyline of downtown Salt Lake City all the way to the orange and yellow hills of the Bingham Canyon Mine. I watched the sun inch its way toward the horizon.

Years ago I reached the conclusion that someone who was dependent on life support for survival wasn't really alive. I resolved that if I ever needed to make such a decision, I'd do it without hesitation. However, the hypothetical person I thought about was a nameless, faceless ghost. I never thought about removing life support from a family member or loved one. And I certainly never thought of making this decision for a baby—let alone one of my own children.

Now that Hope was part of the equation, all my previous reasoning seemed hollow and empty. It didn't matter that Hope was unable to respond to the world around her. Every morning I arrived at the hospital, hoping she had made a miraculous, overnight recovery. But each day as more tests were performed, the true nature of Hope's condition became apparent. She never opened her eyes or voluntarily moved her body. She never gripped my finger or responded when the nurses poked her foot to draw blood. I tried to rationalize away her lack of response by telling myself it was because of the large amounts of painkillers and muscle relaxants that were fed into her body twenty-four hours a day. But my gut told me something else. She was in her current condition because she had been deprived of oxygen for an extended period of time. Her health would never improve. Her life, as long as I chose for it to continue, was going to be lying unconscious in a hospital bed.

Removing Hope from life support was a decision I didn't want to make alone. Hope was part Krista, part myself. More than anything, I wanted Krista by my side. In the seven years I'd known her, Krista always had a unique way of looking at situations and providing valuable insight no matter what the issue. Right now, I desperately wanted her arms around me and to know what she thought the right course of action was.

My thoughts were interrupted by other people talking nearby. The parents of the baby closest to Hope had arrived. They talked in quick, excited voices. The baby cooed and smiled in response to their attention.

"Can you believe we can finally take him home today?" the mother said. There was a joyful lilt in her voice. She squeezed the father's hand. A nurse came and unhooked an IV and handed the baby to the mother. She sat in a rocking chair and began to talk and play with her son.

I tried to ignore the happy couple and their baby, but my attention kept returning to them. The nurse gave them instructions on taking care of their baby, but the mother and father weren't paying attention. Their happiness bubbled all over the room, and I leapt from my chair and walked out the door.

It wasn't until Saturday morning—a week after Hope came into the world—that I made the decision to remove her from life support. Instead of staying late at the hospital like usual, I left early. At the time I told myself I needed to be alone to make sure I was taking the right course of action. Looking back, I was already starting to say good-bye. I worried that if I stayed by Hope's side for too long, I would change my mind.

Mom seemed surprised to see me when I walked in the door early that afternoon. I told her I wasn't feeling well and needed to rest. I went to the temporary room my parents had set up for me in the basement and lay in bed. I tried to think about Hope and my decision, but my mind was too distracted. My body was sore and lethargic. Exercise, especially running, was a daily requirement for me. I hadn't run since the day Krista died. Perhaps a jog would help clear my mind and focus my thoughts.

I dressed in cold weather running clothes: shorts, running pants, T-shirt, long sleeve T-shirt, sweatshirt, and a hat. Quietly I slipped outside into the cold November air. There was a business park half a mile down the road. Since it was Saturday, I knew it would be quiet and deserted with nothing but miles of empty streets to run on. I could almost feel the solitude of that place pull me to it.

The cold air burned my lungs, nose, ears, and cheeks as I headed into the business park. I ran past warehouses and empty parking lots, abandoned railroad cars, and idle eighteen-wheelers. Soon beads of sweat started to run down my back and chest. For the first time in a week I was flush with energy.

I ran until my legs burned; my lungs felt as if they were going to explode. I stopped and knelt by the side of the road. My breath came in ragged gasps. I had pushed myself too hard. I dry heaved several times before my body began to relax. Cold air crept through my clothes. I looked around to get my bearings and discovered I had run around the entire perimeter of the business park—a little over six miles.

I walked the half mile to my parents' house and showered until the water turned cold. I put on shorts and a T-shirt and went straight to bed. I thought of Hope lying alone in the hospital. I realized I would never have a chance to know my daughter. Hope would never take her first steps or utter her first word. I would never have the opportunity to take her to her first day of school. She would never be anyone's best friend, wife, or mother. I lay on the bed and cried silently. I needed confirmation that removing life support was the right thing to do.

Slowly a warm, peaceful feeling spread through my body. The feeling started in my stomach and spread to my arms and legs. In that moment my mind was opened, and I knew it was Hope's time to go. I had made the right choice.

Despite the feeling of peace, it wasn't the answer I hoped for. My heart was still holding out for a miracle. I wanted to take my daughter home. I wanted her to be healthy. She had done nothing to bring this condition on herself. It wasn't fair that she had to die. In spite of my thoughts, the peaceful feeling remained with me. I closed my eyes and let it fill my body. At some point I fell asleep. It was the most sound, peaceful sleep I had all week.

The next morning I sat next to Hope for several hours, watching her chest move up and down in sync with the respirator. I was looking for any sign of life, but Hope lay just as she always had, still and unmoving.

I told a nurse I wanted to speak with Dr. Green. When he stopped by a few minutes later, I told him I wanted Hope to have a final brain scan. The look on the doctor's face told me he wasn't optimistic that anything had changed.

"Is there a reason you'd like another test?" he said.

"I want to be sure I'm doing the right thing."

"I'll order another one." The doctor picked up the cream-colored phone next to Hope's bed, dialed an extension, and requested a last-minute appointment. He hung up the phone, flipped through Hope's chart, and made a few notes.

"There's an opening in ten minutes," he said. "I'll have the nurses prepare her to be moved."

Two nurses arrived and began adjusting the life support monitors. One of the nurses removed Hope from the normal respirator and quickly attached her to one with wheels. The movable respirator was older and louder. Instead of a quiet whoosh, each breath being forced into Hope's lungs came with a banging noise that reminded me of the knock of a diesel engine.

I kissed Hope's forehead and returned to the waiting room where my family and Krista's best friend, Bekah, were waiting. Mom and Bekah looked like they'd been crying all morning.

"Hope's going to have one last brain scan," I said. "If the results show no activity, I'm going to remove her from life support."

Everyone was quiet.

"I'm going outside. I need some air," I said.

"I'll come with you," Bekah said.

She followed me to a small garden area just outside the hospital's main doors. The garden consisted of wooden benches and an artificial stream. Most of the flowers had wilted and turned brown weeks ago. During the summer, I was sure it had been nicer. I wondered if seeing colorful, live flowers gave more comfort to those in my position. Bekah and I sat on a bench near the head of the stream. The sound of water running over the rocks was soothing.

After a few minutes Bekah said, "Do you think the new scan is going to show any improvement?"

"No."

"Then why do you want one?"

"I need to know nothing's changed."

We sat in silence. I watched cars enter and exit the hospital's parking garage. I sensed Bekah had something to say but wasn't sure of the best way to bring it up. I closed my eyes and listened to the stream. I wondered what part of the hospital Hope was in and how the scan was progressing.

"I just don't understand why she did it," Bekah whispered.

"I don't think anyone does."

"No idea at all?"

I had been thinking about it since the day Krista died, and the only thing that I kept coming back to was that maybe some of her mother's or father's mental illness had trickled down to her. Krista's father was manic depressive and her mother was schizophrenic.

They'd met at a mental hospital, and Krista was conceived several weeks later. As long as I had known her, Krista had always lived with her grandmother. I'd assumed her parents were dead. It wasn't until I was seventeen that I learned she had parents who she visited most weekends. But despite everything, Krista had always seemed normal. I often wondered how the genes of two mentally ill people could combine in such a way to produce a child free of her parents' afflictions. I never told anyone, but as Krista's pregnancy progressed, I would often lie awake late at night wondering if the baby would be more like her mother or her grandparents.

An ambulance turned the corner, sirens wailing, and headed toward the emergency room entrance on the other side of the building. After a moment, the sirens abruptly ended, leaving a chilly silence.

Bekah's voice startled me out of my reverie. "Her grandmother told me at church a few weeks ago that Krista wasn't acting like herself."

"Yeah. She had become really withdrawn, as if she didn't care about anything. But I thought it was just the pregnancy. I thought she would snap out of it."

A family of four walked past the garden. The mother looked like she'd been at the hospital all day, worn out, perhaps grief-stricken. Those two things sometimes appeared the same on people's faces. The dad carried a young girl in his arms, and her head rested on his shoulder. I followed them with my eyes until they walked into the entrance of the parking garage and were enveloped by blackness.

"I should have been more concerned about her behavior," I said. "I should have known it was more than her pregnancy."

When I had mentioned Krista's behavior to friends and coworkers who had kids, one of them told me his wife was a different person when she was pregnant. He told me it was like living with a stranger. That described Krista perfectly—a stranger. For the last two months I didn't know who I was living with. But I was willing to put up with it until the baby came. I thought it would all end when Hope was born.

"Do you think she wanted the baby?" Bekah said quietly, almost hoping I wouldn't catch it. She sounded afraid to hear the answer.

"Krista was so excited to be a mom," I said. I had to stop and compose myself. I had a clear memory of Krista showing me the results of the pregnancy test. She pulled me into the bathroom and enthusiastically showed me the little pink line on a test strip. Her face radiated excitement and she laughed, "We're going to have a baby! We're going to have a baby!" Her blue eyes sparkled, and I saw pure joy in her face.

Bekah put her arms around me. "I can't believe she's gone," she said. "I should've been a better friend."

"You were a good friend, Bekah. Probably the best friend she ever had."

Cold from the bench oozed through my jeans, and I shoved my hands deep inside my coat pockets to keep them warm. A wind blew across the parking lot, chilling my ears and nose. I looked at my watch. I wanted to say, "Hope should be back in the ICU shortly," but I didn't. The next words, "I'm pulling her off life support today," were stuck in my throat and my heart.

"Let's go back inside," I said. "I'm freezing."

The doctor held two scans of Hope's brain, one in each hand. He held the first one up to the window by Hope's bed.

"This is the scan we showed you several days ago," he said. "As you know, the dark area is where there's blood on her brain." He held the second image next to the first. "This is the scan we just completed. Do you notice a difference?"

"The black spots are bigger in today's scan," I said.

The doctor nodded. "Unfortunately this means she's not going to improve. I'm sorry, but with this type of brain damage, the odds for any sort of recovery are very, very small."

The results weren't unexpected, yet I was still consumed by grief. The only thing I wanted now was some time alone with my daughter, though I realized I wanted years with her, not minutes or hours.

"I'd like a few minutes with her," I said.

"Take all the time you need," Dr. Green said. "We're going to move your family to a private room. When you're ready, we'll do everything there."

I held Hope's tiny hand and looked at her. Aside from her size, she looked like a healthy baby. Her skin was pink. The matt of brown hair on her head was soft and thick. She had Krista's sharp chin and heart-shaped face. She had my hair and ears. The doubt inside washed over me like a wave onto a shore. I couldn't stop it. I couldn't control it. I looked out the window. An inversion layer of haze and smog, a common occurrence in the winter, hung over the Salt Lake Valley like a dirty, brown blanket. The world seemed so ugly. I thought about the place where Hope's spirit would soon arrive—a beautiful place where Hope wouldn't have to depend on machines to live. I took one last long look at Hope for any sign of consciousness—anything that would indicate that the doctors and the tests were wrong.

She lay motionless, her face so still, as if she were dreaming of heaven.

My mom, dad, three sisters, a brother, and Bekah were waiting in the same room where the detective had last spoken to me. I sat in the chair where the detective had been, while my family sat on the couch. The nurses worked quickly. One by one they disconnected the electrodes and all of the IVs except for the one that contained painkiller. The last device to be removed was the respirator. When it was turned off, the room was silent, and then it slowly filled with the sounds of my family crying. A nurse wrapped Hope in a white blanket and placed her in my arms. Hope gasped for breath. One of the nurses left. The remaining nurse sat on a stool near the door and looked at the floor.

I kissed Hope's head and combed her brown hair with my fingers. I told her over and over how much I loved her. After ten minutes Bekah stood and kissed Hope and whispered good-bye. She wiped a tear with the back of her hand as she walked out the door. One by one my brother and sisters did the same. Finally, Mom kissed Hope on the forehead. Then it was just Dad, the nurse, myself, and Hope. Her occasional breaths, like small sighs, were the only sound in the room.

"She's beautiful, Abel," my dad said. There were tears in his eyes.

Hope's breaths became farther and farther apart. Within forty minutes it was thirty seconds between breaths. I cradled Hope in my arms and held her close. After an hour, there were minutes between breaths. When five minutes had passed and Hope hadn't taken a breath, I looked at the nurse.

"I'll find a doctor," she said.

She returned with a doctor I hadn't seen before. His beard matched his salt-and-pepper hair. He placed the stethoscope over Hope's heart and listened intently. He moved it around different areas of her chest.

"I can't find a heartbeat," he finally said. He checked his watch. "Time of death is six fifty-three." The nurse wrote the time on Hope's chart.

"You can spend as much time with her as you like," the doctor said. "If you brought something to dress her in, you can do that."

I had brought to the hospital a white dress a neighbor made for Hope. It was intended to be used for her blessing in church after she was born but now would be used for her funeral. The dress was tiny and beautiful and covered with lace. I couldn't bring myself to dress her in it. Looking at my dead daughter was more than I could bear.

"I want to go home," I said.

I handed Hope to the nurse. The nurse unwrapped Hope from the blanket and removed the final IV. She spread out the white dress and unzipped the back. I took one last look at Hope and then walked out the door.

It was dark when we left the hospital. My dad and I made the hour-long drive to Ogden in silence. On the way back, I remember thinking I had left something at the hospital. I kept searching my pockets to make sure I didn't leave my keys, wallet, or new cell phone behind.

I was searching for something I had lost but would never be able to find and take home.

# CHAPTER
## *Four*

Per my request, only close friends and family members were invited to Hope's funeral. After a large funeral for Krista, I wanted to keep this one private. Officially saying good-bye to my daughter was going to be the most difficult thing I had done, and I wanted as few people as possible to witness it.

There was another reason I wanted to keep Hope's funeral small. Krista's suicide had made everyone uncomfortable in my presence. I felt like a leper. People acted as if coming near me would spread some unexpected tragedy into their life. By now, I have realized they hesitated because they didn't know what to say. When a loved one dies from a tragic accident or an illness, most people can find words to express their sympathy: "It must have been his time," or "The doctors did everything they could." With a suicide, everyone avoided me, almost as if they blamed me. Most people couldn't even choke out, "I'm sorry." In place of comforting words were a lot of questions no one dared ask. I saw them in the sad faces of family and friends. They wanted to know why Krista had done it. Why hadn't I prevented it? How could I not know she was suicidal? Everyone looked to me for answers. I had none.

I was beginning to feel isolated. No one knew of a widower under sixty. The term *widower*, for me, was not only remarkably astonishing, but it was almost ironically funny. Almost. And no one had ever heard of a pregnant woman killing herself. Late into the night I scoured the Internet for information or news stories about pregnant women committing suicide. I found nothing. Believing there was no one out there to relate to or to tell me I'd get through this only reinforced my feelings of separation from the world.

Hope's funeral was less than ten minutes. While the bishop spoke, all I could think about was the life Hope never experienced. And as her tiny pink casket was lowered into the same plot as Krista's, I felt something for the first time since Krista's death. Anger. The anger burned inside me like the glowing embers of a fire: small, hot, and waiting to burst into flame.

I went home and mingled with those who'd gone back to the house for lunch and to mourn. All I really wanted, though, was to be left alone. After the guests left, I picked at leftover ham and cheese in the kitchen. I put the food into my mouth but couldn't taste anything.

A pile of pamphlets three inches high was stacked neatly nearby. Grief literature. There were brochures on how to cope with the death of a spouse, the death of a child, and losing a loved one to suicide. Intermingled with the brochures were business cards for grief counselors and therapists.

I skimmed through most of the brochures, finding they were worthless—especially the literature on losing a spouse. Those pamphlets were written for people who were retired, old, and ready to die, or "prepared" to be a widow or widower. They contained such pearls of wisdom as remembering the many years the two of you shared together and tips for spending your retirement years alone. There was nothing in them I could relate to. Krista and I had only been married thirty-four months. I was twenty-six years old. I still had a life ahead of me, though I couldn't picture it without Krista and Hope. My future, which only a few weeks before had looked bright and sunny, was now obscured by a thick, gray fog.

I leafed through one of the brochures, looking at pictures of people being comforted by others who had their hands on the grieving person's shoulder. I would've laughed if it didn't hurt so much. I scooped up pamphlets and dumped them in the trash.

"What are you doing?" My mom stood in the doorway, a half-eaten sandwich on the plate in her hand.

"Throwing this crap away."

I put on my coat and boots and headed toward the door.

"Where are you going?" Her voice sounded worried.

"Out."

"Abel, are you all right?"

"I just need some time alone," I said. People kept asking me if I was okay. Did they really expect me to say yes?

I started my car and cranked up the heat. I wanted to get away from everything that reminded me of Krista. But that was nearly impossible. Ogden was a minefield of memories. Krista was attached to every part of the town. A park reminded me of a date where we'd sat at a picnic table and laughed for hours. I drove by a market and remembered dozens of shopping trips where Krista and I had picked up the essentials and non-essentials that had made up our lives. I drove by a street corner and recalled the time my car broke down on the way home from school. Krista and I had both been late for work that day. Everything was a reminder that she was no longer part of my life but was still there in almost every sense of the word.

After driving aimlessly around for thirty minutes, I ended up by the mall on the south side of town. The parking lot was jammed with the-day-after-Thanksgiving shoppers. I needed to surround myself with people who didn't know me, didn't know my tragedy, or know I was a young widower. The mall seemed like the perfect place to lose myself in a sea of anonymous faces.

It took ten minutes to find a parking space. Inside, the mall was just as packed as the parking lot. Most shoppers carried boxes and bags of presents. Long lines snaked back from the cash registers. Everyone, even those standing in line, had smiles on their faces. It was the beginning of the Christmas season. It was an official holiday. There was no reason not to smile.

I wandered in and out of the stores, all the while fighting the feeling that I should be buying presents for Krista. In each store, I picked out something she'd like: sweaters, jeans, lingerie, books, and jewelry.

My eye became attuned to couples who were shopping. I spotted a man and a woman in their twenties standing in front of the Gap. The woman pointed to a coat the mannequin in the window was wearing. The man nodded his head. They walked into the store, holding hands. Another couple sat nearby drinking large steaming cups of gourmet coffee. The man leaned forward and whispered something in the woman's ear. She smiled and whispered something back. Their intimacy brought feelings of excruciating envy. Still this didn't prevent me from continuing to study them. It was almost a comfort to hurt that much. I wanted someone to whisper words that would bring a smile to my face. I wanted someone to love me. The only woman I had ever loved was gone. And there was nothing I could do to bring her back.

At the far end of the mall, across from the fourteen-screen movie theatre, a bunch of tired-looking shoppers sat on benches. Bags of presents lay at their feet. One or two looked at their watches and then around the mall as if hoping to see someone coming.

As I walked by, a memory flooded my mind. It was seven years ago, mid-December and cold. Krista and I had been dating a few months. We had spent the entire day together in Salt Lake, looking at the Christmas lights downtown. On the way home we stopped at her favorite Italian restaurant near the mall. The hostess informed us in a voice that sounded way too perky that there would be an hour wait. To help pass the time, Krista and I decided to walk through the mall. Tired and hungry, we finally slumped on a bench across from the movie theatres and watched people buy tickets for shows. After a while we started arguing over something. To this day I can't remember what it was about. But I do remember the argument escalated and I decided to leave.

Glaring at Krista, I stood and said, "I'm going home."

"How?" Krista said. "I drove." She pulled a ring of keys from her pocket and shook them. The jingling sound infuriated me.

"I'll take the bus." I was bluffing. I had no idea if there was a bus at this end of town that would take me home. I was hoping that Krista would run after me and concede the argument.

Krista called my bluff. "Fine, I'll just have to find another dashing young man to have dinner with."

Furious, I started toward the exit. I was determined to go home even if that meant walking all the way across town. I had taken no more than five steps when, over the din of the mall, I heard Krista's voice. She was speaking very loudly—loud enough for anyone within fifty feet to clearly hear—but her voice was full of affection and love.

"Abel, I love you! Will you please forgive me?"

People walking past and those in line for movie tickets turned to see what was going on. I could feel the blood rising to my face, not from anger but embarrassment. I turned and saw Krista on her knees. Her arms were outstretched toward me.

"I'm so sorry. Please don't be angry at me. I love you so much!" she said.

My eyes did a quick scan of those who had stopped to watch. Most had amused looks on their faces. Off to my right I heard someone laughing. I felt my face turning redder. I wanted to disappear. I didn't like the attention.

I walked over to Krista and helped her off her knees. I gave her a big hug, hoping this would please the crowd. A few people clapped halfheartedly. An older woman said, "Aren't they a cute couple?" The memory blurred and changed. Instead of hugging Krista in the mall, I was kneeling by her side in our apartment, her body slumped against white packing boxes. Her mouth hung partway open, eyes glazed. Her body trembled.

On the verge of tears, I walked quickly out of the mall. My mind shuffled between the Krista with outstretched arms and the one that put a gun to her head. The latter one seemed foreign and unfamiliar. As I unlocked the car, my thoughts turned to Hope dying in my arms. I got in and slammed the door.

"I hate you! I hate you!" I screamed. I pounded the steering wheel with my fists until my hands hurt. Then I allowed myself to cry—something I hadn't done at either funeral. I cried, great heaving sobs, until my head throbbed and the tears wouldn't fall anymore. Then I wiped the tears and mucus off the steering wheel with my sleeve.

"I hate you!" I said again. It felt good to say it.

My anger had just burst into flame.

I was furious at Krista in a way I had never felt toward anyone. I could make the fifty-mile drive to work and do nothing but curse her under my breath. Even after an hour of this, the anger really never subsided. It was always just below the surface, waiting to explode. Krista took the blame for all of my difficulties. If traffic was bad, I blamed Krista. When a deadline at work forced me to stay late, it was her fault. And when the Denver Broncos missed the game-winning field goal one Sunday afternoon, I found a way to blame that on Krista too.

Despite the anger, I still loved her immensely. My rage stemmed from wanting to know why she would take her own life—especially when she was seven months pregnant. I thought a reason for her suicide would go a long way to soothing my rage. The only rational explanation for her death was that she had an undiagnosed mental illness. The theory wasn't a reach since mental illness was prominent in her family. Coming from mentally ill parents, it had always been a wonder to me that Krista was so normal.

I read a lot about schizophrenia. Some of the signs Krista exhibited in the months before her death matched up well. There was the talking nonsense, not having the energy to do anything, not wanting to talk to others, and not caring about her appearance. But many of these were also symptoms of depression. Krista had taken Prozac on and off since we were married but had discontinued it once we tried to conceive. Usually I could detect a difference in her moods after a few days when she stopped taking her medication. This time—at least through the first months of her pregnancy—I hadn't noticed a change in her attitude or behavior. It wasn't until her pregnancy was well underway that her demeanor changed.

And Krista was nothing like her mother, Susan, who was schizophrenic. I had seen Susan in dozens of full schizophrenic attacks. She would rave about the voices inside her head or the police who she claimed were watching her through the television. During these episodes she would scream at the top of her lungs and had a psychotic look in her eyes—the look I always imagined a serial killer having before murdering his victims. If I hadn't known Susan was schizophrenic, I would have mistaken those episodes for drug-induced psychosis. Susan's schizophrenic attacks always terrified me, and I was hesitant to go over to their home when one of them was occurring. Krista, however, always thought she could help. I accompanied her only because I worried about her safety. Susan's more severe schizophrenic episodes would lead to hospitalization for several weeks. Once she was back on her medications she would return home, stop taking her medicine, and let the cycle repeat itself.

Krista's father, Todd, was manic depressive. He sat in his overstuffed rocking chair all day, chain smoking and drinking tall glasses of diet Mountain Dew. The rift between Todd and me came from the way Todd treated Krista. Every day there was a phone call from him asking for food or money or for Krista to pick up one of his many prescriptions at the pharmacy. He expected Krista to be at his beck and call twenty-four hours a day. If Krista did not agree to help, he would call her ungrateful and a lousy daughter and verbally abuse her until she would agree to help or until she would slam down the phone in tears.

Todd and Susan had the means to support themselves. Their monthly social security and state aid checks were enough to survive. It was their spending habits that were horrible. Within days of their checks arriving, most of the money was spent on cigarettes and alcohol. According to Todd, their inability to save money, their addiction to tobacco and booze, and any other thing they were unable to do for themselves were all caused by their mental illness.

Her parents hadn't always been so dependent—or so Krista said. When things would become very frustrating with them, Krista would tell me how life had been different when she was growing up. She had memories of her dad coming back from work and late at night studying to become a police officer. Her mother did her best to keep house and raise Krista and her younger brother, Scott. When she told me these memories, it was as if she believed her parents could turn their lives around and become productive members of society again, not the people who chain smoked and watched television all day.

Krista said when she was about eight, something happened. Todd stopped working, and Susan began to spend time in and out of mental institutions. Unable or unwilling to care for their children—depending on who you asked—Krista and Scott went to live with their grandmother. Krista never lived with her parents again, though once things calmed down a little and her parents were able to find a government subsidized home to live in, Krista spent most weekends with them.

Logically it made sense that schizophrenia or some other mental illness could have scrambled Krista's brain enough for her to take her own life. But I wasn't totally convinced. And without Krista to evaluate in person, I started to wonder if the cause of her suicide would ever be known.

After church the next Sunday I went for a walk. I needed to separate myself from the lingering sadness that seemed to occupy every corner of my parents' house. Though I understood their feelings, I was done being sad.

I stopped in front of a small abandoned house next to my parents' home. A large For Sale sign leaned crookedly in the front yard. I walked to the side door and threw my weight against it. The door swung open and I walked inside.

I stood in the kitchen. A broken dishwasher hung partway out of its crawl space. There were empty spots where a refrigerator and stove once stood. The cupboards were the color of coffee beans and covered with a thick layer of dust. Thousands of box elder bug and fly carcasses covered the floor, their legs curled at odd angles. Insects crunched underfoot with each step.

Each room had at least one hole in the drywall. Broken blinds hung crookedly from the windows. A dilapidated waterbed frame sat in the master bedroom. A partly disassembled washer and dryer lay on their sides in a second bedroom. In the bathroom, the bathtub was an old cast-iron monster. The cheap protective covering that had been used to protect the walls from water had long ago peeled away, leaving behind a warped, water-stained mess. The toilet looked like it hadn't been cleaned in years. The entire house smelled of dust and neglect.

Growing up, this was the only home on the street I'd never entered. The outside of the house was an eyesore. It was covered with brown and white siding that wouldn't have looked good no matter what decade it came from. The box elder tree in front of the house was overgrown. Its branches reached for the power lines above like long slender fingers. The yard usually contained more weeds than grass. The occupants were always renters who never stayed more than a couple of months. Eventually the house was abandoned and taken over by the bank. Soon after, a For Sale sign was put up and remained for years. I wondered if the realtor even remembered it was for sale.

The first time I entered the house was with Krista the previous summer. We were taking a walk one evening when Krista asked about the house as we passed. I told her about its history of renters and its deplorable condition. To prove it to her, I took her to one of the windows to take a look.

"Let's find a way inside," Krista said after she had scanned the interior.

"We can't just break into the house," I said, a little surprised at the suggestion.

"I just want to look around."

Krista tried the front door and then walked around the house, attempting to open the windows. I looked around nervously as I followed her.

"The house is a dump. Why do you want to go inside?" I said.

"I think it has potential."

"Sure, if you have twenty thousand dollars to put into it."

"I think twenty thousand is a bit high. I think it could be fixed up nice for twelve or fifteen grand."

By this point, we'd reached the kitchen door. Krista turned the knob to no avail. She pushed the door and it opened slightly. She pushed again. The door didn't budge.

"It seems to be stuck," she said.

She threw her weight against the door and it flew open. Krista shrieked as she fell onto the dusty, insect-ridden floor. I helped her to her feet and brushed the dust off her clothes and picked dead bugs out of her blonde hair.

"Since we're in, we might as well look around," Krista said, giggling.

As we walked through each room, Krista talked about what she'd do to fix it up, what color she'd paint the walls, and what each room would be used for. An office. An exercise room. A nursery. I kept my mouth shut, hoping that one walk through would be enough to indulge her fantasy. It wasn't. Every time we stopped by my parents' home, Krista would take me through the abandoned house, telling me about the promise the house had. Even though I didn't want to buy the house, I liked how Krista saw potential in old, broken things and wanted to make them new again.

The sound of someone opening the kitchen door brought me back to the present.

"Abel, are you here?" My dad's voice echoed off the old, dirty walls.

I walked down the hall to the kitchen. My dad was still dressed in his Sunday shirt and tie. A few flakes of snow were stuck to his hair. He stood looking at the dilapidated kitchen as if the empty room might hold all the answers.

"I didn't see you at home when we came back from church."

"I'm fine, Dad."

He wiped some dust off one of the cupboards.

"Are you still thinking about buying this place?"

"I don't know."

"If you do decide to buy it, I'll come over when I'm in town and help you fix it up."

"I know you will."

"When do you have to decide?"

"Soon."

"I think the whole family would like it if you bought it."

Neither one of us said anything for a long moment.

"Did you ever tell Krista you made an offer on this place?" he asked.

"I told her two days before she died. I thought she'd be excited about it. But, she didn't really seem to care."

"That doesn't seem like her."

"I know."

Silence enveloped the kitchen. I felt uncomfortable. I knew where the conversation was heading.

My dad's voice sounded as downtrodden as the house. "I feel terrible that I never told Krista how much I loved her. I never told her how happy it made me that she was part of the family."

"Krista knew you loved her, Dad."

"I had so many opportunities and I never told her . . ." My dad's voice trailed off. He looked far away, lost in thought.

I tried to think of a way to change the subject. It was painful because it brought back memories of things I wished I would have done differently when Krista was alive.

"I should have been around more. All my work . . . " My dad didn't continue the sentence. He looked around the kitchen absentmindedly and wiped some dust off one of the counters.

I shifted my weight from one leg to another. I didn't want to talk about the past, Krista, or anything else I couldn't change.

Sensing my unease, Dad finally said, "I'm going to head back to the house. You want to come?"

"Not yet. I want to be alone a little longer."

I listened to the sound of the snow crunching under Dad's feet as he walked by the side of the house. When his footsteps faded away, I leaned against a dusty wall and slid down to the floor. I didn't bother clearing the bugs out of the way. I tilted my head back and closed my eyes.

I felt as if I should buy the house. The feeling was strong and reverberated through my entire body. I had been taught to recognize this feeling as a spiritual impression telling me whether or not to do something.

In this case, I felt buying the house was the right thing to do. Despite the prompting, I didn't want to buy it. It would take months to make the place livable. It would mean a one-hundred-mile round trip commute to work every day. And I didn't have the time or energy for either of those. It was Krista's house. She was the one who liked it. As far as I was concerned, the house's potential had died with Krista. I knew that if I bought it, my family and friends would think I was doing it because it was what Krista would have wanted. I saw no reason to do anything in her memory. What I wanted right then was to move far away from everything associated with her.

I looked at the six-inch hole in the far wall. "Why'd you do it, Krista?" I asked the empty room. "This place could have been yours." I slammed my fist on the carpet. Dead bugs scattered from the force of the blow.

I thought back to the morning Krista died—something I often did when I was alone. When I had returned from running errands, the first thing I noticed was the absence of Krista's car in the driveway. I immediately called the apartment. Krista had answered on the first ring.

"What are you doing?" I said. "I thought we were spending the day at your grandmother's."

"Unpacking," Krista said. "I'll be back soon."

Her comment had struck me as odd. Since we had moved into the apartment a week earlier, Krista had had an aversion to staying there alone. She never told me why, but after I left for work in the morning, Krista would drive over to her grandmother's and spend the day with her.

"I'll help you unpack," I said. I pulled the keys from my pocket and started toward the door.

"I'll be back in an hour."

There was something in Krista's voice that wasn't right. Again I told her I was on my way, but Krista strongly insisted that I stay. Finally I gave in.

"I'll see you soon," I said.

"Tell me that you love me," Krista said.

"What?"

"Tell me that you love me," she repeated.

"I love you," I said,

The line went dead.

When an hour had passed and she hadn't arrived, I called the apartment again. Krista said she would leave momentarily. And like the previous conversation, she ended it by saying, "Tell me that you love me."

The calls went back and forth every thirty minutes for another two hours. Each conversation would end with Krista asking me to tell her I loved her. Toward the end of our last conversation, our words became heated, and Krista insisted she was really leaving this time. But her voice had the same faraway quality it had all morning. I knew it was a lie. When thirty minutes passed, I called again. There was no answer. Even the answering machine didn't click on. At the time my mind wasn't focused on the answering machine. I thought Krista was actually on her way over. I turned on the TV and watched a movie. At the slightest noise outside, I looked toward the driveway, hoping it was the sound of her car pulling in. Occasionally I walked to the kitchen window and looked down the road, waiting to see her red car. But Krista never came. When I called again and no one answered, I drove to the apartment.

Thoughts of that morning always brought out a lot of guilt. I blamed myself and my inaction as a reason Krista may have died. Finally I grew tired and cold sitting on the floor. I stood, wiping the dust and dead insects from my pants and coat.

"There is no way I'm *ever* buying this house," I said loudly. My voice echoed off the bare walls. I slammed the kitchen door as I left.

But in the end I did buy the house. The gentle prodding I felt each time I thought about purchasing it convinced me this was something I needed to do. Four days before Christmas, the woman at the title company slid another form across the desk for me to sign. Each time, I told myself I was making a tragic mistake. *Stand up*, I thought. *Tell the woman this is all a misunderstanding. This is a move based on feelings, not logic. Think of the commute and the wear on your car. Think of the work the house needs. Don't do this.*

Even so, the woman continued to give me papers and I continued to sign. Thirty minutes after the flurry of paperwork started, the house was mine.

The woman stood up and shook my hand. "Congratulations on being a homeowner," she said.

"Thanks." I gave her a weak smile.

"I wasn't given any keys for the property," she said.

"That's all right," I said. "I know how to get in."

I drove home in a daze. When I arrived at the house, there were blue, yellow, and red balloons tied to the mailbox, and a sign that read "Congratulations, Abel!" was taped to the front window. My mom was standing outside with a camera, ready to take pictures of what, to her, was an exhilarating moment.

"Are you excited?" she said, her voice strained with her own enthusiasm.

"I'm a little overwhelmed right now," I said.

I stood for a couple of pictures anyway.

When Mom left, I walked through the house with a pen and a notebook, making a list of supplies I needed to pick up at the hardware store. After paying off Hope's hospital bills, I calculated what remained of Krista's life insurance money and figured I'd have just enough to buy what was needed for all the repairs and to hire out the work I would be unable to do myself. What I'd be left with was a house I didn't want to buy in the first place.

My cell phone rang, and the caller ID displayed the name and number of a good friend, Brent, who lived in Phoenix. Since Krista's death, I felt he was the only person who knew how to talk to me. Other than his initial sympathies, he talked about everything except Krista and Hope. Instead he told me what a fun city Phoenix was to visit and invited me to fly down to spend some time with him. He talked about the two years we lived in Bulgaria as missionaries for our church. He was fun to talk with. The few reasons I had to smile since that cold November afternoon were due to his kind words. This conversation wasn't much different. After talking about the house I had just bought, Brent got right to the point.

"I really think you should come down to Phoenix," he said.

"I don't know," I said, even though I wanted to jump at the invitation to get away from everything.

"Winter's a great time to be in Arizona. The temperatures are perfect."

"I have a lot of work to do on the house."

"It doesn't have to be immediately. I was thinking more about the first weekend after the new year."

I told Brent I'd think about it.

51

The next day as I tore up the carpet from the bedrooms and removed the cabinets from the kitchen, I considered Brent's offer. The more I thought about leaving Utah for a couple of days, the better it sounded. Later that night, after a long day of working on the house, I dialed Brent's number. I wanted to make sure he was serious.

# CHAPTER
*Five*

The evening before I flew to Phoenix, I walked through the house and examined the work that had been accomplished. All the walls had been repaired and painted white. The old carpet had been torn out and new floorboards installed. The bathroom had been gutted, and a new shower and toilet had been put in. The house smelled of fresh paint and was finally looking habitable. I was pleased with the progress.

As I paused in each room, I realized Krista had been right. The house had great potential. She had been able to look past the dead insects and neglect to see its true beauty. I had been too preoccupied with its disrepair to see that a little work could make the place livable.

I stopped in one of the bedrooms and thought about what I was going to do with it. This was supposed to be Hope's nursery. I could see her crib in one corner and a shelf full of dolls and toys against the far wall. This was the room in which I had imagined playing with her and tucking her in at night. I had planned on painting the walls pink. Instead they glistened with a new coat of white paint. I felt a lump rise in my throat and quickly left the room.

There was a knock at the back door. Before I could answer it, my mom entered. She held a plate of steaming pepperoni pizza and had a smile fastened to her face. As I wolfed down the pizza, my mom walked through the house. I listened to her footsteps echo off the walls as she went from room to room and examined the day's progress. Her footsteps reinforced how empty the house was, and I wondered if it would ever feel full without someone to share it with.

"You've finished painting," she said when she finished touring the house.

"The family's been a lot of help," I said. "Couldn't have made it this far without them."

"As I walked through the house, I felt that Krista has seen what you've done. I believe she's happy with the way it's turning out."

I looked down at the floor as I always seemed to do when someone talked about Krista. Though well-intentioned, my mom's comment made me uncomfortable. It wasn't the first time she had said something like that. A few weeks earlier the family had gone on a trip to Salt Lake. After we returned, she told me she had felt Krista was sitting in the van with the family, enjoying the conversation, wishing she could be part of it.

"She probably would be happy with the house," I said. "Too bad she decided not to stick around for it." I said the last part under my breath. I was counting on my mom, who had always been a little hard of hearing, not to catch it. Mom didn't seem to notice the comment, but I regretted the remark as soon as I said it. "I'm sorry, Krista," I said quietly. "I didn't mean that."

Whether or not my mom actually sensed Krista had seen the progress on the house, I knew Krista would be happy with the improvement. I only wished she had seen the same potential with her life.

I finished the last of the pizza and waited for my mom to leave. I wanted to be alone. A death might have brought most people closer to their family, but it had driven me farther from mine. After the initial shock of her death had worn off, Krista had become a saint. No one seemed to remember the odd behavior she exhibited before she died or the fact that she killed herself and—as far as I was concerned—Hope. There were times I felt I was the only one still angry or upset about it. Because of this, I was unable to talk with anyone in my immediate family about Krista or anything related to her death.

My mom paced around what would soon be the remodeled kitchen, looking at the walls. I sensed she had something she wanted to say but was unsure how to bring it up. I wasn't in the mood to wait. I still needed to clean the paint brushes and pack for my trip.

"Do you have something you want to tell me?" I said.

"Bridget finally developed some pictures," she said. "There's some of you and Krista." Bridget was my sister and an aspiring photographer.

"Oh?" I said. "Did you bring them over?" I thought the least I could do was act interested in them even if they were the last thing I wanted to see.

"They were taken a week before Krista died—at that Sunday cookout. Remember?"

I knew what day she was talking about. My family had decided to have a final barbeque before the weather turned too cold. Bridget had taken some pictures of the two of us with a new camera she had purchased.

My mom took an envelope out of her pocket and removed a photograph from it. "Look at this one," she said.

In the photograph Krista was wearing the blue flower print dress she had worn to church that Sunday. She was sitting on a white plastic lawn chair. I was squatting next to the chair, looking at her pregnant belly. My right arm was around her shoulders. My left hand rested on her tummy, and I remembered I had been hoping to feel the baby move while Bridget snapped pictures. Krista's face was turned away from the camera, nestled into my shoulder.

I turned and wiped away a tear. Seeing a photograph of Krista pregnant brought back too many memories. I looked at my mom, hoping my expression would ask her why she had shown me the photo. My face seemed to say she still hadn't told me what was on her mind.

"Do you see it?" she asked.

"See what?"

"Look again."

I glanced at the picture. I didn't see anything significant about it other than the fact it was probably the last photograph taken of the two of us.

"Look at Krista," my mom said. "She's not looking at the camera."

"So?" I didn't understand where she was going with this.

"Her head is turned in all of the pictures."

"Krista wasn't feeling well that day," I said.

"But do you ever remember her not smiling for a photograph?"

My mom was right. Krista had always smiled for the camera. She was usually quite photogenic. Even so, I didn't see the point she was trying to make.

"What are you getting at, Mom?"

"Look at her face again. It's so unlike her not to smile. She wasn't herself. I really think she was mentally ill."

I turned away again, this time to stop myself from saying something I'd regret. Now that Krista was dead, everyone had turned into psychiatrists and knew the reason Krista had killed herself. If it was so obvious, I always thought, then why hadn't anyone said anything while she was alive? The photograph was not enough evidence for me.

"We don't know why she did it," I said. "We probably never will."

"I don't think the photograph's a coincidence," my mom said. "I think some things happen for a reason."

I wasn't in the mood to hear my mom's "There Are No Coincidences" speech. According to her, everything happened for a reason—usually a spiritual one.

"It's a photograph," I said. "Nothing more."

"Just look at it, Abel."

I took the picture from her outstretched arm and set it on the paper plate covered with pizza crumbs.

"When I look at that picture, I see a woman who's tired of life. She's sad in a way I don't think any of us can understand. But I don't see the ravages of schizophrenia or any other mental illness." I sat back down on the chair and tried to calm down. I hoped that my mom would leave.

"Why must you be so angry?" my mom said. "It was her time to go."

Her last comment sent me over the edge.

"It wasn't her time!" I said. "It wasn't Hope's time either! They're both dead because Krista made the choice to put a gun to her head!"

I threw the photograph to the floor. It landed upside down between a tool box and a circular saw.

"Abel—"

"I don't want to hear it!"

My mom put on her coat and gloves without saying a word. She opened the back door to leave. I could feel cold air filling the kitchen. I felt I should apologize or say something so she wouldn't think I was angry at her while I was in Phoenix.

"Mom," I said as she stepped into the cold. "Thanks for the pizza."

It was a weak attempt to smooth things over. She closed the door without saying good-bye.

I sat on the chair for several minutes and then picked up the photograph up from the floor. I brushed the pizza crumbs and dust off it and set it on the kitchen counter. Then I did one final check of the house, making sure everything was in order. I turned off the lights one room at a time. Even though I was proud of the way the house was looking, I still regretted buying it. I didn't relish the thought of living in a home, a neighborhood, and a city that constantly reminded me of Krista. I wanted to live in a place that wasn't riddled with memories. That's why I was looking forward to the trip to Phoenix—it was a place where, for a few days, I could forget about everything.

That night I took a long, hot shower. I scrubbed hard, making sure to remove all flecks of paint from my face, arms, and hair. I wanted to go to Phoenix without any traces of Utah on me. I realized as I scrubbed, however, that a part of Utah would always stay with me. Inside I would always carry the constant ache that Krista and Hope were dead.

The sun was low in the sky as the plane descended into Sky Harbor International Airport.

From several thousand feet above Phoenix, it seemed that every other house in the sprawling metropolis had a swimming pool. There were palm trees and cacti growing in most of the yards. Everything about the city looked warm and inviting.

Brent was waiting on the other side of the security checkpoint. He looked exactly the same as I remembered him when I had last seen him four years ago: tall and thin as a rail with short, light brown hair, narrow blue eyes, and a big smile.

We spent the drive to his house catching up on each other's lives. Brent told me about going to school and working to complete his degree in criminal justice. He told me about meeting his wife, Bethany, their courtship, and how much he was enjoying married life.

"You sound like you found your soul mate," I said.

"Yeah, I did," Brent said.

Hearing about Brent's happy marriage made me jealous. I rolled down the window and let the warm evening air blow though the cab of Brent's truck. A convertible roared past us, the long, dark hair of the driver flailing straight out behind her.

Fifteen minutes from the airport we exited the freeway and drove into a quiet residential area. We drove by homes with cacti and gravel for front yards and groves of orange and grapefruit trees, their branches heavy with fruit. A few minutes later we turned into a community of white townhomes with orange Spanish-styled roofs. Brent parked his truck at the far end of the parking lot. I grabbed my duffle bag from the back of the truck and followed him to the center of the complex past a large swimming pool. The blue water looked cool and inviting.

Brent's townhome faced the pool. We were met at the door by a woman of medium height. Her hair was a rich, dark brown color, as were her large, doe-like eyes. Her skin was pale and flawless. Brent had done more than find a soul mate; he had married one of the most beautiful women I had ever seen.

"Abel, this is my wife, Bethany," Brent said.

We shook hands. Her hand was warm and smooth.

"Brent's told me a lot about you," Bethany said.

"Nothing too bad, I hope."

"Actually I was hoping to hear some stories about him."

"I'm sure I have a story or two you haven't heard yet."

Bethany looked at my baseball hat. "The Detroit Tigers," she said.

Her comment caught me off guard. Tiger fans were rare out West, and outside of baseball fans, few even knew what the Old English D represented.

"You like the Tigers?" I said hopefully.

"No, but I'm from Michigan," she said. "People wear hats like yours all the time in my hometown."

"Well, maybe you can convert your husband," I said.

"Fat chance," she replied. "He prefers to root for a winning team."

I felt the laughter inside me before it burst out. *I'm laughing*, I thought. I wanted to get down on my knees and thank this beautiful woman for her gift of making me laugh and making me feel safe and accepted, not the pariah of being a widower.

The three of us spent the rest of the evening talking. As we chatted, I watched as Bethany stroked Brent's arm with her long, slender fingers or playfully hit him when he told a joke. Her actions made me long for Krista in ways that hadn't manifested themselves until then. I missed the way Krista would stroke the back of my neck when we were watching television or the smell of her hair when she would lean her head on my shoulder. I missed putting my arms around her and feeling the familiar curves of her body. That evening I would have done anything to have her again at my side.

Shortly after midnight, Bethany yawned and excused herself. I watched as she walked up the stairs to their bedroom.

"You're a lucky man," I said, looking back at Brent.

"I know it," Brent said. "I don't deserve her."

My eyes wandered to the photographs of Brent and Bethany hanging on the wall. There was one of them on their wedding day. In the photograph they were holding hands and had smiles as big as the picture. The photo brought back memories of my own wedding. Krista and I were married on a freezing December morning, but I don't remember feeling cold. Instead I felt thrilled and lucky to have someone as beautiful and perfect as Krista as my wife. I caught myself smiling for a moment, waiting for Krista to walk into Brent's front door, as if she had just arrived late, or had run out to get something from his truck. I felt like half of a whole, and the other half was gone forever. The feeling burned inside me. It made me want to cry or vomit or rewind time. I glanced back at Brent. The happy look on his face that was there only moments before was gone.

"Are you all right?" I asked. The sadness was etched deep into his blue eyes. I thought he was going to tell me something was seriously wrong with his marriage, or maybe he was dying from some incurable disease.

"How did she die?" Brent said quietly. "What happened?"

His comment left me momentarily speechless. How could Brent not know? My mind raced through the phone calls we had over the last two months. I thought I had told him about Krista but couldn't be sure.

"What do you know?" I said.

"All I know is that she died unexpectedly."

My stomach lurched. "I'm sorry," I said. "I thought I told you. I've told the story so many times that I just assumed you knew."

"I wanted to ask, but it didn't seem right to do it over the phone."

"Brent," I said, "my wife took my handgun and shot herself in the head." Those words stood in the room as big as a building. The clock in the kitchen ticked so loudly you could hear it over the hum of the air conditioning. Miraculously, as I told Brent about Krista's suicide and Hope's brief life, I didn't shed a tear. A part of me wanted to tell him every detail, to unload it all on him, and cry. But I kept much of it to myself. I gave him the newspaper account story, as if I was telling this sad tale about someone I knew, not about myself.

Brent didn't say anything while I talked. He simply stared at me with the same sad look. When I finished, there was silence for a long moment.

"I'm sorry you had to go through that," Brent finally said.

"You don't have anything to be sorry about."

"Can I ask a question about that day?" Brent's words were barely audible. It sounded like he was whispering, afraid to speak in case someone should overhear his question.

"Ask whatever you want," I said.

"You don't have to answer it."

"Ask away."

There was a pause. Then the question came out.

"Do you think Krista waited for you to come home before she pulled the trigger?"

It was one of those questions until now, no one had dared ask. I closed my eyes. The events of that afternoon replayed themselves over in my mind.

"Yes, I think she waited," I said, opening my eyes. "It seems too much of a coincidence that I arrived home just as she decided to pull the trigger."

"Why do you think she waited?" There was a little hesitation in Brent's voice. He seemed unsure how deep he could probe.

"Maybe she was hoping the baby could be saved," I said. "Perhaps she thought letting me witness her death would put an exclamation point on her suicide. The truth is, I don't know."

What I didn't say was I really didn't want to know the answer to that question. If Krista had waited so I would be the one to find her, so my last memory of her was one with a bullet in her head, then knowing that truth would be hard to live with. It was better to let it go.

"When you were driving back to your apartment, did you have any inkling she was suicidal?" Brent's voice had more confidence this time, but he still looked at me for some kind of reassurance that the question was okay to ask.

I took a deep breath and then slowly exhaled. There were parts of that day I hadn't told anyone—not even family members. I considered telling Brent the lie I had so convincingly told since the day Krista died—that her suicide had been completely unexpected. The truth was I had been warned three times something was amiss, and I had ignored each warning.

I cleared my throat and rearranged the couch pillows I had been leaning on. I opened my mouth to speak but stopped. I felt my throat tighten. I closed my eyes and fought back the tears. In the silence that followed I again thought about telling the lie I had repeated so many times. It was the easy way out. The one thing I had learned since Krista's death was that no one was ever going to question my version of events. But there was something about telling a lie that ate at my very soul. My life, already a daily struggle, was made even more unbearable because I refused to tell the truth. In that moment, I made the decision to tell Brent everything.

"You know those strong, spiritual impressions you receive occasionally?"

Brent nodded.

"I had three of them before she died. Odds are if I had acted upon any of them, Krista would still be alive right now."

I let my words hang in the air for a minute before continuing.

"The day before she died, Krista called me at work and said she wanted to spend the night at her grandmother's house. She didn't give a reason why."

I remembered that conversation clearly because Krista had been calling at least once an hour. She never gave a reason for her calls that day other than she just wanted to see how I was doing. By the time she called with the request to spend the night at her grandmother's, I was so annoyed with her constant interruptions I had agreed to her request just to get her off the phone.

"After work I stopped by the apartment to pick up a change of clothes and a few other items. As I was putting everything in the trunk, I felt a distinct impression I should go back to the house, retrieve my gun, and give it to my brother for safe keeping. Even though the feeling was very powerful, I ignored it."

I could remember standing by the car, my left hand on the trunk, ready to shut it when the feeling hit me. I looked back at the dark apartment windows. My gun was locked in a case and, at the time, I thought I had all the keys. Besides, it was late and I was hungry. I brushed the feeling aside, shut the trunk, and drove away.

"The next morning I awoke early to run errands. Krista was still asleep. As I pulled out of the driveway, I received another strong impression. Only this time I felt that instead of going to the store, I should drive straight to the apartment. Again, I ignored what my gut was telling me."

I had told myself there was no reason to go to the apartment. Krista was at her grandmother's house. There was nothing to do at the apartment except finish unpacking. As I arrived at a major intersection, I felt strongly I should drive to the apartment. Going straight through the light would take me home. Turning left would allow me to run my errands. I didn't know what to do. The closer I came to the intersection, the stronger the impression became. It was like the feeling was being blared into me by someone with a loudspeaker, though I didn't hear anything. I just felt it. Finally, I had to make a choice: drive straight or turn left. I turned left.

"The third impression came as I was walking up the stairs to our apartment. This one was much stronger than the previous two. I felt that I should open the apartment door very quietly and not say anything once I walked inside. But I ignored that feeling too. I opened the door . . ."

There was no need to continue. I stared at the rug on the floor and traced its intricate pattern with my eyes. I felt too ashamed and embarrassed to look at Brent.

"You know what I think about every day?" I said. "I wonder how different my life would be if I had listened to those promptings. Every morning I wake up and my first thought is, why did I ignore them?"

More silence. A tear ran slowly down my cheek to my chin. I felt it land on my shirt.

"The funny thing is that now when I think about Krista, I get angry. I'm furious that she killed herself. I hate her for taking Hope's life and her own. But I feel so responsible for everything. If only I had listened to those feelings, Krista would still be alive."

I waited for Brent to say something—anything. When I finally got the courage to look at him, I saw his expression was full of compassion. For some reason I expected anyone who knew the full story to be appalled and revolted at me.

"I'm so sorry, Abel," Brent said. "I don't know what to say."

"You don't have to say anything," I said. "It feels good to finally tell someone the whole story."

That night for the first time since Krista died, I didn't have to fight off memories of her suicide. Instead I thought back to the promptings and how little, sometimes seemingly insignificant choices can have the biggest impact on one's life. Over the coming months I would tell what I had told Brent to my family and close friends. And as I stared at the dark ceiling and waited for sleep to overtake me, I knew that telling them was going to be the easy part. The hardest part was still to come. I needed to forgive myself for my inaction.

The next morning Brent and I drove to Mesa Community College to run. I had always lived in places with cold, snowy winters. In Phoenix it was clear and sunny, and temperatures were in the low sixties. It was perfect running weather. It was a nice change to wear running shorts and a T-shirt in January.

I tightened my running shoes and started around the track. Brent stayed with me for a few laps. Then he slowed and eventually stopped after I lapped him twice. He sat on a long wooden bench next to the track and watched me run the final laps. I finished the four-mile run in thirty-one minutes and forty-seven seconds—a personal best. Breathing hard, I walked slowly over to the bench where Brent was resting.

"You're in good shape," Brent said. "I wish I could run like that."

I sat next to him and slowed my breathing. I leaned back, closed my eyes, and let my skin soak up the sun. There was a slight breeze, which felt good.

After several minutes I became aware of the presence of someone nearby. I opened by eyes and saw a woman on the far end of the bench, stretching. She had long legs and jet black hair that hung just past her shoulders. She was wearing blue running shorts and a matching tank top. When the woman stretched her arms above her head, her tank top pulled up just enough to reveal a flat, well-toned stomach. The woman looked at me and smiled. I smiled back. She pulled her hair into a ponytail and put it through the back of a white baseball cap. I always found it attractive when a woman wore her hair in that fashion.

I followed the woman with my eyes as she ran. She was clocking in at just under two minutes per lap. After five minutes of running, her skin shone with a thin layer of sweat. It made her body look sleek and oiled. I found myself wishing I had some energy left to run. It would be fun to try and keep up with her. By this time Brent was watching her too.

"She's hot," I said. I regretted the words as soon as they left my mouth. It seemed inappropriate to say something like that less than two months after Krista's death. I looked away, embarrassed.

"Do you think about getting married again?" Brent asked.

The question surprised me. The few times that I had tried to imagine myself with someone else, it always ended up being a slightly different version of Krista. Sometimes the person had a different hair or eye color, but in the end it was Krista's face I always saw myself looking at.

"It's crossed my mind once or twice," I said.

"If Bethany died, I don't think I could marry someone else."

"Why not?" I asked.

"She's perfect for me."

I watched the woman complete another lap. Her ponytail bounced with each stride. I tried to picture myself in that woman's arms. Each time, the woman's face would turn into Krista's. I could see Krista's bright blue eyes, small nose, and mouth that would melt into mine when we kissed. Again I tried to imagine myself with the track woman. I couldn't make it work. Krista had been my wife and closest friend. She was the only person I could see myself with.

I took one last hard look at the woman as we headed to Brent's truck. I still found myself in Krista's arms.

On the way back to Brent's house, I leaned my head against the window and watched the sun-drenched streets of Phoenix roll past. My thoughts were on Krista. Her outlook on life had always been so positive. What had changed? I thought back to September and how, almost overnight, she had stopped caring about things she had been passionate about such as work and her poetry. Nothing mattered to her anymore. The energy and joy which was part of her everyday life had vanished.

"I was such a rotten husband the last few months of her life," I said. I hadn't meant to say that out loud. I hadn't been thinking those words, but they came out anyway.

"You had no way of knowing what she was going through," Brent said after several moments of silence.

"I never tried to understand her, Brent. When she started acting weird, I just became upset."

Brent stopped at a light. A black Honda Accord pulled up next to us. A baby girl lay in a rear-facing car seat in the back seat. She looked like she was crying. The woman who was driving picked up a doll from the floor and handed it to the baby girl. The baby shook the doll and smiled. The light turned green and Brent accelerated, leaving the black Honda behind.

"There are times I haven't been the best husband either," Brent said.

"You ever hit Bethany?" I asked

Brent shook his head. "No, I've never touched her."

"I shook Krista once," I said. "Violently. I might as well have hit her."

I looked back out the window. There was no way I could look someone in the eye and admit what I had done.

"A few weeks before she died," I said, "I reached the breaking point. Krista was brushing off appointments with friends. She kept skipping her prenatal checkups. Then one day she unexpectedly quit her job as a court clerk."

I remembered calling Krista during my lunch break, only to be told by one of her coworkers that she had quit her job that morning without giving notice. Stunned, I called her at home. Krista had refused to tell me anything other than she couldn't put on a happy face for people at work anymore. Neither of us expected Krista to work after the baby was born, but we had been planning on her working long enough so we could use her health insurance and save a little money for some baby-related expenses. But it wasn't the money or loss of benefits that bothered me. It was Krista's continued irresponsibility. She didn't care about anyone—even herself. Most days she sat around in her pajamas and did nothing.

Traffic slowed in Brent's lane and the Honda drove past. I tried to get a look at the baby girl and see if she had the doll, but the car passed too quickly.

"The next day Krista kept muttering under her breath about living in a dark and unjust world. I ignored her, hoping her mood would lighten as it usually did. But this time it went on all day. I should have ignored it, but every time she walked past, I felt anger building inside me. At first I was able to keep it bottled up. Finally, I had enough. I remember thinking I didn't want Krista raising our baby. I was worried she wouldn't be able to care for it. I grabbed her by the shoulders and shook her as hard as I could."

The moment was vivid in my mind. I could see Krista's limp body in my hands, her head flailing back and forth as I shook her. My voice was loud, demanding to know what was wrong with her and why she was behaving so oddly. When it was over, her eyes stared right at me in shock, as if she couldn't believe what I had just done. I let her go and she slumped to her knees.

Brent slowed for another light and stopped right next to the black Honda. The baby in the back seat clutched her doll tightly to her chest. The woman driving the car looked at her watch and tapped the steering wheel impatiently.

"After I shook her," I continued, "I took a few steps back in disbelief at what I had just done. I opened my mouth to apologize, but nothing came out. We just stared at each other for what seemed like several minutes. Finally, Krista stood up and walked to our bedroom and locked the door."

I had knocked on the door and pleaded with her to forgive me to no avail. Krista had remained locked in our room for hours. When she finally came out, she didn't say anything to me the rest of the evening.

I felt warm. I rolled down the window and let the cool air fill the cab.

"It must have been frustrating living with someone whose behavior changed from day to day," Brent said.

"I should never have shook Krista," I said. "I should have been in control."

The woman in the black Honda picked up her cell phone. Hearing her mother's voice, the baby girl tried to find her. Unable to see her from the rear-facing car seat, she twisted her head, trying to catch a glimpse of her mother. The light turned green, but this time the Honda pulled ahead of the truck. At the next intersection the car slowed and turned right.

"You want to know what hell is, Brent? It's not a place with fire and a bunch of red devils with pointy tails and pitchforks. Hell is being separated from the love of your life and looking back on your own actions and wishing you had done things differently."

"I've made mistakes with Bethany," Brent said.

"You can still ask Bethany for forgiveness," I said. "You can try to be a better husband. I can't tell Krista I'm sorry about the time I shook her. I can't apologize for not being more understanding or patient when she was off her rocker. You're going to wake up tomorrow, and Bethany is going to be lying in your arms. You're so incredibly lucky, Brent. You can still be a better husband. I would do anything to be in your shoes right now."

My last words put an end to the conversation. I could tell by the way Brent pursed his lips that he was frustrated. I felt bad. Brent had only been trying to comfort me, and I had pushed him away, telling him that he didn't get it. At that moment I wanted someone I could relate to. Someone who could tell me that what I was going through, what I was feeling, and how I was reacting was normal. The problem was, I doubted that there was anyone out there who could help.

We drove in silence until Brent pulled into the parking lot of the townhomes.

"I'm sorry," I said. "I didn't mean to unload on you like that. You invited me down to get away from everything, and I end up spilling my guts and yelling at you. You've given up a weekend with your wife to spend some time with me. I really appreciate that."

"There's no need to apologize," Brent said. "I have no idea how you're holding everything together as well as you are. If talking about it helps, then talk all you want." He put the truck in park and turned off the engine. "Do you still feel like having lunch with Jennifer?"

Lunch with Jennifer. I had forgotten about that. Jennifer was a mutual friend who lived in Mesa. We had talked a handful of times since Krista's death. When she learned I was coming to Phoenix for a few days, she had suggested that the three of us do lunch one day.

Brent and I cleaned up and then drove across town to pick up Jennifer. She was taller and more pear-shaped than I remembered. Her curly blonde hair hung down to her shoulders, and her light blue eyes radiated her happiness. She had a sharp nose and a big smile.

"Abel," she said in her perky voice. "Come in!" She pulled me into a friendly embrace and said, "It's so nice to see you after all these years."

I pulled away. I was happy to see Jennifer, but I wasn't in a hugging mood. Jennifer didn't seem to notice and turned her attention to Brent, whom she hugged as well.

Brent had suggested lunch at Bank One Ballpark—home of the Arizona Diamondbacks. There was a restaurant in the ballpark that overlooked left field. He said it was worth going to, if not for the food, at least for the view of the field.

Jennifer was chatty, something else I had forgotten about her. By the time we arrived at the restaurant, she had told us about finishing college two years ago with a degree in history and economics. She'd returned to Phoenix, her hometown, and after working for awhile in the real world, she found herself unhappy with where her life was going. She had moved back in with her parents and returned to school to earn her teaching certificate. By September she hoped to be employed as a high school economics and history teacher.

We were seated near the window that overlooked left field. The roof of the ballpark was retracted, and sunlight filled the stadium. The waters of a swimming pool glistened behind the wall of right-center field. I looked over the empty sea of green seats, wishing it was summer and that there was a game we could attend.

As we ate, I noticed how Jennifer's blonde hair brushed her shoulders every time she moved her head. I found it subtly attractive. As we talked, I sometimes thought I was looking at a taller, rounder version of Krista.

We talked baseball and the potential for our teams this year. It turned out that Jennifer was a rabid Cubs fan. She rooted as passionately for the Cubs as I did the Tigers. Brent, a Diamondback fan, was the most optimistic about his team's chances this year, seeing how they had just won the World Series in October. He was looking forward to the upcoming season.

"How long has it been since the Tigers have had a winning season?" Brent said. "Twenty years?"

"Eight," I said. "It's been eight years."

"Yeah, but I bet it seems like twenty," Jennifer said and gave my shoulder a playful shove.

The playful touch of her hand on my shoulder felt surprisingly comforting. I found myself wishing she'd do it again.

"This could be their year," I said, even though I wasn't optimistic things would be any different for the Tigers this year or anytime in the near future.

"Yeah, and maybe Babe Ruth will rise from the dead," Brent said.

Jennifer laughed. "Don't be so hard on him, Brent. The Tigers have that all-star on their team. What's his name?" She looked at me expectantly for the answer.

"What all-star?" I said.

"Exactly," Jennifer said. Her cackling laugh echoed through the restaurant.

Talking baseball put me in a good mood. I took a bite of my hamburger. It was thick and juicy. I looked over the ballpark and imagined a game being played on the field, the seats filled with fans.

"You go to many Diamondback games?" I asked Brent.

"Two or three a year, if I'm lucky."

"That must be nice."

"You're always welcome to come down for a game," Brent said. "I'd love to go to one with a serious fan."

"Doesn't Bethany go with you?"

Brent shook is head and looked away. It seemed like that was something he wished he could share with her.

I steered the topic back to the Tigers. "Too bad the Tigers play in the American League," I said. "If they didn't, I'd come down for sure."

"Interleague play will bring them here one day," Brent said.

"Well, if the Tigers ever have a game in Arizona, I'll buy some tickets and take you and Jennifer," I said.

At some point during the meal I remember looking over the ball park and realizing for the first time in months that I was happy and relaxed. Phoenix was a city without memories, and I found myself wishing I could start a new life in this sprawling desert town. If it wasn't for the fact I had just bought a house in Ogden, I might have done just that.

# CHAPTER
## Six

In a college communications class, I had read about couples who spent most of their lives together. After one died, it was common for the other to pass on soon after, even if he or she was in good health. At the time I couldn't comprehend how someone could lose their will to live after their spouse was gone. But I began, at least partially, to understand how they felt. Krista had been a significant part of my life for seven years—four as my girlfriend and nearly three as my wife. My life had become completely entwined with hers. Now that she was gone, I didn't feel complete. I had to force myself to live.

Things I had done willingly before Krista died, like going to work, became a chore. Though my job hadn't changed, without the prospect of supporting a family, work was boring. There was no incentive for me to put extra effort into my projects. I did just enough to get by. I didn't care if there were any raises or bonuses in my future. I resisted the urge to walk into my supervisor's office and quit only because I knew being unemployed and doing nothing would ultimately be worse.

The battle began every morning at five. I'd stare at the ceiling and say, "Abel, get out of bed." This was something I had to say a lot, as if hearing a voice, even my own, helped give me the push to face another day. Once I convinced myself I could do it, I went running.

Running in Ogden was a solitary activity. I never saw other joggers. Ogden was a blue-collar town, and my course weaved through blue-collar neighborhoods. Most of the people up at this hour were warming their cars and scraping frost from their windshields before heading to work.

I came to relish the solitude. My four-mile runs were the only time I let my thoughts focus solely on Krista and Hope. Pushing my body to its limits helped dull the sorrow that always seemed just about to burst to the surface. And having a set time to channel my thoughts on my dead wife and daughter allowed me to better concentrate on other things throughout the rest of the day. I made it a point to run every morning, no matter what the weather was. It gave me the extra energy I needed to make it through another day.

A late January snowstorm dumped six inches of heavy, wet snow on northern Utah, making the drive home from work slow and tedious. As tired as I was from work and the commute, I knew I had to shovel the sidewalk and driveway so it wouldn't become an icy mess.

I was halfway through when my mom drove down the street, headed in the direction of home. She honked as she passed and then did a U-turn and parked in front of my house. I knew why she stopped. She was returning from her latest session with a grief counselor and was coming to tell me about it. I was surprised when she first mentioned she was seeing one because, until that point, I thought she had been handling Krista's death rather well. For the last month, after each visit, she would tell me about what they had discussed and then try to convince me to see the counselor too.

I kept shoveling as she got out of the car. To avoid the ice, I needed to have the driveway cleared before the sun set.

"I had such a good session today," she said, her voice bubbling.

"I'm glad," I said. I scraped a long section of the driveway with the shovel and threw the snow onto a pile in the yard. My hands were cold, and I wished I had worn gloves.

My mom told me about some of the insight the counselor had provided. "You should take some time off work and talk to him," Mom said, her voice losing some of its ebullience and taking on her motherly tone.

I wanted to say, "I'm doing fine without him." Instead I said, "Between work and trying to finish the house, I don't have time." Working on the house had become a therapy of sorts. Being occupied with painting, hanging drywall, and installing floorboards when I came home from work prevented me from dwelling on my sorrows. Sometimes I felt if I started crying, I wouldn't be able to stop.

But Mom kept insisting. "I've told him about you," she said. "He'd really like to talk with you."

"I'm sure he would," I said. "Every hour he spends with me is another seventy-five dollars for him."

My mom was quiet for a few moments. I knew my comment had upset her. I kept my eyes on the snow.

"I wish you'd stop being so cynical," she finally said. "He just wants to help."

"I don't doubt his intentions, Mom."

"Then why won't you see him?"

I stopped shoveling and looked my mom directly in the eye. "What is he going to tell me? That Krista's suicide isn't my fault? That I need to accept my loss and move on? I know all this, Mom. Besides, I think I'm doing fine without him." I was tired of everyone telling me what was or wasn't good for me or what they knew I needed. How could anyone relate to what I had gone through?

"I just think talking with someone would be good for you."

"Listen," I said, starting to feel annoyed. "I'm not going to tell a complete stranger about the most horrible experience of my life. Dwelling on something that neither you nor I can change isn't going to make it any better." I said the last part rather sternly. I tapped the shovel on the driveway three times. Clumps of snow fell to the concrete.

"Okay," my mom said. "I just want you to know that there are people that are willing to listen."

She walked back to the car and drove home. I cupped my hands together and breathed on them to warm them before finishing the driveway.

I wanted someone to talk with, but a counselor wasn't that person. I needed someone who had lost a pregnant wife to suicide, or at the very least, a young widower. I needed someone who could really understand what I was going through, not the trained, sterile words of a professional. Since finding a young widower wasn't going to happen, I was determined to tough it out alone, one day at a time.

For a month I debated whether or not to continue wearing my wedding ring. It had become a sad reminder of what was missing from my life. Even so, the thought of removing the ring from my finger filled me with guilt. It seemed like an act of infidelity—rejecting the vows Krista and I exchanged on a cold winter morning and disavowing the years we had spent together as husband and wife.

The tipping point came when I was looking at linoleum samples for the kitchen floor. I had narrowed my choices to two: a blue-gray pattern designed to resemble tile and one the color of desert sand. As I stood deciding which one I wanted, the salesman asked if I wanted to take the two samples home and have my wife look at them.

I picked up the blue-gray sample and ran my fingers over it, feeling its texture. "I'm not married," I said.

"You're wearing a wedding ring," the salesman said.

The linoleum sample now felt like dead weight in my hands. I set it down.

"My wife passed away two months ago," I said without looking at the salesman. I couldn't think of another way to say it. My words were followed by an uncomfortable silence. I never realized the complications of wearing a wedding ring while being a widower.

I changed the subject and told the salesman I'd take the two samples home so I could make my decision. I could tell he felt bad about his comment, and I told him not to worry. "I create awkward situations wherever I go," I said as I walked out the door.

That evening I removed the wedding ring from my finger as I worked on the house just to see what it would feel like. The world didn't come to an end. Aside from my left hand feeling a little lighter, nothing seemed different. As the night wore on, however, I began to feel that part of me was missing. I fought the temptation to put the ring back on and managed to go to bed and fall asleep without it. The next morning, my alarm didn't go off, and in my rush to head to work, I forgot about the ring. It wasn't until I was well into my commute that I realized I had forgotten to put it back on. The rest of the day was a loss. I couldn't concentrate on work. The missing ring was too much of a distraction. I needed it back on my hand. It was a relief to go home and put it back on. Something needed to be done, but I didn't want any more awkward moments from wearing it.

The solution to my dilemma came that weekend. I passed a jewelry store in the mall and out of the corner of my eye noticed some gold chains. The idea came to me that I could put my wedding ring on a chain around my neck. I found one I liked and put my wedding ring on it. The chain was long enough that the wedding ring rested on the center of my chest.

On the drive home I kept tracing the ring with my finger. It would take some time to get used to having the ring there instead of on my hand, but it was something I thought I could adjust to. Besides, it felt good to have the ring close to my heart.

The major repair projects on the house were completed the first week of February. It was a relief to have it done, not only because the work had left me drained both mentally and physically but also because I was tired of living at my parents' house. Staying with my family had become a tedious affair. I was used to having more space and freedom. And there was a continual sadness at their home that permeated everything. My new house would give me the quiet solitude I so desperately sought.

I moved in the following Saturday. With the exception of the couch and bed, I hauled what remained of the life Krista and I had shared together myself. There wasn't much to move. Krista and I had never had much time or money to accumulate many things, and most of Krista's possessions had been given away to family members, close friends, and thrift stores in the weeks after her death. The only belongings of Krista's I kept were photographs from our life together, her journals, poetry, books, and a few small personal items.

By the end of the day, the entire house was unpacked, except for the room I planned to turn into an office. I wandered in there and stared at the few boxes of Krista's things that were piled in the middle of the floor. *Should I dig into this tonight?* I wondered. My shoulders ached with the exhaustion of moving and unpacking. I knew, too, those boxes represented more burden than I wanted to go through that day. They were filled with memories that could weigh as much as the whole world. I sighed and walked out of the room. The boxes would sit untouched for weeks.

With the major work on the house completed, my evenings became free. It was the time alone each night I found the most difficult. The loneliness of the house was oftentimes unbearable, the silence unnerving. Every quiet minute alone reinforced the emptiness that consumed my life. To cope, I often turned on the radio in a far room to provide enough background noise so it felt like there was someone else in the house. I also started watching three to four hours of television every night. After a few weeks, however, I found this too isolating. I missed interacting with other people. I wanted to feel like I was still part of the human family.

To fight the seclusion, I joined a church basketball league that played on Tuesday nights. Thursday evenings I had dinner with James and Grace—two good friends Krista and I had met at college. Dinner with them quickly became the highlight of my week. Most of the meals I cooked at home, when I bothered to make something, were simple— canned soup or chili, eggs and toast, or tuna fish sandwiches. I usually ate them over the sink because eating at the kitchen table alone was another reminder of who was missing from my life. Conversely, I loved talking with my two friends over a good meal. Basketball games and dinner became small events that helped me through each week.

Friday nights I forced myself out of the house no matter how tired I was. Most of the time this meant going to a movie—one of the few activities I didn't mind doing alone. Movies were a great way to lose myself in the lives of the characters on the screen. For two hours I could escape the dark reality of my own life and experience the trials and joys of another person. I tried to fill the remaining evenings with other activities: I went grocery shopping, cleaned the house, or finished the remaining small projects on the house. It wasn't enough. There were still broad swaths of time when I was alone with nothing but memories for company.

But it was weekend mornings that were the most difficult. There was no hurry to get out of bed and run, no work to contend with. No alarm clock to wake me. In those first moments of weekend consciousness, I reached to Krista's side of the bed, searching between the sheets for her warm, familiar body. When the fog of sleep finally drifted from my eyes, it took only a moment for that longing to be replaced with a deep sadness. I missed awaking to Krista's kisses on my neck, holding her close, and nuzzling my face into her hair and breathing in her presence.

To fight the longing and loneliness that accompanied these mornings, I began running six or seven miles. I loved the longer weekend runs more than my regular weekday jogs since the sun was up and the temperatures were warmer. And the streets were quiet as they only can be on Saturday mornings. By the time I finished those longer runs, the sadness and yearning had been flushed out of my system.

One day after an invigorating seven-mile run, I found myself remembering my recent trip to Phoenix. I was thinking about Jennifer and the way her hair would brush against her shoulders or the playful shove she gave me during our lunch at the ballpark. Since my return to Utah, thoughts of her had crossed my mind occasionally, and I considered calling her just to see how things were going. I hadn't called even though she had given me her phone number and said we should keep in touch.

That morning, however, as I lay on the living room floor, letting my body recover from the run, I picked up the phone and dialed her number. Jennifer seemed surprised by the call, but we talked for over an hour. She told me about the long, frustrating process of applying for jobs at local high schools and how excited she was to finally enter the world of teaching. Teaching was something, she said, she had wanted to do ever since she was young.

I don't remember saying much during that call. Mostly I listened to Jennifer talk about her life. I do remember hanging up the phone and feeling elated that I just had a real conversation with someone— one where the subject of Krista didn't threaten to arise. The phone call made me feel that I could be myself with Jennifer.

The next weekend I called her again. This time it was after Sunday services. We talked for over an hour. Jennifer gave me the latest information on obtaining her teaching certificate and her night out with her girlfriends on Saturday. I told her about the then undefeated season of my church basketball team and minor work I was doing on the house. That second call established the pattern of the two of us talking for an hour or two each weekend. It quickly became the part of my week I looked forward to the most. I anticipated those calls because I always hung up feeling happy that I had spoken with her.

One Sunday our conversation became more serious. Instead of her usual, cheerful self, Jennifer sounded downtrodden and depressed.

"Everything all right?" I asked.

"One of my good friends got engaged yesterday," Jennifer said. There was an envious quality to her voice.

"Aren't you happy for her?" I asked and then cringed, realizing this probably wasn't the right thing to say.

"Of course I'm happy for her, it's just that . . ." Jennifer's voice trailed off into silence. I listened to her soft breathing on the other end of the phone, wishing I could be there to comfort her. "I turn thirty in July. I'm not anywhere close to getting married or even dating for that matter. Do you know the last time I went out on a date? It was over a year ago."

"What about lunch at the ballpark with Brent and me?" I was trying to lighten her spirit a little, hoping she recalled that afternoon as fondly as I.

"I take it back. My only date in the last year was with a married man and a recent widower."

"At least one of us was single," I said and chuckled. Jennifer didn't seem to appreciate the remark.

"Don't you understand, Abel?" she said. "Now that she's engaged, I don't have any single friends. It's just me. Why don't I buy a house full of cats and accept spinsterhood right now?"

"You're only twenty-nine," I said.

"If I could just fall in love, I'd be so much happier."

Her remark floored me. "Love has its own set of challenges," I said. "And it doesn't guarantee happiness." I thought back to some of the struggles Krista and I had in our marriage. Though we always seemed to work through the problems that arose, there were times I remember feeling sad and depressed.

"I know the challenges that come with love," Jennifer said. "I was engaged once." She said the word *engaged* the way someone would say the word *murderer*.

"Look, Jennifer, I didn't mean—"

"Don't worry about it, Abel. You didn't know."

I debated whether to cut my losses and end the conversation early.

"His name was Steve," Jennifer said. "I thought he was perfect." The way she said it made me think this was a recent event.

"I didn't know you were engaged," I said. "When did this happen?"

"It all ended last year," Jennifer said. "I was to be married last April."

I returned home from work one cold February evening feeling sick. I had a pounding headache and an upset stomach. Usually quite healthy, I thought that the stress of the last several months was finally catching up to me. I skipped dinner and went straight to bed, hoping I'd feel better in the morning.

I awoke suddenly several hours later. In the moonlight I could see Krista's college graduation picture hanging on the wall. I was a sound sleeper and rarely woke up during the night without cause. There must have been something—a noise perhaps—that awoke me. The alarm clock read 12:43. I listened intently for any kind of noise. Nothing.

I was about to lie back down when the doorbell rang. In the dark I picked up my sweatshirt and jeans off the floor and put them on as I made my way to the front door. As I groped the walls of the dark hall, the thought came to me that perhaps my friend Nash was looking for a place to spend the night. His marriage to his wife, Heather, had been going through a rough patch, and he had stopped over on occasion when things were going bad, though he had never stopped by this late.

I looked through the living room window. There was no one on the porch. By the pale orange light of a nearby streetlight, I could just make out a small, unfamiliar car parked in front of my house. I waited a few moments, trying to see if anyone was lurking nearby. Then I turned on the porch light.

Halfway between the house and the unfamiliar car, I saw someone walking in the direction of the car. The person turned as the light came on, and then walked back to the front door. The person was a girl who didn't look a day past eighteen. She was dressed in jeans and a denim jacket. The jacket looked old and threadbare. As she approached, she brushed her long, brown hair away from her face, revealing shallow green eyes. When she went to knock on the door, I noticed her hand was shaking. I couldn't tell if it was from cold or fear. Her knock was soft and timid.

"Who's there?" I said.

The girl's voice sounded tired and scared. "My car . . . it broke down in front of your house. I need to use a phone."

I opened the door. Cold air washed over my bare feet.

"Why don't you come in while I get my cell phone?" I said.

The girl shook her head. She looked at the car and back at me. Her eyes pleaded with me to hurry.

As I headed back to my bedroom for the phone, I left the front door open, hoping that the girl would come out of the cold. When I returned, she was still standing on the porch, looking back at the car. I handed her my cell phone. The girl dialed a number and then turned to make her phone call.

I closed the door halfway, in part to give the girl some privacy but also to slow the flow of cold air that was filling the house. I sat on the couch and watched through the window as the girl paced back and forth while she talked. "Please come and get me," she said. "Please." She seemed frustrated by whoever she was talking to and made the request several times. As her frustration grew, her pacing slowed. Finally she stopped in front of the living room window, her back toward me. After another round of pleading, she turned, and I could see a tear streaming down her face. Our eyes met for a split second. Then she wiped her cheek and turned her face from me.

There was a click from the furnace in the basement, and a moment later the heat kicked on. I made a mental note to myself to buy a storm door. Finally the girl finished her call. She looked at the ground as she handed me the phone.

"Thanks," she said.

"Do you want to come in?" I said. "It's warmer here. You can wait inside until your ride arrives."

The girl shook her head. "My two kids are in the car. I want to keep an eye on them."

She headed back to the car, looking at the ground as she walked. I didn't like the idea of this girl sitting in the car alone with her two kids in the cold. Waiting with her was the least I could do. I retrieved a flashlight and a pair of shoes from the closet and headed outside.

It took only seconds for the cold to penetrate my jeans and sweatshirt. The temperature had to be close to zero—cold enough to quickly chill even those with a thick coat. I hadn't bothered to put on socks, and the frosty air ate through my shoes. I hoped that the girl's ride would arrive soon.

When the girl noticed me walking toward the car, she tried to start it. Each time the engine sputtered and died. I tried to imagine what must have been going through her mind. Was I a rapist? A murderer? A child molester? Each step I took toward her direction strengthened her resolve to start the car.

I rapped softly on her window. She rolled it down an inch—just enough space for our words to pass through.

"I'm not going to hurt you," I said.

The girl didn't say anything. Instead she just stared at me. The steam from her breath began to fog the window.

"Look," I said. "Your car isn't pulled off to the side of the road all the way. Why don't you put the car in neutral and I'll push it to the curb?"

The girl nodded and then fumbled with the gearshift. I walked to the back of the car and started to push. In the dark I couldn't tell what model the car was, but its general shape reminded me of a Rabbit or Yugo. Where my hands were pressing against the car's body, I felt pock marks of rust. The car was light, in the cheaply made sense, and I pushed it to the side of the street quickly.

When it was parked safely at the curb, I shined the flashlight around the car. The inside door panels were missing from the back doors. Fast food wrappers, dirty clothes, and a yellowed newspaper littered the floor. An infant, wrapped in a blanket, slept in a worn out car seat. Another child, a boy who looked about two, was sitting in a second car seat on the passenger side. His eyes were big and alert. Both children looked like they were in need of a bath.

"You want to take your kids inside while you wait?" I asked. I knew what her answer would be but asked anyway. Part of me was hoping she'd agree. I wanted this girl and her children to come inside and let me make things better for them. Helping her would help assuage some of the guilt I still felt about Krista. I hadn't been able to help Krista when she needed it, but I could help this girl and her children.

"We'll be okay. Someone should be here soon," the girl said.

"Do you know what's wrong with your car?" I wasn't mechanically inclined but thought there might be an outside chance I could at least take a peek under the hood.

"I'm out of gas."

*That's all?* I thought. *You're out of gas? Why didn't you say something?*

I told the girl that I had some extra gas in the garage. It took only a moment to locate the red five-gallon gas can that was used for the lawnmower. From its weight, it seemed to be half full. I returned to the car. Seeing the gas can, the girl got out and opened the gas cap. We stood in the cold listening to the sound of the gas drain into the fuel tank.

"How long until your ride comes?" I asked.

"Soon," she said. "My grandmother only lives a couple of miles from here."

The gas can gurgled as the final drops emptied into the car.

"Try to start it," I said.

The girl nodded and put her key in the ignition. After a few attempts to start it, the engine sputtered to life. She turned the heat on high and moved the vents so they were blowing toward her children. She checked each child to make sure they were wrapped tightly in their blankets, and after she seemed satisfied they were warm, she stepped out of the car.

"Thanks," she said.

"There was about two gallons in that can. Is that going to be enough to make it home?" I was ready to follow her to the nearest gas station and fill her tank if she had a long way to go.

"I only live about a mile away. I thought I had enough gas to make it home. I was wrong," the girl said.

I wondered if her home was as bad as the car. I wanted to invite them all into my house and feed them and give them all warm clothes. The girl's body was still shaking. I hoped it was only from the cold.

"Why don't you sit in the car?" I said. "It's warmer there."

The girl got back in the car. She rolled her window down a little more and then adjusted one of the vents so some heat blew directly on her.

"I knew I was low on gas when I picked up my kids from the sitter," she said. "I passed a couple of gas stations on my way home. I should have stopped. I'm sorry I had to wake you."

"Don't worry about it," I said, thinking I wanted to give so much more. She seemed so frail, and I worried that her kids were hungry.

"I don't have much money. I don't know when I'll be able to pay you back."

"You don't have to pay me back," I said. "Just take those kids home and put them to bed."

The girl smiled and looked straight ahead. I sensed that she didn't know what to say. It was as if she was not used to receiving things without giving up something in return.

A moment later a late model Cadillac drove down the road, made a U-turn, and parked behind the girl's car. The girl got out of the car and hurried over to the driver's side window. The window rolled down slowly.

The face of the driver was hidden in the shadows. All I could see was the occasional puffs of gray cigarette smoke that floated into the night sky.

The girl said, "Yes, I'm all right." I heard an old, scratchy voice come from the darkened interior of the car, though I couldn't understand what it said. The girl said, "I told you, I'm all right." More words were exchanged. Finally, the window rolled up, and the girl returned to her car.

"Thanks again," she said. She rolled up the window and waved good-bye as she started up the road. The driver of the Cadillac waited a moment before following. I caught a glimpse of the driver as the car passed. It was an older woman. She was bundled up in a coat with a high collar that reached her chin. On the hand atop the steering wheel, I caught the orange glow of her cigarette between her fingers. I watched the taillights of the two cars until they stopped at the corner and turned right.

I hurried back inside. I could feel my headache and nausea growing worse. The time spent in the cold had not been good for me. As I tried to fall back to sleep, my thoughts kept returning to the girl and her two children. I wished I had done more to help or insisted that she bring her kids inside. I felt I was unable to help those who needed it most.

As I lay in bed, the unsettled feeling in my stomach grew. Five minutes later I was in the bathroom, emptying the contents of my stomach in the toilet. After several minutes, I finally felt my stomach was settled enough to let me sleep. I grabbed a cleaning bucket from under the kitchen sink and placed it on the floor next to the bed should I be unable to make it to the bathroom in time. I found myself wishing Krista was here. She had always been a good nurse when I was sick. She never hesitated to bring me books to read, hot bowls of soup, tall glasses of orange juice, or a cold wash cloth to wipe my face.

I tossed and turned but was unable to sleep. Finally I grabbed the cleaning bucket and went to look for something to read. My bookshelves were in the same room as the boxes of Krista's things. As I scanned the shelves, my eyes kept darting back to the boxes, which were still stacked in the middle of the floor. Unable to find anything to read, I opened the flaps of the top box. Inside was a stack of three ring binders—Krista's journals. Krista had always been a regular journal keeper, and her accounts of our life together filled several notebooks. I thought about what I was doing and closed the box. I went to the living room where I tried to interest myself in late-night info-mercials. Between ads for knives, juicers, and cleaning solutions, my thoughts kept drifting back to the journals. Finally I convinced myself it wouldn't hurt to peek inside.

"Just one," I said to myself. "Just read one entry and put it back."

I returned to the room and opened the box. Sitting in a lotus posi-tion, I opened one of the notebooks to a random page and started to read. The entry was dated January 11, 1999. It was the second week of winter semester at school and our third week of marriage. We had been running late that morning, and as we drove to school, we became ensnarled in a traffic jam. When it became apparent we weren't going to make it to class on time, I lost my temper and told Krista it was her fault because she had taken so long to put her makeup on that morning. My words elicited an angry response in return. It was our first fight as a married couple. It wasn't until that afternoon we had apologized and made up.

Krista perfectly described the day, the mood, and my words. Read-ing the entry was like having Krista in the same room, retelling the experience. I turned the page and read her next entry. Smiling, I read another and another. There were tired entries from working late nights as a desk clerk at a local hotel, exasperated entries when days just didn't go as planned, and happy entries when everything seemed to go her way. There were detailed accounts of trips we took to Wyoming, Denver, Las Vegas, and Zion's National Park. Reading her journal was a bittersweet experience. Each entry brought with it a cascade of memories. I found myself engrossed in what I read, reliving our life together, one day at a time. Then I came across an entry that made everything stop.

> May 30, 2001
>
> Today is a day that is written in the stars. I am preg-nant, or in other words, I am going to have a baby. I came home from work today and noticed that my period was late. I thought, I'll just run over to Wangsgard's and pick out a pregnancy test. I did. I took it. I told Abel. I had always dreamed of how I would tell him and I wish I would have waited, but I was so overwhelmed with it that I just didn't wait. He is happy, but I think he would have been happier if I surprised him. Not that it wasn't a surprise, but it is such a big event to just spring on someone in the bathroom. I should have been more patient.

Which is a very funny thing to be thinking when I'm very overwhelmed and happy and peaceful. I think the most wonderful thing about being pregnant is knowing that in order to get through this, I will have to rely on the Lord every minute.

I don't know where to begin other than it will be all right. I know that the Lord will make things all right. This is right. It's a child. My child. My little one, who the Lord will send. My little one who I must protect and teach. My little one who must learn why he or she is here. My little one who will have to be taught everything. It hasn't sunk in. It doesn't seem real. Abel is happy. I am happy too.

To be honest, I am feeling rather peaceful right now. I love the Lord. I love Abel. I pray that great joy will ensue.

I stared at the page, wishing Krista was right there, but for a different reason. I didn't miss her anymore. I hated her. I threw the journal against the wall. Several pages broke free of their binding and floated to the floor like white feathers.

"You did a great job of protecting our baby," I said. I curled up in the fetal position and cried, holding my gut as if my insides might all slide out. The crying didn't help my upset stomach, and a minute later I was back in the bathroom, throwing up.

When it was over, I lay on the bathroom floor, waiting to see if anything else was going to come up. My head throbbed, but it wasn't from being sick. It hurt from being sad and angry. I was tired of feeling this way, tired of snapping at my family and friends. I needed to learn how to enjoy life again despite the tragedy. Some friends and family were slowly moving on with their lives, and I sensed I needed to do the same. I had done a reasonable job to this point, but the time was fast approaching when I needed to start living again. What I had been doing was just hanging on. I needed to have a reason to wake up every morning. I needed to feel alive. The problem was I had no clue how to go about that.

When my stomach felt reasonably settled, I returned to the room and reassembled the scattered pages of Krista's journal. I didn't bother to read other entries or try to put the loose pages in order. I placed the journal back in the box with the intention of never reading it again. There were some things that would always be too painful to relive.

# CHAPTER
## *Seven*

The weather warmed in March, and it seemed everywhere I went, I saw either happy couples walking hand-in-hand or single women, alone and wishing for someone to date. Or so I thought. Maybe it was hope. When I was shopping for groceries, for example, my eyes would roam from one woman to another, and I imagined myself asking out the ones I found attractive. They always said yes, of course, and from there I would conjure up a whole life for me and whoever had caught my eye. From our first date, to falling in love, marrying, and living happily ever after, I planned out my life with each woman at a glance.

The guilt that followed was always thick and heavy. After an afternoon of this, I'd return home feeling like I had cheated on Krista. Once one met the love of his life, he was supposed to be faithful to that person forever. Checking out other women four months after Krista's death seemed wrong. Though I wasn't naive enough to think I would never date again, it was something I thought would happen years, not months, in the future.

But I missed being married. There was something about waking up next to Krista and going through the motions of another day with her that gave life extra richness and meaning. Without anyone to share both the exciting and mundane moments with, life was boring and empty. I longed for the closeness and companionship that had made me happy for many years. Though I desired something serious and beautiful, I would have been happy with one night of dinner and a couple of hours of conversation with an attractive woman.

It had been seven years since I dated someone other than Krista, and the thought of asking another woman out, while not as repulsive as it had been a month before, was still very intimidating. I began browsing online singles sites when I thought no one was looking—during the lunch hour when most of my coworkers were out of the office or when I was at home alone at night. At the time, online single sites were relatively new and hadn't achieved mainstream acceptance. I thought of them as places for people who were unable to find dates in the real world and was embarrassed to even look at them. I wanted to talk to family and friends about wanting to date again, but that would be pointless. I knew what they all would think, even if they didn't verbalize it: Dating this soon after Krista's death? Way too fast, Abel.

In the end, I turned to the only person who I thought would be honest about it: Jennifer. During the last month our friendship had blossomed, and we were now talking on the phone twice a week. And our conversations became more than just a recap of our lives. We started to share personal feelings, thoughts, hopes, and desires with each other. So during a pause in one of our conversations, I breeched the subject.

"I'm thinking about dating again," I said.

There was a surprised silence on the other end of the phone. "Just thinking about it?" Jennifer finally said.

"Seriously thinking about it," I said. "Like possibly asking someone out in the next few weeks." I was lying on my bed as we talked, staring at the ceiling and making shapes from the abstract patterns. There was an elephant, a guitar, and the profile of a bald man with his mouth wide open.

"This is something you're ready to do?" Jennifer asked.

"Do I not seem ready?"

"It's not that. I'm just a little surprised that you're taking this step so soon."

I was disappointed. Those were the words I expected to hear from others. I thought Jennifer would at least give a little encouragement.

"I'm not looking for something serious," I said.

"So why do you want to do it?"

I tried to think of a way to word my answer that wouldn't make me sound desperate. Back on the ceiling, my eyes returned to the patterns. I found one the shape of a pine tree and another of a candle with a burning wick. In the end, I couldn't think of anything to say but the truth.

"I miss having that special someone in my life," I said.

"I completely understand," Jennifer said. "I haven't had anyone serious in my life since the engagement. Going out again might be good for you."

"Do you think women our age would go out with a widower?" That was one of by biggest concerns about dating again. I thought that most women would see me as used goods.

"I think you're making it out to be a bigger issue than it is."

I sat up slowly, not sure I had heard her right.

"Would you go out with a man whose wife passed away four months ago?"

There was another long pause. I was about to tell Jennifer she didn't have to answer the question when she finally spoke.

"I've never thought about it before," she said.

"Most people our age haven't."

"I don't think dating a widower would be a big deal for most women. As long as you make them feel loved, I doubt they'd care."

Though Jennifer's words were comforting, I still lacked the courage to turn my words into actions. So for the next few weeks, I stuck to my regular routine of imagining my life with the attractive women I saw and browsing through online single sites.

Then one evening on the drive home from work, I came across a radio talk show that struck a nerve. An automobile accident had clogged the freeway, and my usual hour-long drive home was looking more like two. Bored of hearing the same songs over and over again, I switched to the AM band, hoping to find something interesting to help pass the time. I scanned through a few stations before one show grabbed my attention.

"—several of the children were upset because she remarried so quickly after her husband's death," the host's voice said. "Many of the children were so upset that they refused to attend the wedding. Other family members told her that by marrying so quickly, she wasn't respecting her late husband or his memory."

I moved my hand away from the radio dial and listened. Though I'd tuned in too late to hear the exact details, the show's host continued to talk about someone famous—I never caught the woman's name—

who remarried six months after the death of her first husband. I found myself engrossed in the story and angry at the woman's children for not supporting their mother.

Before the show cut to a commercial, the host gave a number for people to call. I never had the desire to call into a talk radio show before, but this topic was too close to home. I had to at least try. With one hand on the wheel, I dialed the show's number on my cell phone. Busy. I hit redial. Still busy. Cars slowly inched forward. Up ahead I saw the flashing lights from police cars and an ambulance. I continued to redial the number, pausing only as I passed the accident, but I couldn't get through. The show returned from commercial, and the host took calls from listeners. Most callers were sympathetic to the widow's decision to remarry and thought the woman's children were immature in their decision not to attend the wedding. One caller said, "Shouldn't they be glad their mother has found someone that makes her happy?" Another caller told her story about remarrying several years after her husband passed away and what a blessing her second husband was. The show cut to another string of commercials. I worried the host would change the subject when the show resumed. He didn't. He took another call. I dialed the number again. To my surprise, there was a ringing sound. The call screener answered on the second ring.

"Thank you for calling the Mike Reagan show," a deep, heavy voice said. "What would you like to talk with Mike about?"

I must not have thought I'd actually get through to the show because while I was dialing, I hadn't thought about what I wanted to tell the call screener. Passion and my own tenacity were what kept me hitting redial. It would take something articulate to get me on the air.

"I'm a twenty-seven-year-old widower, and I'd like to tell Mike what I think about widows and widowers remarrying." It wasn't my most eloquent moment, but apparently it was enough for the call screener.

He asked for my first name and where I was calling from. "Okay, I'm going to put you on hold. Please turn off your radio," he said.

I did as he instructed, and a moment later the radio show came in through the phone. Mike took a call from a lady from California. Traffic was picking up now. I set the cruise control at seventy and took some deep breaths to relax. I couldn't believe I'd made it this far. Figuring there were several callers ahead of me, I leaned back in my seat and concentrated on the road. Mike thanked the woman for her call and then said, "Okay, let's go to Abel in Utah. Abel, welcome to the Mike Reagan show."

I sat up straight. I couldn't believe my call was taken so quickly. My mind was blank. I swallowed hard and said, "Hi, Mike."

"Hi, Abel. So do you have an opinion about people who remarry soon after the death of their spouse?"

I told Mike my age and how long I had been a widower. "My perspective on this whole situation has changed since my wife died," I said. "Before her death, if I knew someone who was dating or remarrying within a year after the death of their spouse, I would've thought they didn't love him or her and weren't grieving properly. Now that I'm a widower, I can understand the loneliness and desire to have someone in your life again."

"That's interesting that you bring that up," Mike said. "How many of us actually take the time to think about what we would do if our spouse was to suddenly pass on? So tell me Abel, are you currently dating?"

The question took me by surprise.

"No. Not yet," I said.

"Is dating something you're looking to do in the near future?"

"It's something I'm really thinking about right now."

"And if you start dating again and found the right person, do you see yourself remarrying soon?"

"If I felt she was the right person, I could." I regretted saying those words as soon as they left my mouth. Truthfully, I didn't have an answer to that question. I would hope I'd take some time getting to know the person and not rush into such a commitment just because I felt lonely.

"Now, Abel, you said you lost your wife just a few months ago. Is that correct?"

"Yes."

"And you're twenty-seven?"

"Yes."

"How long were you married?"

"Almost three years."

"I'm sorry to hear that happened. How did your wife die?"

For a brief moment everything stopped. My mind flashed back to Krista's death. I heard the blood gushing from the hole in the back of her head and saw the blue smoke curling from the barrel of the handgun.

"An accident," I lied. "She was killed in an accident."

Long after I hung up the phone, I replayed my last words to Mike over and over in my mind. I still felt a lot of embarrassment and shame about Krista's suicide. I had lied to Mike because I worried he might ask further questions. This wasn't a good sign, especially when I was thinking about dating again. At some point Krista's death was going to come up, and I would have to tell my date what happened. I needed to reach some sort of comfort level about the subject. And for the next three weeks, I dropped the idea of dating altogether and didn't put much thought into actually asking anyone out until I met April.

I met her at the opening night banquet for the National Undergraduate Literature Conference. I had participated in the conference several times as a student and had come back this year because one of my favorite authors, Ethan Canin, was the main author, and my friend James was presenting one of his short stories. The night of the dinner James and I had found seats at one of the tables near the podium. A few minutes before dinner began, the banquet room was packed, and every seat at our table was filled except for the one directly to my left.

Someone tapped me on the shoulder. I looked up to the face of a college-aged student with long tan arms and sun-bleached blonde hair. Her eyes were the color of the sky just before dusk.

"I was wondering if the seat next to you was taken," she said. Her voice had a soft and gentle quality to it. Her tone could have put anyone at ease with just a few words. It sent my head spinning. In a few seconds, I imagined our lives together. We lived happily ever after.

"Have a seat," I said and motioned to the chair. She sat down and looked nervously around the table. She was wearing a dress with large pink flowers. The dress clung to her body in all the right places. Her face and neck had the same dark tan as her arms. There was something about her that sent jolts of excitement through my body. I'd sized up a lot of women over the last month but never had any of them had this effect on me.

She looked at me and smiled. "So are you reading at the conference?"

I shook my head. "I'm here supporting some friends and to listen to Ethan Canin," I said.

"Oh," she said. There was a tinge of disappointment in her voice. "I was hoping to find someone else who was presenting. I've never been to one of these things before, and I'm a little nervous about reading in front of others."

I found myself wishing I was part of the conference. I tried to swing the conversation back to my favor.

"When I presented, I always pretended that I was reading the story with my best friend, not a group of strangers," I said. It was something Krista had taught me, and it had worked well anytime I had to speak in public.

"That's a good idea. Still, it's a little nerve-wracking reading in a different language," she said. "What if I pronounce something wrong?"

"What are you reading?"

"A story I wrote in Spanish."

I was impressed. "You must know Spanish pretty good if you're able to write short stories in it," I said. "Where'd you pick it up?"

"Peru."

"I'm Abel," I said, extending my hand.

"I'm April," she said smiling.

Before I could say anything else, the dinner began. The servers came out with large trays of steaks and chicken. April and I talked all through the dinner. I learned she was a Spanish major at Weber State University and had lived in Peru for a year and a half as a missionary. She was an avid hiker, climber, and skier. By the time dinner was over, I was infatuated. I tried to listen as Ethan Canin read a short story to the audience, but I had a difficult time concentrating. Instead I pushed my chair back from the table far enough that I could look at April's soft hair and the way the dress complimented her slender body.

After the dinner ended, April put on her coat and gathered her keys from her purse. "Maybe I'll see you at the conference tomorrow," she said smiling as she walked out the door and into the night.

I drove James back to his apartment. I must have been thinking a lot about April because when James finally spoke, I had forgotten he was even in the car with me.

"That was a nice-looking girl you were talking to," James said. "Did you ask for her phone number?"

"Why would I do that?"

James laughed. "It was pretty obvious you liked her."

I felt the blood rush to my face. "Was it really?"

I glanced at James. I wondered what he thought of me flirting with someone. He and his wife, Grace, had been good friends of Krista's and mine. He seemed supportive, but I wondered if he was secretly appalled at my actions that evening.

"I think you should ask her out tomorrow if you see her," he said.

"I'm not ready to date again." It was a partial truth. I still hadn't resolved how comfortable I was talking about Krista with others.

"I don't think you'd be flirting with someone if you weren't thinking about asking her out. I was surprised you didn't ask her to do something after dinner."

I didn't say anything. I rolled down the window and let the cool, spring air flow through the car.

"Do you know if she's going to be at the conference tomorrow?" James asked.

"She's reading a story she wrote in Spanish."

"She's multilingual. You can use that to your advantage. Learn how to say 'please have dinner with me' in Spanish. It will sweep her off her feet."

"I'm not interested," I said. But it wasn't the truth. I couldn't get April out of my head. That night all I could think about was her long, sun-bleached hair and bright smile. Even though my attraction to April felt normal, I felt guilty for seriously thinking about dating her. The shame was so strong that the only way I could fall asleep was by telling myself that my feelings for April were a one-time thing and I would never see her again.

But April was there the next morning. She arrived just as the first session of the conference began. James and I had arrived thirty minutes earlier, and I had been watching for her ever since. April sat on the opposite side of the room. For the next hour as I sat and listened to Matthew Klam read his short story "The Royal Palms," I glanced in April's direction every few minutes, trying to think of something to talk with her about. My mind was blank. I hadn't had to worry about things like this for a long time. With Krista I always knew what to say.

The reading ended, and April was out the door before I could make it halfway across the room. I looked for her but was unable to see where she had gone. The conference was breaking up into a half dozen smaller sessions. She could go to any or none of them. Dejected, I decided to attend a short story session at the far end of the building. James opted for a poetry session. We parted and agreed to meet up at the end of the day in the library.

There were five presenters and about twenty-five people in the audience at the first session. I found an empty chair near the back and waited patiently for the readings to begin. To my surprise, April walked in a minute later.

"Hi again," I said. I couldn't believe my good luck.

April smiled and took a seat next to me. She was wearing a short sleeve white blouse and a knee-length black skirt. Around her left ankle she wore a turquoise anklet. There was something about the anklet I found very attractive.

"Enjoying the conference?" I asked.

"I really am. I enjoy hearing authors read their own work." Her voice was soft, and it soothed me just to hear it.

While the presenters read their stories, I glanced over at April, tracing her legs down to the anklet. Instead of listening, I kept thinking of the best way to ask her out. I thought of different and clever things I could say. All the while my heart was pounding in my chest. By the time the session ended, I hadn't found the courage to ask her out.

"What session are you going to next?" I asked. My plan was to go with her to whatever session she wanted to attend.

April lifted the green backpack from the floor and placed it on the table. "I'm behind on my homework," she said. "I'm skipping the next session, but I plan on catching a few poetry sessions later this afternoon."

She smiled before she left. I followed her out of the room and watched her walk down the long hall of the student union building in the direction of the library. I thought about walking after her and talking with her some more but decided against it. I still didn't have the guts to ask her out and didn't want to come across as liking her too much. I figured I would catch her later in the afternoon, by which time I hoped to have found more courage.

I spent the rest of the day in different fiction and poetry sessions. At each one I hoped I would see April. She wasn't anywhere to be found. After the final session of the day ended, I headed to the library to meet up with James.

Outside it was warm and sunny. Students had shed their winter coats for jeans and T-shirts. There were strong memories of Krista associated with Weber State's campus, but I had become better at not letting memories overwhelm me. As I walked, I thought about when Krista and I worked at the university's writing center together, read on the grass during warm spring afternoons, or ran from class to class in the rain. I also remembered one day when we were first dating, heading off to different classes, and I looked over my shoulder at Krista and thought she was the most beautiful woman I'd ever seen.

In the library, the door to the session James was attending was closed. Through the door I could hear the voice of a student reading a story. The session was running late. I sat on an overstuffed couch against the wall and waited.

The library had been refurnished since I was a student. There used to be old, beat up blue couches spaced against the wall behind the rows of bookshelves. Even though they were very worn, I found them extremely comfortable and had spent many hours reading or sleeping on them. The library had replaced them with royal purple couches that matched the school colors. They were nicer but not long enough for me to stretch out on, and I didn't find them as comfy.

As I stared at a row of office doors along the far wall, a memory flashed through my mind. It was finals week. Krista and I had been dating about six months. We had spent the last several hours poring over the books and other study aids for our tests. We took a break and sat on one of the old, blue couches. Krista rested her head on my shoulder and closed her eyes.

"When finals are finished, I'm going to sleep all day," she said.

"If you do that, I won't be able to spend any time with you," I said.

Krista looked at me, smiled, and said, "I love you." We moved toward each other and kissed. A shadow passed in front of us. I opened my eyes just in time to see a librarian walk by. She looked at the two of us, her face hardened into a scowl. Her black hair was pulled tightly back into a ponytail. I had seen this librarian several times before and had never seen her smile. Her constant frowning soured what was otherwise an attractive face. She walked into one of the nearby offices. The door shut with a loud click.

"Did you see the way she looked at us?" Krista said.

I nodded and moved in to kiss Krista again. I decided not to take the librarian's scowl personally. Krista pushed me away and walked back to the table that was piled with our books.

"She needs to be cheered up," Krista said.

"Come back to the couch," I coaxed. "Don't worry about the sour-faced librarian."

Krista tore a blank piece of paper out of her notebook. She rummaged through her backpack, found a blue highlighter, and began to draw. Reluctantly I sat next to her at the table and watched as she drew a picture of a bird. I knew Krista well enough to know what she was doing but asked anyway.

"Why are you drawing a bird?"

"It's the bluebird of happiness," Krista said. She shaded in the head and the body with the highlighter. "I'm going to give it to the librarian to cheer her up."

Under most circumstances I would have laughed along with Krista, but today I was tired and just wanted to cuddle with her. "Forget it," I said. "We should be snuggling on the couch."

Krista ignored my comment and continued to draw. With an orange highlighter she added a beak and two skinny legs. Then with a black marker she wrote in big, bold letters: THE BLUEBIRD OF HAPPINESS VISITS YOU! She started toward the librarian's door, drawing in hand. I grabbed her free arm and looked her right in the eyes.

"Listen to me. *Do not* give the bluebird of happiness to that woman."

"Why not?" Krista asked in a playful voice. She continued toward the librarian's office, dragging me behind her.

"She might be having a very emotional day. Your bluebird could cause her to fly into a psychotic rage."

Krista stopped. "You're just embarrassed. You don't want her to know that her sour look bothered me."

I was running out of ideas to stop Krista. We were twenty feet from the librarian's door. Then fifteen. Then ten. I grabbed Krista and spun her around so she was facing me.

"Your drawing's not going to cheer her up," I said.

"You don't know that," Krista said. She grabbed my arm and gave it a playful squeeze.

Before I could reply, the door to the librarian's office opened. The librarian emerged with a black purse over her shoulder. Her eyes went from us to the drawing in Krista's hand. The bluebird was in plain view for her to see. The librarian refocused her icy stare on the two of us. Krista smiled broadly. I looked at the gray carpet and wished I could disappear. The librarian turned and walked up a nearby flight of stairs in a huff. The high heels of her shoes clicked loudly on the concrete.

To my relief Krista returned to our study table. I thought the era of the bluebird was over. But instead of sitting down, Krista rummaged through her backpack and pulled out a roll of clear tape. She taped the corners of her drawing and before I could protest, ran quickly over to the librarian's office and taped the bluebird of happiness to the middle of the door. She returned to the table, laughing.

"I can't wait to see the librarian's face when she returns," she said.

"We're not waiting for her to come back." I picked up my books and walked over to a table on the far side of the room. It offered a view of the librarian's door but was far enough away that we'd be hard to spot. Krista looked at the door, then back at me. She slowly gathered up her books and joined me at the new table.

"We'll never see her face from here," she said.

In the end it didn't matter. The librarian never returned.

Sounds of talking and laughing brought me back to the present. People walked by holding conference programs. I took one last look at the brown, sterile-looking door where Krista placed the bluebird of happiness. I wondered if the librarian still worked there. I wondered if she smiled when she saw Krista's drawing or if she simply threw it in the trash.

My stomach rumbled. I wanted something to eat. Other people walked by. I didn't see James. As I walked toward the room where the reading had taken place, I nearly bumped into April. She looked up at me and smiled.

"Did you enjoy the conference?" I asked. My mind started racing. The few hours since I had last seen her had not increased my confidence in asking her out.

"I did. I'm thinking about participating again next year." She folded the schedule and put it in her pocket. She looked at her watch. "I have to run to work. Maybe I'll see you around sometime."

"Yeah, that would be nice."

She turned and started to walk toward the exit. I watched her long, tan legs take one step, then another. If I was going to ask her out, it was going to be now or never.

"April," I said. April turned and looked back expectantly. I opened my mouth to ask if she had any plans this weekend. But before the words could come out, memories of Krista flashed through my mind. Our first kiss. Our wedding day. The bluebird of happiness. The desire to ask April out disappeared.

"Maybe I'll see you next year," I said.

For a brief moment, a disappointed look crossed her face. "Yeah," she said. "Maybe next year."

She walked toward the exit. She opened the door and stepped out into the bright spring sunlight. In the brief moment before the door began to close, the sun caught her hair just right, giving it the appearance of strands of gold. Then the door closed and she was gone.

# CHAPTER
## *Eight*

It wasn't until the end of April that I swallowed my pride and posted a profile on an online dating site. It was frustrating being able to post only a few paragraphs and a photo. I had no idea how to show I was just a normal twenty-seven-year-old who happened to be a widower. In my mind, each time I looked at the profile, the only thing I could see was the line that said "widower." Everything else seemed irrelevant.

Despite my trepidation, I began emailing women who seemed to have a lot in common with me. One of them was a twenty-nine-year-old teacher named Michelle. She had short, black hair and liked to read, watch movies, and run. After two weeks of exchanging emails we agreed to a date the next Saturday.

I mentioned my upcoming date to Jennifer that evening. She was the only person I felt comfortable telling about it. My family wasn't an option to talk with, and I was too excited about the upcoming date to ruin it with an argument. Jennifer was safe. Of all my friends, she would be the most receptive to the news. Jennifer was excited, though it took her a minute to find something to say. The news seemed to have caught her by surprise.

"That's wonderful," she finally said. "When are you going out?"

"Saturday."

"What are you going to do?"

"Lunch."

"Is that all?"

"I hadn't thought about that yet."

"Be sure you have a plan, Abel. There's nothing worse than going out with someone who doesn't know what they want to do."

"I'll come up with something," I said. I wasn't worried. I had three days to think of another activity.

"Are you sure you're ready to take this step?" There was an anxious sound to her voice, as if she was worried I would be heartbroken by Saturday night.

"I am," I said. "I'm looking forward to it."

I spent Friday evening with my sister Clare and her husband, Dan. They had invited me over for dinner and to spend the night at their place. My sister was a resident hall advisor for a dorm at Brigham Young University. She had graduated the previous year and was using this job to put her husband through his last year of school. The apartment was small: one bedroom, a kitchen, and a living room all crammed into about six hundred square feet. She was seven months pregnant their first child, a girl.

It had been several months since I had seen my sister, so when she opened the door, I couldn't believe how big her belly had become. It was about as big as Krista's the day she died.

Clare led me in to their small living room. There was a computer and desk in one corner that my sister used for her resident advisor job. On the far wall was an eight-foot sofa covered with a quilt. There was a small television and a stereo that faced the couch. Between all this, there was just enough room to walk to the kitchen. My sister's apartment always reminded me of the first place Krista and I shared: small and cramped. But that small apartment was full of some of my happiest memories of her.

I laid my jacket and overnight bag on the couch and followed my sister to the kitchen. I pulled the table out to the middle of the dining room to make room for a third plate. As we set the table, Clare talked about their upcoming plans for the baby and was a little concerned that they still hadn't settled on a name. "We don't even have three or four we can agree on," she said.

Listening to her talk about the baby was bittersweet. Her excitement reminded me of my own enthusiasm when Hope was on the way. As she talked, I closed my eyes and imagined that Krista was talking to me, telling me about plans for the baby. It was difficult, but I managed to keep my emotions under control. In situations like these, I tried not to let my feelings dampen the anticipation of others. Just because my daughter was dead was no reason to stop others from having joy about their future child.

"So what are your plans for tomorrow?" Clare asked. Her voice cut through my memories. I opened my eyes. She pulled three glass cups from the cupboard and handed them to me.

"Did you have something in mind?" I said. I arranged the cups on the table, hoping I wouldn't have to tell Clare about my date with Michelle.

"Dan and I were thinking about going to see a movie tomorrow," Clare said. She patted her belly. "After the baby comes we won't be going out as much. We thought it would be fun if you joined us."

"I already have plans."

"What are you doing?"

I debated what to tell her. Of all my family members, Clare seemed to be coping with Krista's death the best and was the one I thought would be the most open to me dating again. I told her the truth.

"I have a date."

Clare stopped. She held the plate she was about to set down a few inches above the table.

"You asked someone out?"

"Yeah," I said.

"How did you meet her?"

I decided not to say I met the woman online. I didn't want Clare thinking desperation had driven me to dating. "It's kind of a blind date," I said. "I haven't met her yet." I hoped Clare would assume someone had set me up.

Clare seemed to get over her initial shock. "That's great you have a date. You'll have to call me tomorrow night and tell me about it."

I looked at Clare's face. She seemed to be sincere in her interest. If she was upset or thought it was too early, she hid it well.

"Does anyone in the family know?" she asked.

"No. And please don't tell anyone. I don't think they're quite ready for me to take this step."

Clare finished setting the table then checked the casserole in the oven. She sat next to me in one of the old wooden chairs in the dining room.

"Are you excited?"

"Just nervous. Really nervous, actually. I feel like I'm back in high school dating for the first time. I don't know what to say or how to act."

"What are you going to do?"

"Lunch. If that goes well, maybe we'll do something else."

"You don't have a plan?" she said. She seemed a little surprised.

"When I think of something to do, the only things that come to mind are what Krista enjoyed," I said. "I knew Krista's favorite restaurants and activities. I know nothing about this woman. I'm just hoping I can get to know her better over lunch and think of something to do after. Right now my goal is to just make it through the date without throwing up."

Clare laughed. "I think you'll do fine."

"I hope so," I said. But the image of me puking at the lunch table made my stomach flip.

It was raining steadily when I left my sister's apartment the next afternoon. By the time I reached I-15 ten minutes later, the steady rain had turned into a downpour. Traffic crawled along the freeway, and I was glad I had given myself a twenty-minute cushion to reach Michelle's apartment. Long, hard rains like this were rare in Utah, and I kept thinking it would stop any minute.

When I drove over the point of the mountain into the Salt Lake Valley, the rain was falling so hard that even with my wipers set to the fastest speed, I had difficulty seeing past the taillights of cars in front of me. I looked in the rearview mirror. Water poured from the roof down the rear window, making it impossible to see anything behind me. I tapped the steering wheel impatiently and turned to a news station on the radio, hoping to hear some more positive news about the weather.

I stroked my chin and was surprised to feel two days of stubble. I adjusted the rearview mirror and took a quick look at my face. Somehow in the midst of getting ready that morning I had forgotten to shave. Shaving was something I was not fond of, not because I looked good with whiskers, but because my skin was sensitive to razors. Shaving daily was something I had stopped doing soon after Krista died. On a good week, I shaved every other morning. Taking another quick look in the mirror, I realized two days of growth didn't make me very presentable. A clean-shaven look would definitely go over better with Michelle.

The green numbers of the dashboard clock showed I was still running ahead of schedule. I took the next exit and pulled into the parking lot of a convenience store. I opened the trunk and sorted through my overnight bag. After a thorough search, I realized I had forgotten to pack my shaving equipment. I slammed the trunk shut and cursed under my breath. The rain was falling hard and steady, and I could feel water running from my head and down my face. Through the gray clouds and rain I noticed a ShopKo sign about a quarter mile down the road. The store gave me an idea. I drove to the store and ran inside. I found the shaving section and purchased a cheap bottle of shaving cream and a pack of five disposable razors. I paid cash at the express checkout and then hurried into the bathroom.

I placed the shaving cream on the side of the chipped sink and turned on the water. I held my fingers under the faucet as I waited for it to warm up. The water didn't warm up; it was still as cold as ice. I turned on the hot water on another sink and waited. Nothing. I looked at my watch. I was running out of time. I splashed cold water on my face and then lathered up. I gave the shaving cream a good thirty seconds to soften up my whiskers. Then I started to shave as fast as I possibly dared. The new razor pulled at the stubble on my face. I winced and thought about how pleasant it was to shave with an electric razor.

An employee wearing a blue vest and a white name tag entered the bathroom. He gave me a funny look before he entered one of the stalls. I ignored him. I had taken things very slowly around my chin. If there was one place I risked cutting myself, this was the most dangerous. I finished a minute later and then rinsed my face in the still cold water. I looked myself over. I only had one small nick on my neck. I pulled one of the rough, brown paper towels from the dispenser and dried my face and applied a small corner of the paper towel to my cut. In a moment a small red dot appeared and slowly spread. I made a mental note to remove it before I met up with Michelle. I threw the shaving cream and the rest of the disposable razors into the trash on my way out.

It was still raining when I left the store, but instead of a downpour, it was sprinkling. Traffic on the freeway was back to normal. Ten minutes later I drove into a large apartment complex. Each of the buildings looked identical: gray siding and white trim around the windows and doors. The grounds were green and well maintained.

I navigated my way through the complex to her building. I was in luck and found an empty visitor parking stall nearby. I checked my watch on the way to her door. 1:05 PM. Five minutes late. Not bad, considering the weather and my unexpected stop. I felt my face and realized the bit of brown paper towel was still attached to my neck. I removed it and took the stairs one at a time to Michelle's apartment.

I paused and took a deep breath to calm my nerves before I rang her doorbell. I heard the faint sound of the ding dong echo through the apartment. A moment later the yellow light from the peephole went dark. There was the sound of a deadbolt sliding back and the door opened.

A woman with large green eyes opened the door. She looked similar to Michelle, but there was something different about her that I couldn't put my finger on. My eyes traveled from her face to the rest of her body. She was wearing a dark green sweater that was a little big for her. She wore black jeans that fit her trim figure and long legs quite well. Her feet were bare. Her toenails were painted the same dark red as her hair. Then it hit me. Her hair. That's what was different. The photograph on the Internet showed her with black hair.

"Are you Abel?"

I nodded.

"I'm Michelle," she said.

We stood staring at each other for several awkward seconds.

"Sorry," I said. "The color of your hair threw me off."

"Oh, what color was I online?"

"Black."

"I like dying it different colors. I just changed it last week." She gave me a halting look. "Would you rather be dating a raven-haired woman?"

"I'd go out with you no matter what color your hair was," I said.

"Really? Well, I suppose if we have a second date I'll dye it green and then see how you feel." Michelle let out a short laugh. "I should invite you in instead of leaving you standing in the cold," Michelle said. She stood to the side of the door. "Come in for a minute. Let me put my shoes on and we can go."

I found myself inside a nicely furnished and immaculately clean apartment. It had a warm, homey feeling to it—something I was finding hard to do with my house. Michelle walked down the hall into a bedroom. I heard a door open and close. On a lamp table next to the entranceway was a photograph. Michelle and another woman were standing on what appeared to be the top of a mountain. Behind them was blue sky, and in the valley below, pine trees. Both Michelle and the other girl had smiles that beamed pride of a big accomplishment.

Michelle returned a moment later wearing black low-heeled shoes. "That's me and my roommate at the top of King's Peak," she said. "Ever hiked it?"

"No," I said. "Always wanted to."

"Life's short," Michelle said. She grabbed her purse from the kitchen counter. "You should do it while you have the chance." She reached inside and I heard the tinkling of keys. "Mind if I drive?"

"That's fine," I said. I was a little relieved at her offer. I was unfamiliar with this part of town, and trying to drive in the rain and trying to carry on a conversation was more than I thought I could handle.

As we descended the metal stairs toward the parking lot, I found myself wanting to reach out and hold her hand. This desire wasn't from the physical attraction I had for her but because holding hands was something I had always done when Krista and I walked down stairs together. It was protective and instinctual. I found myself reaching out toward her anyway but pulled back at the last minute. I balled my fist up and shoved it in my jacket pocket.

Michelle's car was a dark blue Subaru with a ski rack on the top. Like her apartment, her car was spotless. A rainbow-colored air freshener that smelled like vanilla hung from the rearview mirror.

"So where would you like to eat?" she asked as she started the car.

"I'm not familiar with the restaurants in this area. Why don't you pick something and I'll pay for it."

"There's a good Mexican and Italian restaurant nearby. Any of those sound appealing?"

"They both sound good."

"Let's see how crowded the Italian place is. It's mid-afternoon. It's shouldn't be too busy."

As Michelle navigated her way out of the apartment complex, I tried to think of something to say. Conversation had come so naturally with Krista. Had my first date with her been this difficult for me to talk? I couldn't remember.

104

"Can you believe this rain? I've lived here ten years, and I don't think I've ever seen a rainstorm like this one," Michelle said as she pulled out of the apartment complex. We were already talking about the weather. Not a good sign.

"It doesn't rain like this where you're from?"

"In Boise? No, it never rains like this."

"What brought you to Utah?"

"School, initially."

"And now?"

Michelle shrugged her shoulders. "For some reason I keep thinking I'll find my soul mate."

The rain was falling harder. When it hit the roof of the car, it sounded like a room full of people clapping. I looked over at Michelle and noticed that she had the beginning of crow's feet under her eyes—a reminder that I was dating a woman who was almost thirty. I tried not to think about Michelle's age because it made me feel old. I touched my own face and wondered what signs of age were there.

Much to our surprise, the Italian restaurant was crowded, and the hostess informed us there'd be a ten-minute wait. We sat on a hard, plastic bench in the lobby. I felt uncomfortable sitting and waiting where everyone could see us. I kept looking at people as they walked in and out of the restaurant. Even though I was fifty miles from home, I worried someone would see me with Michelle and tell Krista what I was up to. I wondered if this was what men who cheated on their wives felt like. Or if, by the time they had reached the stage where they were comfortable going out with someone other than their wife, they were past feelings of guilt.

Michelle leaned closer to me, and I caught the faint scent of her perfume. It smelled like roses. I found it subtly attractive. "You look a little nervous," she said.

"First date jitters," I said.

She brushed a strand of hair from her eyes. "I've had a tendency to make men nervous, you know."

I didn't want to ask why, but since I was struggling for conversation, I decided to play along. "Why's that?"

"I don't know," she said. "They find me intimidating for some reason." She sighed and leaned back on the bench. "So, how's dating the second time around?"

"Different. There are some adjustments I have to make." I looked at a couple that had come in from the rain. I wanted to see if I recognized them. I didn't. Smiling and laughing, the man gave a name to the hostess and sat on the bench next to us. Drops of water fell from their jackets to the tile floor, creating a narrow trail of water.

"Like what?" Her green eyes were piercing.

I wasn't sure how to answer since I had only been dating again for twenty minutes. Before I could say anything, the hostess called out my name. We were seated at a table in the far corner of the restaurant. The waitress told us about the soups and specials of the day and then handed us our menus. I hoped Michelle had forgotten what we were talking about. She hadn't.

"You still haven't answered my question," she said as she opened her menu.

My eyes scanned the list of entrees, but I wasn't reading anything. I was too preoccupied with the question. I could only think of one answer. "I think the biggest adjustment about dating again is learning to be comfortable in the presence of another woman."

Michelle set the menu down next to her plate. "Are you comfortable with me?" she said. She gave me the same intense look she had given me in the lobby.

This time I met her stare. "Like I said, it's an adjustment."

Michelle rapped her long, well-manicured fingernails on the menu and then picked it back up. "I think I'll have the lasagna," she said.

An older couple was seated at the table next to us. I glanced at them as they ate to see if I knew them. I still felt like I was cheating on Krista.

*You're not doing anything wrong,* I told myself. *It's okay to date again.*

The waitress came and took our orders. While we waited for the food to arrive, Michelle continued to probe.

"So what about my profile intrigued you enough to contact me?"

I took a sip of water. The truth was I couldn't think of a reason I had picked her out of several hundred profiles. Her photograph had simply stood out.

"You looked like an interesting person," I said. "Someone I thought would be fun to know more."

"And am I everything you thought I would be?"

I smiled. "I'll let you know."

The old man at the table next to us said something, and the woman he was with laughed. They seemed comfortable with each other. I was envious. I wished Michelle and I could talk to each other that easily.

"What made you respond to my initial email?" I said.

"To be honest with you, I usually don't date people who've been married before," she said. "Too many issues."

I nodded slowly, trying to understand why she decided to go out with me.

"But you were a widower," Michelle continued, "and that changed things a little. I figured there wasn't much you could do about that. So I threw caution to the wind and here we are."

"And, how is it?"

"It's more difficult than I thought it would be. There are a lot of questions running through my head. I want to know about your wife. I want to know why you're dating again five months after she died. I don't expect you to answer these questions or anything. I'm just telling you what I'm thinking."

The waitress arrived with plates of steaming food. I took a bite of my lasagna, and the hot sauce warmed my tongue. It was spiced well and had several kinds of cheese on it. Better than standard restaurant fare.

"This place is good," I said.

Michelle smiled. "I come here as often as I can."

Michelle did most of the talking during lunch. She seemed to sense, or at least I thought she did, that this date was difficult for me. She kept the rest of the conversation light and regaled me with funny stories from her childhood. The rain had almost stopped when we left the restaurant. It was still drizzling, falling like a fine mist. The clouds were slowly moving their way down the mountains, a sign that more rain was on its way.

"What do you think of dreadlocks?" Michelle asked.

"What do I think of them?"

"Yes. Do you think they look good?"

"It depends on who's wearing them."

"How do you think they'd look on me?"

I looked at Michelle and tried to picture her with auburn dread-locks. I didn't think they'd look very flattering.

"Are you thinking about them?"

"Haven't decided yet."

Michelle drove back in the general direction of her apartment. I was unsure whether to ask if she wanted to do anything else. I decided to let her drive and see if she gave any hint of how she was feeling. She drove back to the apartment and parked in her assigned parking spot.

"Thanks for lunch. It was nice getting to know you better," Michelle said.

If I was going to ask her to do something else, this would be the time to do it. We stared at each other for a long moment. Even though I wanted to spend more time with her, I lacked the courage to say anything.

"Email me next week. Maybe we can do something again soon," Michelle finally said.

"I'll be in touch."

Michelle took the stairs to her apartment. As she shut the door, my gut told me there wouldn't be a second date.

Back on the freeway, heading home, I replayed the afternoon in my mind. It had been very awkward and difficult, but it wasn't a disaster either. I felt it was something I needed to keep doing. Going out with someone, enjoying the company of a woman, gave me a feeling of normalcy—something I hadn't felt in months. Lunch with Michelle made me feel that I was part of the real world again, if only for a couple hours.

The rain fell harder. Traffic slowed. I turned the wipers on high. It was going to be a long drive back to Ogden, but for once I didn't mind. I had a lot to think about.

# CHAPTER
# *Nine*

The first time I saw Julianna Taylor, I was sitting on the back pew of the chapel where the few single people in our church tended to congregate. The Sunday service had ended, and the congregation began to move toward the exits. Through the crowd I noticed a tall woman walking up the aisle in my general direction. She wore a long yellow dress, with small green flowers, that clung to the curves of her body perfectly. Her curly hair was the color of corn silk and fell just past her shoulders. As she drew closer, my fingers and toes tingled, and my heart rate quickened. I looked at her hand to see if she was wearing a ring and then scanned the people around her to see if she had come to church with another guy. As far as I could tell, she was single and alone. Though I attended church weekly, I had never noticed her before and wondered if she was visiting

Sitting next to me was the church's clerk. One of his responsibilities was to keep track of the new members in the congregation. If anyone would know if she was a regular, he would.

"Do you know who that woman is?" I asked. He was engrossed in paperwork, and it took him a moment to look up. By this time the woman was almost to the exit and would soon be out the door.

"Who?" he said. He squinted his eyes as he looked at the crowd leaving the chapel.

"The tall one with the yellow dress and curly hair," I said.

"Oh her," he said. "That's Julianna Taylor." His gaze returned to his paperwork.

"Julianna," I said. "Beautiful name." I watched her until she turned down a nearby hallway. "How long has she been coming to church?"

The clerk stopped writing and looked up at the ceiling. He chewed on the end of his pen. "I'm not sure."

"What do you know about her?" The clerk was only a few years older than I, and I thought perhaps being single he would have already gathered enough information about Julianna to see if he'd consider dating her.

The clerk stroked his beard for a moment, lost in thought. "I believe she's a chemist or scientist or something like that." He returned to the stack of paperwork on his lap.

I thanked the clerk and then worked my way through the crowded hallways, trying to locate Julianna. I found her in one of the Sunday School classes sitting alone. She had her scriptures open on her lap and was reading from them. I sat in an empty seat directly behind her and spent the next hour staring at her long, blonde curls and trying to think of an excuse to talk to her. I found it hard to believe that someone this beautiful didn't have a boyfriend. By the time Sunday School ended, I had convinced myself that she did have one and asking her out would only lead to an awkward moment for both of us.

Julianna stood to leave. Our eyes met briefly. I smiled. Julianna smiled back.

"Hi," I said.

She nodded hello and then picked up her scriptures and left. The last thing I saw was her yellow dress flowing around her long legs.

I walked through the halls, looking for Bekah, who could usually be found trying to put her one-year-old son, Anderson, to sleep about this time. I found her sitting on a couch in the foyer, rocking Anderson in her arms. I engaged in small talk for a minute and then asked if she knew Julianna.

"I know who you're talking about," Bekah said.

"What do you know about her?"

"Not much," Bekah said. "I just know who she is."

Anderson raised his head at the sound of his mother's voice and smiled, then nuzzled his face back into her shoulder. Bekah pulled the blanket from around his body so it covered his head.

"Why do you want to know more about her?" Bekah said. She whispered the words and looked down to make sure she hadn't disturbed Anderson.

This is where the situation became tricky. Bekah had been Krista's best friend, and seeing if she would find out whether or not Julianna had a boyfriend was a lot to ask.

"I need to know if she's seeing anyone," I said.

"Seeing anyone?"

"You know. A boyfriend."

There was a pained look on Bekah's face. It lasted only a moment and then was gone.

"I didn't know you were interested in getting back into the dating game," she said.

"I've already been on a couple dates," I said.

"You have?" Bekah looked as if she was calculating the time since Krista's death in her head. "How long have you been doing it?"

"Several weeks."

Anderson snored softly. Bekah pulled the blanket back far enough so she could see his eyes. She leaned back into the couch and sighed.

"Why not ask her yourself?" Bekah said.

A door down the hall opened and Julianna emerged. She walked down the hall in our general direction.

"That's her," I said.

Bekah and I sat silently looking at the floor as Julianna passed. I noticed Julianna was wearing brown Doc Martens shoes and white socks. My eyes didn't go any higher. Instead they followed her feet out the main entrance of the church.

"It would mean a lot to me," I said after Julianna was gone.

"I'll talk to her next Sunday," Bekah said.

"Thanks," I said. "I appreciate it."

I headed to the parking lot, hoping to catch a final glimpse of Julianna before she left. I made it just in time to see her drive away in a bronze-colored Saturn. I made a mental note of the car so I would know if she was at church next Sunday.

As it turned out, Julianna wasn't dating anyone. At least that's what Bekah told me from the casual conversations she had with Julianna at church over the next few weeks. This good news, however, didn't give me the necessary courage to ask Julianna out. I still feared rejection. Each Sunday I looked longingly after her, wishing I could find the strength to say a few words to her.

In the meantime, I continued to date women I met online. There was one date with an artist who sculpted cowboys and horses but was so shy she could barely put two sentences together, one with an unemployed administrative assistant who was more interested in knowing if I knew of any job opportunities, and one with an interior designer who had silky black hair and large, brown eyes. I found her drop dead gorgeous. Unfortunately, her looks were all she had going for her. She had recently broken up with her boyfriend and spent the entire date complaining about him.

The feeling that I was somehow cheating on Krista diminished each time I went out. I was learning to relax and was being myself more. And even if the time we shared wasn't the best time for either me or the woman I took out, I enjoyed spending an evening out with someone.

I wanted to tell my family that I was dating again but didn't know how to explain to them that what I was doing wasn't a rejection of Krista or our marriage. Since Jennifer was the only person I could talk with, she became the play-by-play recipient of every date and laughed and cringed along with me. It felt good to have someone to talk with. It made the whole dating experience seem more real.

Then came the Sunday that changed everything. It was warm for an early May morning, or at least it felt warmer than usual when I walked outside to retrieve the newspaper from the driveway. All morning I had been thinking of Julianna and wondered if this would be the day I'd have the courage to talk to her.

Sitting at the kitchen table with a plate of scrambled eggs, I pulled out the sports page, eager to look over the latest baseball scores. The main picture above the fold made me stop. It was of a woman in a white running singlet crossing the finish line of the Ogden Marathon. She looked tired, exhausted, and very familiar. I scrutinized the woman's face. She looked just like Julianna. I flipped to the bottom half of the page to read the caption. It read: *Julianna Taylor crosses the finish line in downtown Ogden as the woman's marathon winner.*

I was dumbfounded. I read the article about the marathon and checked the results. It really was Julianna. She had won the Ogden Marathon in three hours and six minutes. The baseball scores were forgotten. I kept looking at the photograph and rereading the article. I now had a reason to talk to her and, if things went well, ask her out. I wondered if she would still come to church after running the marathon.

So I wouldn't miss her, I arrived at church thirty-five minutes early. I sat in the middle of the back row so I would have a clear view of both doors leading into the chapel. Slowly congregation members arrived. Old couples arm in arm, teenagers, families. Everyone but Julianna. Just as the service began, Julianna walked in. She was wearing a white blouse and plaid skirt that went to her knees. She looked stunning. She walked with a slight limp and took a seat near the front.

The only thing I remember about the service that day is that it seemed to drag on forever. The entire time I kept looking at Julianna, psyching myself up to talk to her. When the meeting finally ended, I worked my way through the crowded hallways and caught up with her before she entered the Sunday School classroom.

"Congratulations on winning the marathon yesterday," I said.

Julianna's face turned red and she looked away. "Thanks," she said.

"It was quite a surprise to see your picture in the sports page," I said. "I didn't know you run."

"Now the whole world knows," Julianna said. She looked back at me and met my gaze. Her green eyes were big and beautiful and made my stomach do flips.

The Sunday School class started. We found our seats.

"There's a social after church," I whispered. "I'd love to hear how you managed to win a marathon."

Our eyes locked for several seconds. Then Julianna looked away.

"Do you run?" she whispered back.

"Every morning." I patted my stomach. "It keeps the weight off."

"I usually don't go to the social. I don't like big gatherings."

"I don't like to go either," I said. "But if you show up, at least I'll have someone to talk to."

Julianna pursed her lips and then said, "All right. I'll go."

I was late to the social. By the time I arrived, everyone was milling about and having a good time. Everyone, that is, except Julianna. She stood in a far corner by herself. She leaned against a wall and looked at the floor. When someone walked past, she looked up as if she was afraid they would talk to her. Apparently she wasn't kidding when she said she didn't like large gatherings. She smiled, however, when she saw me approaching.

"Tell me about the race," I said. My tongue felt dry and thick, and it sounded like I was stammering all over the place. I thought back to when Krista and I were first dating but couldn't remember if I had ever been that nervous with her.

Julianna told me how she had run one of the best races of her life and overtook the woman in first place with about two miles to go. She seemed almost embarrassed when she talked about her accomplishment. She kept downplaying her achievement and saying there was nothing very impressive about winning the Ogden Marathon even though it was only the third marathon she had ever run. As we talked, I had the feeling that running was something she really loved. I knew a lot of runners, but Julianna had a passion for it that surpassed all of theirs. Then it hit me. If I was going to ask Julianna out, I might as well ask her to go running.

"We should go running together sometime," I said. "I'd like to see if I can keep up with you."

Julianna smiled. I couldn't tell if it was because she was excited about the date or the prospect of beating me in a run.

"How about Friday evening," I said. "There's a nice four-mile course near my place."

"I'd like that."

We agreed to meet at my place after work.

Julianna looked at her watch. "I need to go," she said. "I have dinner with my family tonight."

"See you Friday," I said.

Julianna flashed me a smile as she walked out the door.

"I see you finally found the courage to talk to her."

I turned to see Bekah standing behind me. Anderson squirmed in her arms, trying to break free from her grasp. He tugged at Bekah's hair. "No, Anderson," she said and slowly worked his fingers free. She turned Anderson sideways, which made grabbing her hair impossible and made Anderson a little grumpy.

"So, did you ask her out?" Bekah asked.

"We have a running date for Friday," I said. "But keep it to yourself."

"You'd be surprised how many people at church know you like her," Bekah said.

My stomach tightened. Who else knew how I felt about Julianna? Was my family aware of it? I looked nervously around the room. No one seemed to be paying attention to us.

Anderson started crying before I could ask Bekah to elaborate. She tried to comfort him, but his crying turned into a loud, piercing wail. "It's his lunchtime," she said. "You'll have to tell me about your date next Sunday."

The rest of the afternoon my mind was occupied with my upcoming date with Julianna. Back at home I kept looking at the picture of her on the sports page crossing the finish line. Running a marathon that fast took a lot of time, training, and dedication. I was impressed. And for the first time, I thought she just might run me into the ground on Friday. My thoughts were interrupted by the chirping of my cell phone. I looked at the caller ID. It was Jennifer.

"Did you forget about our afternoon chat?" she said. "You usually call the moment you get home from church." There was a flirtatious sound to her voice.

"Sorry," I said. "It's been a busy day."

"You mean a phone call with your favorite Arizona girl wasn't your top priority?"

"I didn't forget about you, Jennifer."

"You better not. Who else is going to talk to you after church every Sunday?"

"I'm sure Brent would."

Jennifer laughed. "I think you'd rather spend the day with me."

"Your voice is a little more pleasant than his."

"Really," she said. "Why didn't you call?"

I told Jennifer about seeing Julianna's picture in the paper and our impending date. It wasn't the first time we had talked about Julianna. In previous conversations I had mentioned how much I wanted to ask her out.

"It looks like fate gave you the chance to see if the two of you click," Jennifer said. Her voice had lost its playful tone. It was now serious and sober—almost jealous.

I tried to ease any concerns she might have about Julianna.

"If this date's anything like my previous ones, I'll only go out once with her."

"I hope it's a little more enjoyable than some of the dates you've had recently," Jennifer said.

I smiled. Jennifer seemed to be okay with everything.

"If you want, I'll give you a call Saturday morning with all the details," I said.

"Promise?"

"I promise."

At exactly four o'clock that Friday, Julianna knocked on my door. The knock came as a surprise since I had not heard a car in the driveway. When I opened the door, I found Julianna dressed in a white sleeveless shirt and purple shorts. Her hair was pulled back into a ponytail. Her arms and legs had a nice tan and were covered with a light film of sweat.

"Ready to run?" Julianna said.

I looked past her to the driveway and then to the empty street.

"Did you run to my house?" I asked.

"Of course," she said. "I only live a mile away." She wiped a bead of sweat from her forehead and smiled.

I should have been surprised, but I wasn't. Julianna could run twenty-six miles faster than anyone. Why would she balk at running the mile to my house?

I put on my shoes, and then the two of us started down the road. Since Julianna was unfamiliar with the course, she followed my lead, which meant I set the pace. The pace was slightly faster than what I was used to, but it wasn't anything I couldn't handle. I was sure Julianna could handle it too, but then I thought this might not even be close to what she was used to.

"Is the pace too slow?"

"It's fine."

"You sure? You're the one that won a marathon in three hours."

"My body's still recovering. This pace feels great."

We turned right down a street that wound its way though a new subdivision of townhomes.

"I hear you work in the business park," I said.

"Yeah."

"And you're a chemist?"

"A criminalist, actually."

"What's a criminalist?"

"I analyze forensic evidence. Drugs mostly."

I had to take several deep breaths before I asked another question. I wasn't used to talking and running at the same time, and with the faster than usual pace, doing both was difficult. Julianna, however, didn't even look tired.

"Is it anything like that television show, *CSI*?"

Julianna laughed. "Not really. We mostly do lab work. It's rare that we spend any time at crime scenes. We don't wear sexy tank tops to work or carry a gun. And we never interview suspects. That's a detective's job."

I had to stop talking and concentrate on running. The pace had picked up slightly, and talking had zapped a lot of my strength.

"How far have we run?" she asked.

I pointed down the road. "That stop sign is two miles," I said.

Julianna looked at her watch.

"Are you timing us?" I asked.

Julianna seemed a little surprised at the question. "I usually time my runs, don't you?"

"Sometimes."

The truth was, I rarely timed them anymore unless I was trying to achieve a specific goal.

"Seeing how fast I'm going is habit of mine. I always need to know what my pace is."

We only said a few more words the rest of the run. The second half of the course took us into a neighborhood of split-level homes and tall, mature trees. I used the time to think of the best way to ask Julianna out to dinner after the run.

About a hundred yards from my house, Julianna looked at her watch and increased her speed dramatically. I tried to keep up with her but had to slow down with thirty yards to go. As Julianna surged ahead of me, my eyes followed the curves of her body and watched as her ponytail bounced from side to side. It was all very attractive.

Julianna looked back over her shoulder.

"Am I running too fast?" she yelled. There was a big smile on her face. She crossed the finish line a good five seconds before me. We walked slowly in the direction of my house. My lungs and throat burned. Julianna didn't even seem out of breath. After cooling down, I invited her inside for a drink of cold water.

"Does running make you hungry?" I asked as I handed her a cup.

Julianna nodded and took a long drink of her water.

"Would you like to have dinner after we clean up?"

"I'd like that." She looked at her watch. "Pick me up in an hour."

I nodded. "I can do that."

"Great. I'll see you then."

Julianna made a move for the door.

"Are you going to run home?"

"It's only a mile away."

"I can drive you."

"I'll be fine, Abel." She opened the door and stepped outside. "See you in an hour," she said.

I watched her ponytail bounce from side to side as she ran down the driveway and up the street and out of sight.

On the drive to Julianna's apartment, I was excited and nervous all at once. There was a level of anticipation to having dinner with her that I hadn't felt since Krista and I had first started dating. There had been similar feelings of eagerness and expectation every time we went out together. The feeling was almost electric. It made everything seem more vibrant and full of energy.

Julianna looked stunning. She wore a yellow formfitting T-shirt and jeans. Her hair was curled, the same way I remembered it looking the first time I saw her. At the time it all seemed like a dream. I couldn't believe I was fortunate enough to have the company of this beautiful woman for the evening.

I walked Julianna to my car and got in. Julianna hesitated outside the passenger door for a minute before she opened it. Though I didn't know it, I had just made my first mistake. Julianna had been raised in a family where her dad had always opened the car door for her mother and had never been on a date where the man didn't open the car door for her. But I was too caught up in my euphoria of being with her to notice that she was a little put off by this. As far as I was concerned, the date was off to a great start.

Dinner was at a restaurant called the Bluebird. It was located in Logan, a forty-minute drive to the north. I had chosen this restaurant mainly because it would give me a chance to spend the drive time getting to know her better. I wanted to learn as much as I could about the beautiful, quiet woman who ran marathons.

The date was going well as we entered Cache Valley. Fields of alfalfa and corn were spread out like squares on a green quilt. We were talking about our families—specifically, which of our siblings were still at home and which ones were out on their own. I was telling Julianna about Clare and how she had recently given birth to a girl when Julianna said, "Is that your parents' first grandchild?"

Her question stuck me as odd. No, Fiona wasn't the first grandchild for my parents. Hope was. Didn't she know that? Then it hit me. Did Julianna even know I was a widower? Because we had attended the same church for several months, I assumed she knew everything. My mind went over the bits of conversation we had shared. I couldn't think of any specific comment that indicated she knew I had been married.

I said something about Fiona being spoiled rotten since my parents had no other grandchildren to spoil. The city of Logan was slowly creeping up on us. Amid wooden barns and farm homes, a new subdivision was being built in the middle of a green field on our left.

"How long have you been coming to our church?" I said. I needed to know what she knew about my past.

"Since January."

She hadn't been attending our church when Krista died. I tried another question.

"And did you talk to anyone at church about me before we went out?"

"No. Why would I do that?"

"You know, to make sure I was a decent guy."

"Are you?"

"Most of the time."

Something about the comment struck Julianna funny and she laughed softly. Even her laugh I found attractive. Could she be any more perfect?

We came upon a slow-moving trailer loaded with hay bales. The first cut of the season. Bits of hay swirled around the car as we passed. I knew I was going to have to tell Julianna about Krista before the evening was over. I had heard horror stories from friends who had gone on several dates with someone before they discovered their date was still married, had kids, or had some other issue that would have been good to know on the first date. The one advantage about finding dates online is that women knew I was a widower in advance. As far as I could tell, Julianna thought I was single. She might not have even agreed to go out with me if she knew I had been married before.

Looking back, I should have told her while we were still in the car on our way to dinner. I didn't, of course. I was too worried about her reaction. Had it been anyone else, I think I would have been all right with them not being happy at the news. But Julianna was different. I had strong feelings for her that I couldn't explain. Any hint of rejection from her was going to sting.

When I did finally get the courage to tell Julianna, I picked the most inopportune time. We were halfway through dinner. Julianna was in the middle of a bite of chicken parmesan when I said, "There's something I need to tell you. I'm a widower. My wife passed away six months ago."

"Oh," she said. She swallowed her food and wiped her mouth with her napkin. She looked down at her plate.

There wasn't much conversation the rest of the evening. I tried restarting it a couple times, but the most the two of us could manage was the occasional string of sentences. Julianna refused to look at me on the drive back to Ogden. Instead, she kept her gaze focused on the mountainsides of Sardine Canyon. I couldn't tell if it was what I had told her or how I had done it. This wasn't the way I envisioned our first date going. During the quiet moments, of which there were plenty, I tried to think of ways to apologize to her and set things right. But by the time we arrived at her apartment, I hadn't thought of anything.

I parked the car, but before I could get out to walk her to the door, Julianna opened the door and exited the car. She bent down and said, "Thanks for dinner." Then she was gone. In the rearview mirror I watched her walk to her apartment and close the door.

For the rest of that evening, I thought of ways to apologize. If a date with anyone else had gone this poorly, I wouldn't have cared. But thoughts of Julianna kept gnawing at me. There was something about her that made me feel alive and happy again. I just couldn't figure out exactly what it was.

# CHAPTER
## *Ten*

The 2002 Major League Baseball season came with a pleasant surprise. The Detroit Tigers were scheduled to play a three-game series against the Arizona Diamondbacks in Phoenix. Watching the Tigers play in person was something I'd always wanted to do, but I'd never had the opportunity. Since Phoenix was only an hour away by plane, I started making plans to attend at least one game.

I was excited not only to see the Tigers play but at the chance to see Jennifer again. Over the last few months our friendship had deepened. We spent about an hour a day talking on the phone and sent several emails to each other while at work.

When I told Jennifer about my impending trip, I thought there was a hint of excitement in her voice. As we talked, the trip grew in scope, and we decided that I should stay a few extra days and take a trip with her to see the Grand Canyon.

I looked forward to the trip like I had no other. This five-day trip to Arizona was a chance to see if our friendship would blossom into something more serious and beautiful.

The morning I was to fly to Phoenix, I arrived at the cemetery with flowers—a mix of daises and lilies—and feelings of guilt for having not visited Krista and Hope's grave for five weeks. In the months following their deaths, I made weekly visits to the cemetery, braving the snow and wind to spend fifteen minutes at their headstone. I felt a need to be close to them. As the months passed, these feelings weakened, and weekly visits became biweekly. Once I started dating, the time between visits increased even more.

I placed the flowers in a small glass vase near the headstone. With the exception of two robins hopping about the lawn looking for worms, I was alone. I sat on the dew-covered grass and looked over the valley. The cemetery was located in the foothills of the northeast corner of Ogden. On a clear day one could look to the west and see all the way to the mountains on the far side of the Great Salt Lake. This was one of those mornings. The sun was just cresting above Lewis Peak, bringing with it the dry heat of the desert. The salty waters of the Great Salt Lake sparkled on the horizon.

Normally I was selective in what I thought about at the cemetery. The next life and Krista were acceptable. Thoughts of Krista's suicide or Hope were not because they brought up strong emotions I preferred not to deal with. The irony of this wasn't lost on me. Of all places where I should be willing to let my emotions and thoughts go, the cemetery should have been one I felt most comfortable doing this.

But that day my thoughts were on Julianna and Jennifer. Despite a horrible first date, Julianna and I had gone out twice more. I had been floored when she had agreed at church the following Sunday to a second date. I had expected her to say no and had an apology ready to give her. But when I asked her to go out with me again, she agreed. I was too stunned to say anything other than, "I'll see you Saturday." Our second and third dates were better than the first, but they weren't great either. We never discussed Krista or my previous marriage. Those subjects became the proverbial elephant in the room. They hung over everything we did. Once or twice I tried to find ways to bring up the subject but never thought of a good way to do it. Julianna seemed content not talking about them.

I wondered what Krista thought about me dating again or if she even cared. Occasionally I speculated how often she checked in on her loved ones in this life from heaven or wherever she was. Since the other side was supposedly a more beautiful place—one where there were no tears or sorrow—I often thought she had more pressing things to do than worry about my life. But on the off chance Krista took a moment to stop and see what I was up to, I wondered if she was disappointed. I had promised to love Krista forever, and seven months after her death I was spending practically every weekend in the company of one woman or another. Knowing how jealous she could be, I didn't think she'd be very happy about it. Maybe things were different once you passed on. Maybe jealousy wasn't a part of her world now. Maybe she didn't care and was simply waiting for my time to come so I could be with her again.

A 737, heading south on its way to the Salt Lake airport, glittered in the sky. The sun had caught the side of the jet just right, and its body reflected the light like a mirror. I watched the plane until it was out of view. Then I looked at my watch. It was time to go. In a few hours, I'd be on my way to Phoenix. And that night I'd be attending my first Detroit Tigers game.

I rearranged the flowers in the vase. Before I left, I said out loud to Krista on the off chance she was listening, "I promise I'll visit again soon."

Jennifer's smile was visible from the other side of the security checkpoint twenty yards away. She waved excitedly when she spotted me. As soon as I walked past the bored-looking security guards, Jennifer flung open her arms and we embraced.

"I'm glad you're finally here," she said and gave me another hug. That additional hug was all it took for me to know that there was something between the two of us. The flirting we expressed on the phone and through email was real. This came as a relief. On the flight to Phoenix, as I looked at the sweeping deserts of southern Utah and northern Arizona, I wondered if the signs of affection I had picked up were simply something I imagined because I wanted it to be true.

We took the freeway from the airport to her parents' house. The plan was to wait there until Brent got off work. That meant three hours of uninterrupted time together.

"My family is so excited to meet you," Jennifer said. "They won't be home now, but Sunday night you're invited to dinner. You haven't already made plans with Brent for that night, have you?"

Even though Jennifer was the main reason for my trip to Arizona, I had made plans to stay at Brent's house. Despite my growing feelings for Jennifer, I worried about arriving in Phoenix and finding out that my feelings for Jennifer were nonexistent. I had decided to attend the ballgame Friday night alone with Brent. I was worried I was heading into the relationship too fast. I thought at least spending some time with Brent would give me some time to think and make sure a relationship with Jennifer was what I wanted.

"I think Sunday evening is free," I said. I wondered what Jennifer had been telling her family about me. I hadn't breathed a word about Jennifer to mine.

We drove through an older neighborhood filled with rambler-style homes. Unlike the newer suburbs of Phoenix, most of these homes had grass for lawns, though they weren't the same rich green color I was used to seeing in Utah. The grass was wilting in the stifling Phoenix heat.

"I grew up in this neighborhood," Jennifer said. "I love it here. I'd love to spend the rest of my life in Mesa, close to my family."

Jennifer's words made me pause. Krista had often uttered similar statements about her family. One of the few things we constantly argued about was my desire to move away from Ogden and closer to work. But Krista didn't have the desire to live far from her family. It was an issue she wouldn't budge on, and as a result I endured a daily one-hundred-mile round trip commute to work most of our married life. I shook the comparison from my mind. *Don't compare,* I thought. *Jennifer isn't Krista.*

Jennifer stopped in front of a red-bricked rambler. We entered in through the side door that led to a family room. One wall was covered with bookshelves where books of all types and sizes were stacked. There seemed to be little or no order to them. In the corner was a desk piled high with papers. A framed picture of a couple in their fifties that I assumed to be Jennifer's parents hung above the desk.

I sat on the couch while Jennifer went to the kitchen for water. She returned a minute later and handed me a tall, cold glass. Then she sat next to me, so close that our legs were pressing against each other. It was a little too close for me. I moved a few inches away. It wasn't that I didn't want to be near Jennifer. I wanted to take it slowly and make sure that a relationship with her was right. I was also wrestling with my feelings for Krista. Despite the anger I often felt toward her, I loved her dearly. I didn't know if there was room in my heart for two people. If the relationship with Jennifer was going to become more serious, I wanted to make sure it was a step I was ready to take.

Jennifer slid closer so that our legs were touching again. "You seem lost in thought," she said. "What are you thinking?"

I couldn't tell her what I was really thinking, how I was trying to determine the best way to have a little more room on the couch. Instead I said, "I'm thinking how nice it is to be back in Phoenix."

Four hours later Brent and I were on our way to the ballpark. A bank sign near the ballpark flashed the time and temperature; it was one hundred and fourteen degrees. How did people live in this heat? Ever since we left the air-conditioned comfort of Brent's truck, I felt like I was standing next to an open oven. Across the street from the ballpark we bought frozen two-liter bottles of water, which Brent said we'd need to keep us hydrated through the game.

The ballpark was kept at a cool eighty-five degrees. We arrived just as the Tigers were finishing batting practice. This early, we were practically the only people in the stands. We walked around the mezzanine, checking out the different views of the field before we found our seats. They were located on the lower deck twenty-five rows back on the first base side of the field. If we looked straight ahead, we could see directly down the third base line.

"I've never sat so close before," Brent said. "These are really good seats."

The Tiger player in the batting cage smacked a ball into deep center field. A player in the outfield ran after it and made a diving catch to the applause of his teammates.

"How's the dating game going?" Brent asked.

I smiled. "It's going."

"Anyone special I should know about?"

I wanted to tell Brent about Jennifer but decided against it. Brent had never liked her much and wasn't thrilled that she was accompanying us to the game the next day. I also didn't want to jinx what might happen between Jennifer and me. Aside from some flirting on the couch that afternoon, little had transpired. I had the feeling we were both waiting for Sunday to see what would happen. So instead of Jennifer, I talked about the only other girl I thought about on a regular basis: Julianna.

"I've gone on three dates with a girl who runs marathons," I said.

"Tell me about this marathon girl," Brent said.

"Not much to tell. Our first date was absolutely horrible, Brent. She didn't know I was a widower, and I ended up telling her midway through dinner. She had a mouthful of chicken when I sprung it on her."

Brent laughed. "And she agreed to a second date?"

"And a third. To be honest, I'm still a little shocked she said yes."

"Maybe she has a thing for you. Maybe she can't get you out of her mind."

I shook my head and watched as a new Tiger player took his turn in the batting cage. He swung hard at the first pitch and drove the ball deep into right field. The ball bounced off the warning track and rolled onto the grass. The player slammed his black bat on the ground in disgust. The next pitch he hit into the left field bleachers. The dozen or so kids hoping for a ball to come their way chased after it.

"I usually don't ask a girl out after a bad date. But there's something about Julianna. She's always somewhere in the back of my head."

"Once I dated a girl I couldn't get out of my mind," Brent said.

"What happened?"

"I married her."

I laughed. "That's encouraging."

"Best thing that ever happened to me."

A player in the outfield threw a ball high in the air. I followed the ball as it fell back into his glove.

"Well, this girl must like you a little bit," Brent said.

"I don't think so."

"Why not?"

"She goes running every morning," I said. "Five o'clock just like me. If she had any feelings for me, she'd ask me to run with her."

"Maybe she doesn't want to humiliate you by kicking your butt," Brent said.

"She loves running, Brent. I've never met anyone who enjoys it like Julianna. She knows I run. If she liked me, it would be something she'd want to share."

The player in the batting cage took one last swing and hit a foul ball into the upper deck of the ballpark.

"Has your family met her?"

"Briefly. At church."

"They like her?"

"I don't know. They don't understand why I'm even dating again. Most of them are still grieving for Krista."

The Tiger players on the field jogged toward the visitor's dugout while the grounds crew dismantled the batting cage and started raking the infield dirt with long, silver rakes.

"What makes you think they're not moving on?" Brent said.

"They talk about Krista all the time. They ask me questions about the day she died. It's the way they talk about her that makes me think they aren't ready to see me with someone else."

"Are you still grieving?" Brent said.

I looked over at Brent. Our eyes met for a moment and then returned to the field. The grounds crew had reached first base and was making its way to second.

"Not a day goes by that I don't think about Krista or Hope. I wonder all the time what my life would be like if they had lived. I miss them more than anyone will ever know."

The ice in my bottle had melted enough that there was several ounces of water. I took a long drink and rubbed the condensation on the outside of the bottle over my neck. Several drops of cold water ran down my back, giving me chills.

"I've spent the last few months trying to put my life back together," I said. "I can't begin to explain how hard that's been. Every day I've battled the guilt and responsibility I feel for Krista's death. But it's always there gnawing at my heart. I don't know if it will ever go away. I imagine I'll carry some of those feelings around for the rest of my life."

I caught a whiff of popcorn and Polish dogs. On the field someone from the grounds crew was chalking out the batter's boxes.

"I know people who have made a mistake and have spent the rest of their life regretting it. My dad took a job in Wyoming nine years ago. To this day he regrets taking that job. I can't remember the last time we had a conversation where he didn't bring it up, wishing he hadn't moved to Casper. I have a hard time understanding why he feels that way. I don't want to be like that—especially when it comes to Krista. It's a waste to spend your life wishing you could have done things differently. Life's about learning from your mistakes and making better choices. Even though I wish I could go back to the day Krista died and save her, I can't do that. Both she and Hope are dead, and there's nothing I can do to bring them back."

"It seems to me like you've made good progress," Brent said. "I'm surprised how well you're holding up."

"It helps that I can fly to Phoenix every six months," I said.

A middle-aged couple carrying hotdogs and beers sat a few rows in front of us. They both wore black Diamondback hats. I looked around the ballpark. The green seats were slowly being filled by fans. I checked my watch. Game time was only thirty minutes away.

Our talk shifted to baseball. The Tigers came into the game with a 23–41 record. The Diamondbacks, however, were headed in the opposite direction. They had just won the World Series in October, and there was no reason to think they couldn't repeat as champions. That night Randy Johnson, one of the top pitchers in baseball, was starting for the Diamondbacks. The Tigers started Mike Maroth, a rookie pitcher who was making his second major league start. Though I hoped for a good game, I wasn't overly optimistic about the Tigers' chances of winning.

"Don't count the Tigers out," Brent said when I told him about my concerns. "The Diamondbacks often have problems with young pitchers that no one has heard of."

As the game started, I didn't care if the Tigers won or lost. For the next few hours I was going to fulfill a lifelong dream, and I wasn't going to let anything stop me from enjoying it.

Brent was right about the Diamondbacks. The young Tigers' pitcher gave the Diamondback batters fits all night. He pitched eight innings and allowed only three runs. It was a good effort and enough for the Tigers to win the game 6–3.

On the drive back to Mesa, Brent said, "You look happy."

"The Tigers just won."

"It's more than that. You seem genuinely happy tonight."

Brent had seen something I didn't think was visible. For the first time since Krista died, I was truly happy. I had been able to spend the last several hours without thinking about Krista or Hope. It felt good. It was a feeling I wanted to have every day.

"I am happy," I said. "This has been a wonderful day."

The next evening Brent and I were leaning against the top of the right field fence, fifteen feet from the foul pole. We had been standing in the bleachers for forty minutes, hoping that a Tiger player would hit a ball in our direction before batting practice wrapped up. On either side, children and adults stood two deep, hoping the same thing. During batting practice only a few balls had been hit over the right field wall, and of those, only one had landed within thirty feet of where we were standing.

I took the baseball glove off my left hand and handed it to Brent. "You want a turn?" It was Brent's glove. I had forgotten to pack mine.

Brent shook his head. "They'll be stopping any minute now."

I put the glove back on and glanced back at Jennifer. She was sitting ten rows back. She was wearing jeans and a white blouse and a Cubs baseball hat. Her blonde curls hung down below the hat. She waved when she saw me looking back at her. I smiled and waved back before returning my attention to the field.

Brent looked at Jennifer and then back to me. "I think Jennifer likes you," he said.

I kept my eyes on the field. I still hadn't said anything to Brent about Jennifer. "Why do you say that?"

"She was flirting with you like crazy at my place this afternoon."

"Was she?" I said.

Jennifer had gone over to Brent's house thirty minutes before we left for the game. She sat close to me the entire time and would occasionally touch my shoulder or arm as we talked. Each time she touched me, I found myself smiling. It felt good to have someone who wanted to show affection. I could feel the blood rising to my face. If Brent had noticed Jennifer flirting with me, had he also noticed when I flirted back?

I watched as the Tiger player taking batting practice hit a ground ball in our general direction. It rolled all the way to the warning track. Another Tiger player picked it up, and the kids next to us yelled for the player to throw it to them. He ignored their cries and threw the ball back to the infield.

The crack of wood on leather turned my attention back to the field. A ball arced high in the air, heading in our general direction. It had enough height and speed that it looked like it might make it to the bleachers.

"It's heading straight to you!" Brent said.

"No, it's not," I said.

"Yes, it is!"

I looked at the ball that was now on the downward part of its arc. Brent was right. The ball was heading right to me. I held the baseball glove high in the air, ready to catch it. As the ball sped toward my open glove, I did the first thing you're taught not to do in little league when catching a baseball: I closed my eyes. For a moment my world was quiet and black. The noise of the ballpark and those next to me were gone. All I could feel was my heart thumping in my chest. Then with a smack, the baseball landed in the glove's webbing. I instinctively closed the glove around it. I opened my eyes. The noise and lights of the ballpark returned. I checked the glove to make sure the ball was there. It was.

Brent was ecstatic. "I can't believe it. That ball was hit right to you!"

I was too shocked to say anything. I held the ball in my free hand and turned it over to examine it. There were some general scuff marks and a black streak where the bat connected with the ball. Then it sunk in. I had just caught a Major League Baseball—something every baseball fan dreams of.

Brent's voice was still loud and excited. "Can I see it?"

I gave the ball to Brent. He held it like it was a piece of valuable jewelry. "That was amazing," he said. "I've never been near someone who's caught a ball before." He handed the ball back to me. I turned toward Jennifer and held the ball high in the air. Jennifer clapped her hands and smiled.

I took the glove off my hand and handed it to Brent. "Your turn," I said. Brent shook his head and looked at the infield where the grounds crew was dismantling the batting cage. "Batting practice is over."

We returned to our seats. I sat between Brent and Jennifer, who took turns examining the ball and talking about my catch.

I liked attending a baseball game with Jennifer. She could keep up with the baseball talk. Though Krista and I would attend two or three Minor League Baseball games a year, Krista went simply because she wanted to be with me. She never paid attention to the game but instead would use the game as a chance to talk to me or whatever friends we happened to go with. I was glad that she came to games with me but sometimes wished she had more of an interest in the action on the field. But Jennifer understood the rules and the subtleties of the game. It was a nice change.

It was sometime during the top of the third inning when our hands touched. I don't remember who made the first move or if it was something that we both did simultaneously. But I do know it took place underneath the scorecard I was filling out. I remember thinking when I first held her hands that they were incredibly soft— quite a contrast from Krista's, which, no matter how much lotion she used, always felt rough and calloused. I kept my eyes on the field, not daring to look at Jennifer. I waited for her to pull her hand away but she didn't move it. I looked over at Brent. His attention was riveted on the field.

Jennifer and I held hands on and off through the rest of the game. Brent seemed unaware of what transpired right next to him. During this time Jennifer and I barely spoke a word to each other. All of our communication went on underneath the scorecard. It was wonderful. I had forgotten how powerful a simple thing like holding hands could be. At that moment the sadness involving Krista seemed far away and distant.

With most of my attention focused on Jennifer, the details of that game were forgotten. I remember the game seemed slower than usual, and the Tigers' bats had lost the punch they had the previous night. I also remember that the Tigers lost 3–2 and that I didn't care. I was happy things had progressed so nicely with Jennifer and was looking forward to spending more time with her. I also remember on the way to the parking lot we walked two steps behind Brent and held hands all the way to the car.

When I awoke the next morning, sunlight was streaming in through the window, and my watch read a quarter past nine. The house was quiet except for the faint hum of the central air. Church was not for another two hours, and figuring I had at least another hour until I needed to get ready, I stared at the ceiling and thought of Jennifer and having dinner with her family that evening. Looking back, I think it was the first morning since that fateful November day that my waking thoughts hadn't been of Krista.

Around nine thirty I heard sounds of someone in the hallway. A soft knock on the door brought me out of my daydream. Brent slowly opened the door and peeked in.

"You awake?" he said. He was wearing pajamas and his eyes looked tired. "I have a church meeting at ten. Do you want to come with me or go later with Bethany?"

What I wanted to do was stay in bed until Jennifer came to pick me up for dinner. I was too comfortable and happy to do anything else. But I said, "I'll go with you."

Brent closed the door, and a minute later I heard the sound of the shower starting. I stood up and stretched my arms and back, trying to wake myself. When Brent was done, I took a quick shower and changed into my church clothes: white shirt, tan slacks, and yellow tie. By nine fifty-five Brent and I were driving through the Arizona sunshine on our way to church. Outside it was already ninety degrees.

We arrived at church, and Brent went to his meeting while I sat on the last row of the chapel. The organist was practicing the three hymns we'd sing during the service. I found it comforting and repeated the words of the hymns in my mind as she practiced.

After the organist had gone through each hymn twice, a hunched old man wearing a dark blue suit walked into the chapel with a stack of programs in one hand. Seeing me sitting on the back bench, he walked over and offered me one. "Program?" he said in a quiet, raspy voice.

I took one from his outstretched hand and thanked him. The man nodded and walked away. He stood at the door, waiting to hand one to the next person who entered. I glanced at the front page. The headline, printed in big, bold letters jumped out at me: FATHER'S DAY.

The whole world stopped.

Somewhere in the back of my mind I knew Father's Day was this weekend. However, the fun of the last few days had pushed those thoughts to the far recesses of my mind. Now all I could think about was Hope. Tears welled up in my eyes. I tried to think about something else—the baseball games or holding Jennifer's soft hands. It didn't work. The tears fell freely.

On the way to the bathroom, I thought of how different my life would be if Hope had lived. I wouldn't be in Phoenix—that was for sure. Instead, I thought of holding Hope as a blue-eyed seven-month-old baby and gently rocking her to sleep.

I found an empty stall and sobbed silently. At that moment I wanted to be a father more than anything. Not the father of a dead girl, but a father who had someone to love and protect. I felt cheated out of the opportunity to experience what so many others would take pride in today. My grief turned to anger, and I cursed Krista silently in my mind.

When I was finally ready to leave, I splashed cold water on my face from the sink and looked myself over in the mirror. My eyes were still red, but otherwise I looked fine. By the time I returned to the chapel, it was nearly full. Brent was standing just inside the doors looking for me.

"There you are," he said. "I was starting to get worried you were lost." He looked at my eyes and asked, "Are you okay?"

"I'm fine," I said, but my voice betrayed my true feelings.

I made it through the first half of the service without a problem. Brent kept looking over at me like he knew something was bothering me. I did my best not to make eye contact with him, thinking that my eyes would reveal the grief and envy that weighed heavily on my shoulders.

As the second half of the services began, several members of the congregation spoke on the importance of fathers in their lives. They told stories of their fathers and husbands and what good examples they were to them and to their children. I stared at the carpet until the last speaker finished. As the service came to a close, I began to relax. I had made it through the service without crying.

Then the bishop stood in front of the congregation and made an announcement. "We have a special gift for fathers. Will all the fathers in attendance please stand up?"

All around me, fathers in the congregation stood. The teenagers in the church began to hand out boxes of cookies.

Brent's eyes said, "Stand up." I wanted to stand and be recognized as a father, but I knew that if I did I wouldn't be able to hold back the tears. Instead, I put my head in my hands and stared at the floor. I thought back to Hope's funeral, to the end of the service when her tiny pink casket was lowered into the ground. That moment had been the most difficult of my life. Then my memory flashed to Krista as she lay in our room, blood gushing from the back of her head. The sadness was replaced by hot, intense anger. I closed my eyes and took slow deep breaths and tried to quell the rage that was waiting to explode.

"Abel?" Brent's whisper cracked my dark world. I opened my eyes. Brent was leaning close and had a concerned look on his face.

"I forgot it was Father's Day until I came to church," I whispered back.

Brent put his arm around me. For some reason his action had a profound calming effect and the anger diminished. But the heartache remained. And as the congregation sang the closing hymn, I knew that even if I had the chance to be a father again, Father's Day would always be bittersweet. That day would always be a reminder of Hope and the father I never had the chance to be.

The initial meeting with Jennifer's parents went well. They didn't ask many of the standard questions that I expected, however, like what I did for a living. No doubt Jennifer had filled them in on everything so her parents would know she was bringing home a good man. Instead her parents seemed more interested in learning if I was serious about Jennifer. They asked if I had looked for work in Arizona or if my house in Ogden was big enough to raise a family. Their questioning left me a little uncomfortable. I liked Jennifer but wasn't ready to ask for her hand in marriage.

I was sure they knew about Krista but was surprised when they didn't mention her—especially when, to them anyway, it seemed like a forgone conclusion that Jennifer and I were going to live happily ever after. It was possible they didn't know how to broach the subject. But considering their other questions, I thought they'd want to make sure I was ready to make Jennifer the number one person in my life.

Right before dinner Jennifer and I found ourselves alone in the living room. The sounds of her mother making the final preparations emanated from the kitchen. Jennifer was staring at me intently. I knew she wanted me to kiss her. I wanted to lean into her and kiss her but didn't feel her parents' living room was the best place to do it. I averted my gaze to the framed photographs of Jennifer's family on the top of the piano. Jennifer placed her hand on mine. I squeezed her hand and looked her in the eye. She moved closer and we kissed.

I was unsure what to expect when our lips met, but I was anticipating feelings of elation, joy, and excitement. But with Jennifer, there was nothing. It wasn't because the kiss lacked passion or substance. Everything I wanted physically in a kiss—good lip movement, a brief taste of tongue—was there. But emotionally the kiss didn't excite me.

My first kiss with Krista had been brief but intense. When our lips touched, I was filled with something similar to an electric shock. The feeling grew with our relationship and even after we were married. A passionate kiss from Krista was enough to send those feelings through my body again. I felt bad for comparing my first kiss with Jennifer to my first kiss with Krista, but that was all I could think about.

Jennifer moved in a second time. I closed my eyes, waiting for the sparks to fly. Once again there was nothing. Physically, however, it felt wonderful to kiss someone. Until that moment, I didn't realize how much I had missed it.

Jennifer rested her head on my shoulder. "I love you," she said.

I put my hand on the back of her head and let my fingers brush through her yellow hair. I wanted to say, "I love you too" but the words didn't come.

From the kitchen came the voice of Jennifer's mom announcing dinner was ready.

"Ready for your first official dinner with the family?" Jennifer asked.

I nodded.

We walked into the kitchen together holding hands.

Because I was unfamiliar with the layout of Phoenix, it took me several minutes to realize Jennifer wasn't driving back to Brent's house after dinner.

"Where are we going?" I said.

"There's something I want to show you," Jennifer said.

We drove down the broad, brightly lit streets for several minutes before turning down a dark side street. A minute later Jennifer parked near a large, well-lit granite building.

"We're at the temple," I said.

"It's a nice place to walk at night when it's cool," Jennifer said.

I followed her through the parking lot and then to a sidewalk leading to the temple grounds. The LDS temple was a large, square building covered with eggshell-colored terra cotta tiles with well-manicured grounds. Across the top of the temple, depictions of Mormon pioneers crossing the plains were carved into the building.

To my surprise there were other people walking around—about twenty couples in all. Most of them held hands and from time to time stopped and looked at the temple, no doubt dreaming of being married there. Jennifer took my hand, and we started a slow walk around the temple grounds. We paused every so often for a kiss. I had stopped wondering why I wasn't feeling anything inside when I kissed her. Jennifer was a good kisser, and I enjoyed the kisses for the simple physical pleasure that they were.

After two walks around the temple we sat on a cement bench next to a palm tree. Jennifer put her arms around me and leaned her head on my shoulder. From the bench we could see out the front gates of the temple to a quiet street with old homes lining either side. It was quiet and peaceful. I closed my eyes and breathed in the warm Arizona night.

Suddenly it was the middle of the day. I saw myself standing near the gates of the temple, dressed in a tuxedo. Jennifer was standing next to me. She was wearing a white wedding dress covered in lace. My mom and dad and all of my brothers and sisters stood next to us. Brent, Bethany, and other friends were there too. I saw Jennifer's parents and other people I did not recognize but somehow knew were Jennifer's friends and family. They all congratulated Jennifer and me on our marriage. Everyone was smiling and happy. Everyone, that is, but me. I stood in the midst of them, realizing I had just made the biggest mistake of my life because I knew I was going to spend the rest of my life with a woman I did not love.

Jennifer tugged at my hand, and the image of our wedding day melted away. "Abel?" she said. "What are you thinking about?"

The lights on the temple bathed Jennifer's face in soft, white light. I looked back to the lawn where I had seen the two of us standing. The memory of that image burned into my mind so well I could see Jennifer and the faces and smiles of those in attendance with exquisite detail. Thinking about that day again only intensified the feelings of dread and regret.

Again Jennifer's voice brought me back to the present. "Abel, what's wrong?"

"Nothing," I said. "Everything's fine."

"You spaced out there for a minute."

"Yeah. I'm tired. It's been a long day."

We walked back to the car. Before I opened my door, Jennifer pressed my body against the passenger side of the car and kissed me again.

"Maybe next time we come here, we can do more than walk around the grounds."

"What do you mean?" I said even though I knew exactly what she was implying.

Jennifer put her hand on my chest. "I thought if things worked out between us, it would be a nice place to be married."

I closed my eyes. The vision of our wedding day flashed through my mind a third time. The dark feeling was still there.

Jennifer seemed to sense that something was wrong. She moved her hand from my chest and took a step back. "I don't mean to scare you or anything," she said. "I'm just excited that things have gone so nicely between us."

"It's not that," I said. "I think I've had a little too much Arizona heat the last few days." I pulled Jennifer close and kissed her. "I'm looking forward to our trip to the Grand Canyon tomorrow."

That night I couldn't sleep. I tried reading, writing in my journal, and playing games on my cell phone but nothing worked. My thoughts kept returning to Jennifer, our first kiss, and the vision of our wedding day. I didn't know what to make of it.

After I married Krista I had thought it would be impossible to open my heart to another person. Before I started dating, I had to rethink my position on there being more than one person I could love. Perhaps part of the reason that I was unable to feel the same connection with Jennifer as I did with Krista was that there was only one person out there for me. Though I didn't want to believe it, maybe Krista was that person, and now she was dead, I would be unable to love or be with anyone else.

Around two, sleep slowly overtook my body. I thought about the trip to the Grand Canyon I'd be taking in a couple hours with Jennifer. But my final thoughts as I drifted off to sleep were not of Jennifer or our trip, but of Julianna. I realized that this was the first Sunday in months I hadn't seen or been able to talk to her. I thought it odd that she would pop into my mind at that moment. But then darkness overtook me and I slept.

The trip to the Grand Canyon was perfect. The three-hour drive to the south rim flew by as Jennifer and I talked about whatever was in our minds. I could talk about anything with her—books I had read, my job, or sports—with ease. And I was interested in Jennifer's life and interests too. The only other person I had ever felt this comfortable talking to was Krista. Each mile that brought us closer to the Grand Canyon pushed aside the doubt and confusion that had crept up the previous night.

About thirty minutes from the south rim, Jennifer turned off at an exit. When I asked where we were going, Jennifer smiled and said, "You'll see."

Five minutes later we were driving down a dirt road. Jennifer pulled off near a gate and unlocked it. She drove up a little hill, past some pine trees, and a cabin came into view.

"This is the family cabin," Jennifer said. "I thought I'd show you around before we spent all day at the canyon."

It turned out that the cabin was nothing more than an excuse for the two of us to have thirty minutes where we could make out. When we finally stopped to catch our breath, I wasn't caring much for the Grand Canyon. I would have been happy to stay at the cabin the rest of the day. But Jennifer insisted that we go. "You can't come to Arizona without seeing the Grand Canyon," she said. "It's the most beautiful thing you'll ever see."

Jennifer was right. The Grand Canyon was spectacular. My first look at it, realizing how large and vast it really was, took my breath away. Standing there, looking over the red and yellow walls, I felt like I was standing on the edge of eternity, watching time slowly pass one grain of sand, one gust of wind at a time.

We spent the day hiking along the top of the south rim. I enjoyed the feel of sun and wind and watching the cool green waters of the Colorado push their way along the canyon's floor. As the sun dipped into the western horizon, we headed back to Phoenix, dirty and tired. The Grand Canyon had been a wonderful end to my time in Arizona. I felt like my life was slowly coming back together, one piece at a time.

# CHAPTER
## *Eleven*

On the flight back to Utah, I sat next to a chatty, raven-haired college student who was flying to Salt Lake to spend a week with her fiancé. While she talked about her impending nuptials and plans for the future, I thought about my relationship with Jennifer. I had hoped my visit to Arizona would either solidify my feelings for her or prove that there was nothing between us. But the trip had done neither.

Physically our relationship had taken off. This kissing, the hand holding, and the feeling of her warm body pressed against mine when we hugged was wonderful. Emotionally something was missing. With Krista there had been an invisible, almost magnetic attraction—something that made me want to spend all of my time with her. Even after the initial euphoria of dating and marriage had worn off, long periods of time away from her were difficult. It wasn't like that with Jennifer. After spending several days with her, I felt drained. I was looking forward to the two-week break before she came to Utah.

The thought crossed my mind that perhaps I was pursuing a relationship with Jennifer as a way to stick it to Krista. After a lot of soul searching, I realized that even though I was still mad at Krista, the anger wasn't the catalyst for pursuing Jennifer. That came from my growing desire to move on with my life and have it return to some semblance of normalcy.

And there was one last problem I couldn't resolve: I couldn't stop thinking about Julianna. Since we lived only a mile from each other, every time I went grocery shopping or ran other errands at the nearby shopping center, I hoped to accidentally run into her. Every Sunday I looked forward to seeing and talking to her at church. I thought that part of the reason I was having a hard time connecting to Jennifer emotionally was that my relationship with Julianna was in some kind of indeterminate state. Maybe my emotional attachment to Jennifer would become stronger if I could remove Julianna from the picture. So I did what I thought would be the best way to clear things up: I asked Julianna out.

I envisioned the date going something like this: We'd spend a few hours together and, like most of our other dates, it would be average at best. At that point, I would realize how much fun it was to be around Jennifer and could tell Julianna I had enjoyed dating her but I didn't see the relationship progressing any further.

The moment Julianna opened the door to her apartment, I realized getting her out of my mind wasn't going to be that easy. She wore jeans that accentuated the length of her legs and a tight orange shirt that emphasized the curves of her upper body. Just looking at her made me weak in the knees—a reaction that until then only Krista had been able to elicit. As we drove to the ballpark, I kept sneaking glances at her body. I knew physical attraction wasn't something to solely build a relationship on, but I was almost willing to make an exception with Julianna.

I took Julianna to an Ogden Raptors baseball game, mostly because it would give us two and a half hours of uninterrupted time together—more than enough time, I thought, to prove that we were completely incompatible. There were only about 1,500 people at the game. This turned out to be a good thing. The closest person to us was two rows away. This gave us some privacy we wouldn't have had otherwise.

I told Julianna about my trip to Arizona, the baseball games, catching the baseball in the right field bleachers, and seeing the Grand Canyon. I omitted any reference to Jennifer and only mentioned that I had done all these things with friends who lived in the Phoenix area. Julianna told me about the training she was doing for the marathon she was going to run next month. She said it was one of the more difficult marathons in the country because it snaked its way over the mountains to the east of Salt Lake City before ending in a park near downtown. Tomorrow she was waking up early and running twenty miles.

"Why do you run marathons?" I asked. "There are lots of other races. Shorter ones. Why marathons?"

"There's something about running long distances that I love," Julianna said. "There's a feeling of accomplishment and a physical high I can't achieve any other way."

A Raptor batter took a called third strike and walked dejectedly back to the dugout. There was a smattering of boos from the crowd directed at the umpire.

"You seem happy with life," I said.

"I am."

"Has it turned out the way you expected?"

"Not really."

"Then why are you so happy?"

"I don't let circumstances dictate my happiness," Julianna said. "Just because life isn't going the way I imagined it doesn't mean I can't find joy with what I've been blessed with."

"So how has life not turned out how you planned?"

Julianna took a deep breath and slowly exhaled. I had the feeling she was unsure how much she wanted to tell me. I wished we were close enough that she could feel comfortable telling me what she was really thinking. On the field a batter hit a lazy fly ball into right field. The right fielder caught the ball and jogged toward the dugout. The inning was over.

"I kind of hoped to have found someone by now that I wanted to spend my life with," Julianna finally said.

"You're what, twenty-three? You're still young," I said.

"That's easy advice for you to give," Julianna said. "You've already found someone to marry." Her words cut deep and served as a reminder that there was a part of my life we still hadn't discussed.

"There are advantages to being single," I said. "A lot more freedom." I said those words even though I hadn't minded giving up certain "freedoms" to marry Krista.

"Let's say I never fall in love," Julianna said. "That's not going to stop me from being happy. I want to keep running marathons. I can train as much as I want now. I'm considering applying to medical school. I'd love to be a doctor. There are a lot of things I can do since I'm not attached. But that doesn't mean I want to be single forever."

Julianna had articulated something I had been feeling for a long time. Krista's death had been devastating, but I was doing my best to take advantage of what life had given me even though at times it was difficult. And I felt a little heartened that Julianna was discussing commitment. Perhaps she saw some potential in our relationship.

We sat in silence through the next two innings. During that time I thought of different ways to bring up Krista, but each time I rationalized away the need to talk about it. After all, this was meant to be the date where I was going to end things with Julianna, not talk about the past. By the time our conversation resumed, the openness Julianna had exhibited was gone, and our conversation fell back to generalities. Though I tried to revisit our previous conversation, Julianna would always direct the conversation back to the baseball game. It was as if she didn't want to risk coming any closer to me emotionally.

When I walked Julianna to her door that night, I felt more confused about her than ever. Even though the date wasn't spectacular, it was the best one we'd had so far. Instead of weakening my feelings for Julianna, the date had only strengthened them.

On the drive home I checked my cell phone messages. There were four messages from Jennifer. The first was pleasant, asking where I was and saying that she wanted to talk with me and see how my day at work had gone. Each successive message was a little more anxious, wondering where I was and why I hadn't called. I parked in my driveway and was about to dial her number when the cell phone rang. It was Jennifer.

"I've been trying to call you all night," she said. "Where have you been?"

"I went out with a friend," I said. I didn't feel good about telling her a half-truth. Though we hadn't left with a commitment that we couldn't date anyone else, our actions in Phoenix had suggested we were a serious couple, and I knew that Jennifer wasn't even thinking about asking anyone else out.

"What? You didn't want to talk with me all evening?" Jennifer sounded like she was joking, so I laughed. In the back of my mind, I wondered how serious that comment had been.

"How come you're not out with friends on a Friday night?" I said.

"My friends? They just sit around and complain about their husbands. I don't need to hang around them now that I have you."

"You should still do things with them. We can't be together every day," I said.

"In ten days we'll be together," Jennifer said. "I can't wait to see you again."

Jennifer was scheduled to fly to Utah on the third of July and spend the next five days with me. After my date with Julianna, I was less eager for Jennifer to arrive. It wasn't that I didn't want to be with Jennifer. I knew the two of us would have a good time together no matter what we did, but I felt we were moving too fast. I wished we had taken things slower back in Arizona.

Before Jennifer arrived, there was one order of business I had to take care of: I had to tell my mom about Jennifer's visit. It wasn't going to be easy because I had no idea how she'd react. I wished my dad was in town because his reaction would be easier to read. But since he was in Wyoming, I broke the news of Jennifer's trip three days before she arrived. Mom was washing the dishes after dinner. I sat at the table and watched the air conditioner in the window blow wisps of her salt-and-pepper hair behind her ears. We made small talk while I built up the courage to tell her. When I finally mentioned it, I tried to be as casual about it as I could, hoping it would make the news easier to take.

"I have a friend flying up from Phoenix over the Fourth of July holiday," I said.

"Is it your friend Brent?" my mom said. "I'd like to meet him."

"This is a different friend," I said. "Her name is Jennifer."

My mom stopped washing the dishes and turned off the air conditioner. The silence that filled the kitchen made me want to hide.

"Who's coming?" she said.

"Jennifer."

"The girl you went to the Grand Canyon with?"

"That's her."

My mom grew quiet, as if she was pondering the significance of what I had just told her. "Does she have family in the area she's visiting?" she said.

With that question I knew my mom was hoping that Jennifer's arrival in Utah was a coincidence. In her mind it was impossible for people to become so serious that quickly.

"She's coming to see me."

My mom let the dish she was holding slip from her hand. It disappeared in the soapy water and clunked against the plates in the bottom of the sink.

"To see you?" She said the words slowly, as if what I was telling her wasn't quite sinking in.

"Yes, Mom. To see me."

My mom leaned against the counter and thought for a moment. "How serious are the two of you?"

"Serious enough for her to fly down and spend five days in Utah," I said.

"Oh," Mom said. The way she said "oh" reminded me of the way someone might say it upon learning that a neighbor or distant relative had died. There was no further need to discuss the trip. I started making plans to keep Jennifer as far away from the family as possible.

It was a tradition for my family to have a large Fourth of July barbeque. The annual event attracted upwards of thirty to forty people: extended family, neighbors, and friends. There was lots of good food and conversation to be had. And after dark, everyone would take their chairs out to the side of the road and watch as the teenage boys lit illegal fireworks, smuggled in from Wyoming. For hours after dark the middle of the street would be filled with contraband light. The barbeque was something I usually looked forward to. This year, however, I didn't want to attend. The barbeque meant Jennifer would be introduced to everyone—not just my family.

I thought about skipping the barbeque entirely but knew that wouldn't be the best way to have my family open up to Jennifer. Instead I decided it would be better to arrive at the barbeque late, hoping it would be easier to blend in. By the time Jennifer and I arrived, the party was in full swing. My parents' backyard was filled with family and friends. The younger children had already finished eating and were lighting sparklers or throwing snaps at the ground or each other. Most of the adults were seated in lawn chairs around the fire pit, talking to one another and waving the smoke from the fire out of their faces when the wind shifted.

It didn't matter that we were late. The fact that I was bringing a girl, one who was staying at my house no less, to the barbeque was a show stopper. It seemed, in my mind anyway, when Jennifer and I walked into the backyard, all the conversations abruptly stopped. Maybe it was because I was already worried what people would think about Jennifer and me that I read something into their actions that wasn't there. But it seemed everyone's eyes went from me to Jennifer then back to me, as if they were trying to picture me with someone other than Krista.

I introduced Jennifer to those seated around the fire pit. Everyone was friendly, shook Jennifer's hand, and did their best to make her feel welcome. But I didn't care if the guests liked her. I was more concerned with my family's reaction.

It didn't take long to realize that my family didn't care much for her. The first clue came from my dad. After Jennifer had talked with him for several minutes, my dad joined me at the picnic table where I was loading my plate with baked beans, potato chips, and orange Jell-O. My dad helped himself to a second hamburger and a large serving of three-bean salad.

"Mom said you caught a baseball at one of those games you attended in Arizona," he said. "You need to tell me that story."

My heart fell. The fact that he didn't say anything about Jennifer meant he didn't like her. If my dad liked someone, he always made it a point to say something nice about them to me. With Krista, for example, my dad had told me over and over again what a sweet person she was. This was his way of telling me he approved of our relationship.

It soon became apparent my dad wasn't the only one who wasn't fond of Jennifer. Other family members were polite but standoffish toward her. When I was able to pull them aside and ask what they thought about Jennifer, their answers were diplomatic and noncommittal. "She's an interesting person" or "I need to spend more time with her before I can answer that" were the most common responses. And though it hurt that they didn't like her, it was the fact they wouldn't even tell me this that hurt the most.

As the barbeque progressed, I became more frustrated at my family. I hadn't expected them to embrace Jennifer with open arms, but the level of resentment I felt was surprising. I knew they needed time to adjust to seeing me with someone besides Krista. But at the same time I thought that Jennifer was being unfairly compared to my wife. It was like they expected Jennifer to be Krista—have the same personality and mannerisms. They seemed unwilling to give Jennifer a chance.

Jennifer seemed oblivious to my family's feelings. She enjoyed being the center of attention, and this was her moment to show them that she was the new woman in my life. As the evening progressed and I watched Jennifer interact with my family, it seemed like she was trying too hard to impress them. When my dad told a joke, Jennifer laughed a little too loud. When my mom talked to her about the history project she was working on, Jennifer came across as a little too interested. It bordered on obnoxious, and my family could see right through it.

When it was dark, everyone brought their lawn chairs to the sidewalk to watch fireworks. My seventeen-year-old brother, Liam, and his friends took charge and lit up the night sky with bottle rockets and other fireworks they had purchased in Evanston the week before. Halfway through the show Liam snuck up behind Jennifer and lit a smoke bomb under her chair. Jennifer jumped out of her chair as the smoke billowed around her. She walked over to Liam and began to reprimand him.

"That's not funny," she said. "Fireworks are not toys. You're setting a bad example for the younger kids." She said it in a tone of voice someone might use when scolding a young child.

Her reaction surprised my brother. He was expecting a more playful reaction. In the past years when he had done something similar to Krista, she had jumped out of her chair and good-naturedly chased him up and down the street. Jennifer was simply annoyed. For the rest of the night, Liam made sure he stayed twenty feet from her at all times.

Jennifer's reaction also dampened the festive mood that had been strong until that moment. By the orange streetlight I could see everyone uncomfortably staring at her.

"Liam was only teasing you," I said after the smoke had cleared.

"That doesn't make it right."

"It was just a smoke bomb."

"Someone could have been hurt," she said and then held my hand as Liam and his friends launched more fireworks into the sky.

As we walked back to my house, Jennifer seemed oblivious that no one in my family seemed to like her.

"Your family's wonderful," she said. "And your dad cracked me up with his jokes."

*That's because he didn't have anything else to say to you,* I thought. I decided not to tell Jennifer the truth. There were still four more days for her to spend in Utah. Perhaps there was still enough time for my family to warm up to her.

✦ ✦ ✦

I avoided my family as much as possible for the remainder of Jennifer's visit. We spent a day at Antelope Island walking along the salty shores of the Great Salt Lake. Another day was spent touring the canyons and valleys east of Ogden. And just like our trip to the Grand Canyon, any doubts about our relationship that crept into my mind were pushed aside. We were having a good time together and immensely enjoying each other's company. There was no reason to think we wouldn't spend the rest of our lives together.

Then Sunday came. I awoke that morning with a mix of excitement and trepidation. We were expected to attend church with my family. But that wasn't the part that had me worried. Going to church meant Julianna might see me with Jennifer. One glimpse of Jennifer would be all the excuse Julianna would need not to date me again.

I showered and dressed at my parents' house, where I was staying while Jennifer visited, and walked to my home. Jennifer was running late. She had bags under her eyes and said she hadn't slept well. I sat at the kitchen table and flipped through the Sunday paper while Jennifer finished readying herself. I tried to immerse myself in the baseball news, but I couldn't focus on the game recaps and the box scores. My thoughts were on the upcoming service and a way I could avoid Julianna for three hours.

Jennifer walked into the kitchen. "Can you zip up the back of my dress?" she asked. She turned around to show that the last six inches of her dress needed to be zipped. It was the sweep of her hand to pull back her hair that abruptly drew me back to Krista's same gentle motion, her simple act of trusting intimacy between husband and wife that for me never grew routine. It was something I always enjoyed. She would hold her hair with one hand so it wouldn't be in the way. Instead of immediately zipping up her dress, I would kiss Krista's back and work my way up to her neck. I closed my eyes and smiled, remembering what it felt like to press my lips against Krista's skin.

"Is that runner girl going to be at church?" Jennifer's voice shattered my memory. I opened my eyes and with one quick motion, zipped up her dress.

"Who? Julianna?"

"That's her. Do you think she'll be at church today?"

"I assume so."

"I can't wait to see her."

I didn't understand why Jennifer was so eager to see Julianna. The last time I had even mentioned Julianna to Jennifer was two weeks before my trip to Phoenix.

"Why do you want to see Julianna?" I said.

"I want to drop the J-bomb on her," Jennifer said.

"The J-bomb?"

"The Jennifer bomb." Jennifer's cackling laugh filled the house. "I can't wait to see the look on her face when she sees you with me."

Suddenly, I wasn't interested in going to church. There was a vindictive tone to Jennifer's words that I didn't understand. I didn't see why she viewed Julianna as a threat. "What makes you think Julianna's going to care?" I said.

Jennifer stood close to me. She put her hands on my shoulders and looked me in the eye. "I know you like her, Abel," she said. "When you talked about your dates, I sensed your frustration that things weren't going better with her."

I tried to remember what I had said to Jennifer about my dates with Julianna. I didn't remember telling her I was frustrated about the dates or that I even liked Julianna. I was about to protest, but Jennifer put her finger to my lips and said, "You wouldn't have asked her out three times if you didn't have feelings for her. All I want to do is let her know that you're taken." Jennifer gave me a kiss on the lips. "Now let's go."

I did my best to make sure we were late to church. As we walked out the door, I told Jennifer I had left something at my parents' house and spent several minutes in the basement sitting on the floor while Jennifer waited in the car. By the time we arrived, the service was underway. The only empty seats were the two on the back row my parents had saved for Jennifer and myself.

The first thing I did after we were seated was look for Julianna. It took a few minutes, but I spotted her long, curly hair a few rows from the front of the chapel. For the next hour I kept glancing at her, hoping that by some miracle after the service, she wouldn't notice Jennifer.

After the closing prayer, I stayed in my seat, waiting for the inevitable. Jennifer leaned close and whispered in my ear, "Is Julianna here?" I nodded and pointed her out to Jennifer. Julianna was slowly making her way up the far aisle. She seemed to be lost in thought and wasn't looking around the congregation. I thought I was in the clear until Julianna reached the back of the chapel and looked in my general direction. For a second, I thought I saw her eyes rest on me, then Jennifer, and back to me. But I wasn't sure. Julianna looked away and walked into the foyer.

Jennifer seemed to think that Julianna had seen us. She squeezed my hand and kissed my cheek. "Now you're mine," she said. Her words should have made me happy. I had found someone who loved me and wanted to be with me forever. Why wasn't I excited at this? I managed a smile, took Jennifer's hand, and escorted her to the Sunday School portion of the meeting.

There were two Sunday School classes, and I purposely chose the one I knew Julianna wouldn't attend. For the next hour I tried to think of a way to leave Jennifer's side for a few minutes and talk to Julianna after church even though I had no idea what I would say to her.

After Sunday School I excused myself and went searching for Julianna. I saw her tall, slender body right before she turned the corner. I ran to catch up with her, but as I approached the corner, I nearly ran into Bekah.

Bekah grabbed my arm. "I saw you with someone at sacrament meeting," she said.

"Her name's Jennifer," I said. "She's from Arizona." I looked over Bekah's shoulder, down the hall, hoping to see Julianna. The hallway was filled with people, but Julianna wasn't in sight.

Bekah had a confused look on her face. "I thought you were interested in Julianna."

"It's a long story."

"I have plenty of time," Bekah said.

"Let's talk later," I said.

Bekah looked hurt. It wasn't like me to brush her off like this.

"I'll explain everything to you in a few days," I said. I squeezed through the crowded hallway as fast as I could. I made it to the parking lot just in time to see Julianna drive away.

After church I found myself lying on the couch, resting my head in Jennifer's lap while she ran her fingers through my hair. It was the first time since Jennifer arrived that we had taken time to relax. My mind was preoccupied with Julianna, and I wondered what she thought of seeing me with Jennifer. There were so many things I wanted to explain to her. I closed my eyes and pretended it was Julianna tousling my hair with her long, slender fingers. Slowly I began to relax and sleep overtook me.

The next moment I was running up the cement stairs to the apartment, taking the key out of my pocket and opening the door. I tried to stop the dream, tried to tell myself to wake up, but there was nothing I could do. I heard my voice calling out for Krista, and then a moment later heard the report of the gun. It wasn't until I ran back to our bedroom and saw Krista's body that I was able to wake up.

I sat up straight and cried out. Jennifer was startled, and I could feel her body jump with mine. In a moment her arms were around me, pulling me close to her. I pushed myself away and sat on the far end of the couch, trembling.

"What's wrong?" Jennifer said.

"Nothing," I said. "It was a bad memory. A nightmare."

Jennifer moved closer and again put her arm around me. This time I let her hold me. My heart rate slowed, and I wiped away a few beads of sweat from my forehead.

"Was it about Krista?" Jennifer said.

I nodded and forced the images of Krista's bloody head out of my mind. In the ensuing months, the flashbacks to Krista's death had become less frequent. I now only had to battle them once or sometimes twice a week. Usually I was prepared to deal with them, but this one had caught me by surprise. It was also the first time I experienced them in the presence of another person.

"Relax," Jennifer said. "Everything will be fine."

After a few minutes I again rested my head on her lap. This time I didn't dare close my eyes. I turned my head so I was staring at the coffee table and the front window where the hot July sunlight formed a square puddle of light on the carpet. I was embarrassed about the whole situation. I wanted to talk about what I had dreamed with Jennifer but didn't know how to broach the subject. Instead we sat quietly.

Then it dawned on me that Jennifer had never asked about Krista or brought up concerns about becoming involved with a widower. I thought through all of our conversations, and the only time I could remember us talking about the widower issue was when we talked about the concerns I had about dating again several months ago. We hadn't discussed it at all since then. Something about that didn't seem right. If the situation was reversed, I'd have lots of questions and issues that needed to be resolved before becoming part of a serious relationship. Jennifer seemed fine with everything. I took partial responsibility for the lack of communication about Krista. When I was on a date, I usually waited until the other person started asking questions. I didn't want my dates thinking my dead wife was the only thing I could talk about. But now that Jennifer and I were becoming more serious, I felt there were issues that needed to be discussed.

"I don't have moments like those very often," I said. I thought this would be a good way to bring up Krista.

"It's okay, Abel," Jennifer said. "Relax." She rubbed my chest. "Talking about it will just make it worse."

I lay there, my eyes wide open, my mind churning over the doubts about Jennifer that were again slowly rising to the surface.

# CHAPTER
# *Twelve*

The day after Jennifer returned to Arizona, Bekah invited me to dinner. I had a feeling this wasn't just a friendly dinner invitation but an excuse to talk with me about Jennifer. I was glad for the chance. Since I was unable to talk with my family about Jennifer and wanted a sounding board for my feelings, Bekah was perfect for that.

The meal was simple but one of my favorites: pepperoni pizza and breadsticks. Bekah and I made small talk and watched as Anderson, who was now fifteen months old, ate and played with his food. I was on my third slice of pizza when the subject of Jennifer finally arose.

"Did you have a good time with *that* girl?" Bekah asked. She said it in such a way that let me know she wasn't fond of Jennifer. "The way she was all over you in church, it was obvious she was enjoying herself."

"We had a good time," I said. I summed up the highlights of her visit and emphasized how much we had in common and how comfortable I felt around her. I wanted Bekah to see that the relationship was more than a physical thing.

"And when are you going to see her again?"

I shrugged my shoulders. "Labor Day, maybe."

Bekah looked down at her plate. She had barely touched her food.

"What's wrong?" I said.

"It's just that . . ." Bekah's voice trailed off. She looked unsure how to say what was on her mind. "It seems like it's happening so fast."

I looked out the kitchen window to the horse pasture where a brown mare nibbled at some grass. "A lot of people feel that way," I said. I thought back to the barbeque and my family's reaction to Jennifer.

"How serious are the two of you?" Bekah asked.

I looked back at Bekah. She looked as if she was bracing for bad news.

"I'm not sure," I said. "But if I were to ask Jennifer to marry me, I'm certain she'd say yes."

"You're that serious?"

"*She's* that serious."

"How do you feel about her?"

"I don't know," I said. I looked down at my plate, at the half-eaten piece of pizza. Suddenly I wasn't hungry anymore. I pushed the plate to the middle of the table. With my right hand I played with the lace edge of the tablecloth.

"We have the most amazing time together. It's like we're best friends." I glanced back at Bekah. "But there's something missing that I can't explain."

"Try to explain it to me," Bekah said.

It took a moment to gather my thoughts. "There was something about Krista," I said. "Something that I've never felt for anyone else. I don't know how to begin to describe it other than a very intense attraction. When Krista and I were first dating, she consumed my thoughts. I wanted to be with her every minute of the day. I don't feel that way about Jennifer."

I smiled, remembering the early days in my courtship with Krista. I had fallen in love with her the first time I went out with her, though it took her longer to warm up to me. After our first date I knew I didn't want to be with anyone else. I had found the woman I wanted to spend the rest of my life with.

"If you feel differently about Jennifer, then why are you spending all this time with her?" Bekah said.

"When Jennifer and I go out, we have a fabulous time together. I get along with her just as well as I did with Krista. In some ways, I get along with Jennifer better."

"What are you saying?" Bekah said. "Do you love Jennifer more?" The quiver in Bekah's voice made me think she was about to cry.

"What if those feelings that I had for Krista are something I can only have for one person?" I said. "Does that mean I can't be with anyone ever again? Do I need those same feelings with Jennifer to have a strong relationship with her?"

Anderson picked up a piece of pepperoni, threw it to the floor, and squealed in delight. He had been so quiet, I had nearly forgotten about him. He threw a second piece to the floor before Bekah could stop him. She removed the uneaten pizza from his tray and then wiped his face and hands with a washcloth.

While she was doing this, I looked back at the horse pasture. The brown mare was now walking slowly toward the other side of the field where a large, metal tub was filled with water. She put her nose in the water and took a long drink.

Bekah set Anderson on the floor in the living room with a few toys. He picked up a blue plastic ring and began chewing on it. She sat back at the kitchen table and took another look at Anderson to make sure he was all right.

"It's really none of my business who you date," she said. "I don't mean to pry. It's just that Krista was my best friend, and I have a hard time seeing you with anyone but her."

Anderson crawled into the kitchen. Using the table leg as a balance, he stood up and took two unsteady steps toward Bekah, who picked him up and placed him in her lap.

"Tell me," Bekah said. "If you knew how your marriage to Krista would end, would you still have married her?"

"I'd do it over again a hundred times if it were possible," I said.

"Even if it ended the same way each time?"

"Even if," I said.

Bekah started crying. "It makes me so happy to hear that," she said. She wiped her eyes with a napkin. "Just so you know, I'll support you if you decide to remarry."

I went out with Julianna the following Saturday. We ate dinner at a local pizzeria and then headed back to my place and watched a movie. It was a horrible date. What little conversation we had felt forced. Julianna had always been reserved when we were out, but this evening she was frigid. She said as little as possible during dinner, and, as we watched the movie, she sat on the far end of the couch with her arms folded. About an hour into the show I moved to the chair next to the couch so I could sit closer to her. Julianna slid to the next cushion as if to emphasize she wanted nothing to do with me.

After the movie I drove her back to the apartment and walked her to the door. I tried to coax some final words out of her. The date was frustrating enough that I thought about never asking her out again. I wanted some sign that she was still interested in me or that this evening had been a fluke. But all Julianna said before retreating into her apartment was, "Thanks for dinner."

On the drive home I listened to the three voice messages Jennifer had left on my cell phone. The first two were playful. She sounded annoyed on the final message and wanted to know where I was and why I hadn't returned her calls. I was too irritated from my date with Julianna to talk to anyone and decided not to call her back.

I lay on my bed and thought about Julianna's behavior. Over the last two months we had gone out a total of five times. None of our dates had been spectacular. The first one and this one had been downright awful. Yet Julianna continued to accept every invitation to go out again without hesitation. And despite the less than stellar dates, I couldn't shake the attraction I had to her. I tried to figure out what was going on behind her pretty green eyes. As my eyes grew heavy, I decided that at church the next day I would talk to her and settle things with her once and for all.

The talk almost didn't happen. After the first hour of services, Julianna quickly left the church. I had to run to catch up with her.

"We need to talk," I said.

From the look on her face, talking to me was the last thing she wanted to do.

"I don't have time now," she said. "It's my sister's birthday. I'm late for her party."

We were twenty feet from her car, and Julianna's long strides were rapidly closing the distance.

"I need ten minutes," I said.

Julianna took her keychain from her purse and pushed a button. With a chirp, the car alarm was deactivated. Another three steps and we were at her car.

"I'll call you after the party," Julianna said. "If it's not too late, we can talk then." She got into her car and put the key in the ignition.

"I'll be home all night," I said.

Julianna started the car and drove away without another word.

As the day progressed I grew less confident that Julianna would call. The way she brushed me off in the parking lot made me think she would stay as late as she could at the party, simply so she wouldn't have to talk to me. While waiting for her call, I decided to visit the cemetery. I thought it would be a quiet place to sort out my feelings. And I hoped that if Krista were lingering nearby, she would hear my thoughts and know that even though I was moving on, I still loved and missed her.

I was sitting next to Krista and Hope's headstone when Julianna called. It was dusk, and I was looking over the valley, watching the lights from the city come on like stars, one at a time. I was positive Julianna was going to tell me that she had stayed late in Salt Lake and we wouldn't be able to talk. To my surprise Julianna said she was at her apartment. I told her I'd be there in five minutes.

I stood and took a long look at the headstone. "This talk could change everything," I said. "But it won't change the way I feel about you." My words seemed to disappear into the gathering darkness. I walked back to my car and drove to Julianna's apartment.

Julianna was wearing red-rimmed glasses when she opened the door. I had never seen her with glasses before but thought the small frames looked good on her. It wouldn't be until months later that I would learn she had worn them to help disguise the fact she had been crying while she waited for me to arrive. She invited me inside her sparsely furnished apartment. A worn eight-foot couch lay against one wall, and a small twelve-inch television stood in a far corner on top of a cherry wood chest. The only other furniture in the living room was a bookshelf, half of which was filled with books and the other half with ornate dolls.

"Have a seat," Julianna said. She gestured to the couch. I sat on one end, and Julianna sat on the other. It felt like there were miles between us. Julianna stared at the far wall and looked like she was going to be sick.

"Are you feeling okay?" I said.

"I'm fine," she said.

We both sat in silence, dreading what was coming next.

"Do you like going out with me?" I finally said.

"Sort of." Julianna didn't look at me when she said this. She continued to stare at the wall. I wanted to see her full face while we talked.

"I can never tell how you're doing when we're together," I said. "You hide your feelings well."

"I'm not sure how I feel about you," Julianna said.

More silence. I tried to read Julianna's face. It was expressionless.

"Tell me about her," Julianna said after a minute. She was looking at me now. Even behind the glasses, her green eyes could be piercing.

"Who?" I said, though I was pretty sure she meant Krista.

"Your wife. Tell me about her."

"What do you want to know?"

"What was her name?" Julianna's tone indicated frustration that she had to pull even basic information out of me.

"Krista."

"Krista," Julianna repeated as if the name suddenly added a human element to this previously unknown person. "How long were you married?"

"Almost three years."

"When did she die?"

"November."

Julianna looked at the ceiling as if she was counting the number of months between November and July. "How did she die?" she said after she had reached her answer.

"She took her own life."

Julianna literally shook at the news. It was like she was expecting something else: an automobile accident or a fatal, unexpected disease. Anything but suicide.

"How did she kill herself?"

Now it was my turn to look away. I still felt embarrassed when I told this part of the story. "With a gun. My gun. I came home one afternoon, and as I entered the apartment I heard a gunshot."

Julianna nodded her head slowly. "Did you have any kids?"

"Krista was seven months pregnant when she died," I said. "Our baby, Hope, lived for nine days."

Julianna seemed surprised by this answer too. I couldn't tell if it was from the fact that the child had lived or that Krista was pregnant when she committed suicide. There was a sad but curious look in her eyes that indicated she wanted to ask more questions but was unsure how to proceed. Her gaze returned to the far wall.

"There were too many complications with her coming into the world so early," I said. "I made the decision to remove life support."

Julianna's lips were pursed as if in deep thought.

"I don't know if I can do it," she finally said.

"Do what?"

"Date a widower."

"Why?"

"Why? You have to ask why?"

"Tell me why it would be hard," I said. I could foresee a lot of potential problems but wanted to know if Julianna's concerns were the same as the ones I saw.

"I don't know if I can live with having my every action compared to those of a dead woman," she said. "I don't want to compete with a ghost."

"Have you felt like I've been comparing you to Krista?"

"I don't know you or Krista well enough to answer that question," Julianna said. "But I know when someone dies, they tend to be put on a pedestal. It doesn't matter what they did wrong. All anyone can remember is the good, loving things about them. Meanwhile I'd be with you making mistakes and being compared to a woman who is a saint in some people's minds."

"I never thought about it that way," I said.

"I've thought about it a lot since we've been going out. I almost think it would be easier to date a divorced man. At least then I can assume that there's some sort of hostility toward the previous spouse."

I thought back to my family's reaction to Jennifer at the barbeque. I realized that a lot of their response to Jennifer was because they were comparing her to Krista. This comparison was going to be an issue whoever I dated was going to have to deal with.

"Why are you dating again?" Julianna asked.

I didn't have a good answer to that question. "I enjoy spending time with other people," I said.

"What exactly do you enjoy about it? Being close to someone? Is that the only reason you're dating—to satisfy some physical need?" Julianna looked at me. "I don't want to be a warm body. I want to be loved and appreciated for who I am."

"We really haven't been physical—"

"What did Krista look like?" Julianna said. "Did she have long, blonde hair like me? Did she have my green eyes? Maybe I'm a spitting image of her and that's the only reason you want to date me. I don't even know if you've dated anyone else. I don't want to be the first and only woman you've gone out with."

"I've gone out with other people," I said.

"Then there's the communication issue," she said. "We've gone on five dates, and aside from the bomb you dropped on me during our first date, you've never talked about Krista again."

"I haven't been sure how to bring her up."

"I don't want you to feel that way," Julianna said. "I want you to be comfortable talking about her, and I want to be comfortable asking questions about her and the life the two of you shared."

I leaned back into the soft couch cushions. As far as I could tell, any chance of having another date with Julianna was history.

"Where do you see this relationship going?" I said.

"For now, all we can be is friends."

"Friends," I repeated. I was willing to take that. Perhaps with a little time, we could take another run at the dating thing.

"Just friends," Julianna said.

Julianna still looked like she was going to be sick. Considering how things had gone, I thought this would be a good time to leave. I thanked Julianna for making time for me and told her that being friends would work out fine.

As Julianna followed me to the door, I felt impressed that I should ask her out on a date for Saturday. I quickly brushed the thought from my mind. We had just agreed to be friends. Asking her out could undo everything we had worked toward this evening. I put my hand on the doorknob and again felt that I should ask Julianna for a date. I opened the door and then turned and said, "Would you like to go out on Saturday?" Even as I said those words, I stood there wishing I could take them back.

"Sure," Julianna said. She looked surprised at her response. I thought it best to leave before she changed her mind.

"Plan on dinner," I said.

On the drive home I cursed myself for asking Julianna out. I didn't have the confidence that our date on Saturday, if it happened at all, would go any better than our previous ones. But something about our conversation felt right. The issues she had raised were valid concerns, and I thought if we could find a way to work through those problems, then there might be a chance that things would work out between the two of us.

My cell phone rang as I pulled into the driveway. It was Jennifer. I hadn't spoken to her all day. I put my finger on the button that would send her straight to voice mail. There was so much I wanted to think about, and Jennifer was only going to be a distraction. But if I didn't answer now, she would call back. It wasn't that I didn't want to talk with her. I just wanted some time alone to sort things out.

"I've been waiting for your call," she said when I finally answered the phone.

"I spaced it," I said. "I've had a lot on my mind this evening."

"Is everything all right?"

"Everything's fine," I said. "Things are finally starting to make sense."

Whatever had been stopping Julianna and me from getting along well on our previous dates had disappeared by Saturday. For the first time our conversation flowed. It was as if our talk the previous Sunday made us feel like we could open up with each other about anything.

Julianna excitedly told me about her marathon. She had finished the race in three hours and thirty minutes—twenty minutes slower than her previous marathon—but she seemed happy with her time. And overall she had done well, finishing fifteenth out of 250 female runners.

Several times we swapped jokes and funny stories and found ourselves doubled up with laughter. For the first time together we relaxed and acted like ourselves. And I was sad when the evening had to come to an end.

As I stood outside Julianna's door, we made plans to spend the following Saturday together. My gut told me this was the date that was going to show whether there was a real possibility for us to take the relationship further.

It was. We watched the M. Night Shyamalan movie *Signs* and went hiking. Through the movie I resisted the temptation to hold Julianna's hand, which lay on the armrest. I told myself we needed to take things slow. One wrong move could send our relationship tumbling back to square one. I kept my arms folded, telling myself to be patient.

After the movie we drove to the summit of North Ogden Divide. There was a parking lot where trailheads for several popular hiking trails were located. We each carried backpacks with several bottles of frozen water and lunches of turkey sandwiches, chips, carrot sticks, and chocolate chip cookies that Julianna had prepared.

We started up the trail toward Lewis Peak. Even though the trail snaked along the north edge of the mountain and was shaded by pine trees, it was still hot. We stopped every ten minutes or so and took long drinks of water. I let Julianna set the pace. Mostly I wanted her in front of me so I could look at her long, tan legs without her knowing I was staring. Her legs were strong from running, and I enjoyed watching the muscles in her legs expand and contract with each step she took.

After about a mile and a half, the trees thinned, and the trail leveled out and snaked its way south toward the summit. We followed the trail for another half mile until I spotted an outcropping of rock fifty feet off the trail. The rocks formed a small ledge that extended over the east side of the mountain. I told Julianna that it would be a good place to stop and eat.

Both of us were soaked with sweat. We sat on the ledge that looked over the farms and homes that made up the cities of Huntsville and Eden.

"It's very nice up here," Julianna said after we had rested for several minutes.

"There are many good hiking trails in the area," I said. "My favorite is the one that goes to Ben Lomond." I pointed to the mountain to the north.

"Do you go hiking a lot?" Julianna asked.

"Not as often as I'd like to."

"Why not?"

"I don't like hiking alone. I'd rather do it with someone." My stomach grumbled and I smiled. "We should eat if we're going to have any strength to make it back down."

We unpacked the lunches and started eating. A slight breeze kicked up and felt cool on my shirt, which was still clinging to my back with sweat. While we ate, I took a long look at Julianna. The light gave her hair a gold tinge. Julianna glanced in my direction. I looked away, embarrassed to have been caught staring.

"What are you looking at?" she said.

"You."

"Why are you looking at me?"

"Because you're one of the most beautiful women I've ever seen."

Now it was Julianna's turn to look away. "I'm just plain and ordinary," she said.

"You're anything but."

"How do you know that?" she asked.

"I don't go out with plain and ordinary girls."

Julianna's face reddened. The wind blew a strand of her hair across her face.

"So tell me," I said. "How come a beautiful girl like you doesn't have a boyfriend?"

"Who says I don't have a boyfriend?" She smiled and looked me right in the eye.

Her green eyes let me know that she was serious. I had assumed that since she was always available to go out and never came to church with anyone that she didn't have anyone special in her life.

"Do you have one?" I said.

"I broke up with him three weeks ago."

I waited for her to say more. Instead she pulled a cookie out of her backpack and chewed it slowly.

"Can I ask why?" I said after she had finished the cookie.

"It wasn't because of you," she said. "I broke up with him the day before we had that serious talk at my apartment."

"Are you sure it wasn't because of me?"

Julianna threw a cookie at me. It hit my shoulder and landed on the ledge. I picked it up and took a bite. "Five second rule," I said. Julianna shook her head and looked back over the valley.

"He lived in Provo. That made it hard to see each other on a regular basis. I need to spend time with a person to feel like the relationship is going somewhere. Phone calls and a visit once a week aren't enough for me."

"I can understand that," I said, thinking about Jennifer. I wondered how many messages were going to be on my voice mail when I returned home. "It's hard to know if you want to spend eternity with someone when you're never around them."

Julianna finished the water in her first bottle. She pulled the second one out of her bag and took another drink before continuing. "He wasn't ready or willing to commit to a serious relationship, anyway. He seemed happy living apart and seeing each other once a week. I think a relationship should be moving forward or backward. Our relationship hadn't been going anywhere for several months so I ended it."

I chewed on a carrot stick, pondering what Julianna had just shared with me.

"So if you had a boyfriend, why did you keep agreeing to go out with me?" I said.

"Honestly?"

I nodded. Julianna brushed her hair away from her face and looked down at the valley. She pulled her legs up to her chest and rested her chin on her knees.

"After our first date I was ready to be done. I drove to my parents' house that night and told them about how awful it was. When I was done with the story my dad told me I should give you a second chance."

"Why did he say that?"

"I don't know. It was a strange thing for him to say. He's the type who wants to make sure his daughters are dating men who will treat them right."

"Did he tell you to give me a third and fourth chance too?"

Julianna shook her head. "I don't know why I kept going out with you. I wanted to say no but felt I should do it."

We heard the sound of voices and turned as two teenage boys ran down the trail. The wind carried their voices back up the mountain long after they disappeared.

"Since we're on the question of past loves," Julianna said. "How long did you wait to date again after Krista died?" Julianna kept her eyes on the valley below, her face expressionless. I was learning she could hide her body language when she had to.

"About five months."

"Have you been dating regularly since then?"

"As often as I can."

"And how often is that?"

"Just about every weekend."

Down in the valley a black pickup drove along a dirt road, leaving a trail of brown dust. It turned into a long driveway of a ranch-styled house that was surrounded by several pastures. I looked back at Julianna for any clue on what she was thinking or feeling. Her poker face remained intact.

"Am I the only person you've dated more than once?"

"No."

"Have you been serious with anyone since your wife died?"

The pause before I answered made Julianna look at me. "Actually, there's someone else I've been seeing while we've been dating," I said.

Julianna raised her eyebrows for a split second. That was an answer she wasn't expecting.

"You're with someone?"

"Yeah. For the last two months."

Silence. My eyes wandered from Julianna back to the black pickup truck. The driver lowered the truck's tailgate and lifted something that looked like a long rectangular piece of plywood out of the back and carried it to the garage.

"She lives in Phoenix. I brought her to church about a month ago. I thought you saw the two of us together."

"I wasn't paying close attention to you a month ago," Julianna said. "If I would have seen you with someone else, I would have been glad for an excuse to turn you down."

"I'm glad you weren't paying attention."

"What are you going to do about your girlfriend in Phoenix?"

"I don't think it's going to last much longer," I said. "I think I've found someone better. Someone I've wanted to know more about since the first time I laid eyes on her."

Julianna blushed and looked away. I rummaged through my backpack and found a cookie. I moved closer to her and said, "Have a cookie."

We talked for the next hour. It was as open and honest a conversation as I've ever had with anyone. It was during this talk I knew without a doubt that I wanted to spend the rest of my life with Julianna.

The shadows of the bushes and few trees grew long. It was at least a thirty-minute hike to the parking lot. To be in the car before dark, we'd have to leave soon. But I didn't want to leave. I would have preferred to stay on that ledge with her all night.

The wind caught a plastic sandwich bag. I grabbed it before it went over the ledge and put it in my pocket. "We should get going," I said. I picked up the remains of our lunch and put it in my backpack. But Julianna didn't move. She sat, looking over the green valley. A gust of wind caught her hair and blew it over the side of her face, obscuring it from my view.

"Everything okay?" I said.

"I've really enjoyed this afternoon," Julianna said. She pulled her hair out of her face and tucked it behind her ear. "But before we go, there's something I have to tell you."

I set the backpack on the ground. There was something about her tone that indicated this was something important. I braced myself for bad news.

"I suffer from depression," she said.

A memory of Krista flashed through my mind. She was having one of her bad days and telling me that there was no hope for anyone and that we were all going to die. The look in her eyes was dark and dreadful.

"How bad is it?" I said without looking at her.

"I'm not suicidal. I've never thought about killing myself," she said. "Considering your history, I think it's something you need to know."

"Do you do anything to treat it?" Though I doubted Julianna's depression would lead to any dark episodes like I experienced with Krista, it was enough to make me pause and wonder if it was something I was willing to live with.

"I've been off and on medication for several years."

I looked back up at Julianna. "Off and on?"

"I've always believed that you are responsible for your own happiness. No matter what happens you should try to make the best of the situation. Sometimes medication is necessary, but I'd rather try to be happy on my own."

Her answer intrigued me. Maybe it was because I spent so much time with Krista's family, where prescriptions were preached as the cure-all for every ailment; this was the first time I had heard someone say they'd rather not be on anti-depressants.

"What do you do to make yourself happy?" I said.

"That's part of the reason I run marathons. The endorphins running releases make me feel better. I also try and do things for others when I'm feeling bad. And I try to concentrate on the positive when bad things happen." Julianna looked up at me. "It's not easy. It seems like when life is going good, I stop taking the pills. Then something bad happens, and soon after, I'm back on them."

"Some people would say that there's nothing you can do about the way you feel," I said. "Take a pill and enjoy the ride."

"I'm not saying that medication isn't helpful. I just think that people have more control over the way they behave and act than they think."

I looked at the ground. An ant approached one of several cookie crumbs in the dirt. He picked one up in his pinchers and turned back to the direction he had come. Krista's dark days had been difficult. There was no guarantee that Julianna wouldn't act similar or that one day she could wake up and her depression would be much worse. I had to decide if this was something I could live with. It was tempting to simply give up and find someone who didn't have depression. I'd been through a lot. Who would blame me if I decided to throw in the towel?

Then my mind went back to Krista. Despite those hard days, I never once thought about giving up on her. I wanted to see her through those hard times because I loved her. She had meant more to me than anyone else, and I was willing to help no matter how bad the situation became. And in that moment I realized it didn't matter if Julianna would have good days or bad. She was trying her best to work through her depression, and I was willing to take a chance and love her no matter what lay ahead.

"Thanks for telling me," I said. "There are a lot of people who think if they don't take a pill every morning, they can't be happy. I think it's great you're doing your best to resolve these issues on your own."

Julianna smiled. "Thanks," she said. "That means a lot."

We gathered our things and headed down the mountain. When we walked by some mountain flowers by the side of the trail, I picked one and handed it to Julianna. She took the flower and smiled. And with that smile I knew there would be many more days together in our future.

It wasn't until we were on our way home, warm night air blowing through the car, that I realized I needed to call Jennifer and end things. I hadn't been honest with Jennifer about our relationship. All that needed to change. It was time to come clean.

After dropping Julianna off at her apartment, I turned on my cell phone. There were three messages on my voice mail—all from Jennifer.

In the messages she sounded happy and eager to talk to me. I sat in the driveway and brought up Jennifer's number. I imagined myself pushing the call button and hearing Jennifer's voice answer. I went through a dozen different ways of telling Jennifer our relationship was over. I tried to think of the kindest, nicest way possible to end it until I realized there was nothing I could say that would ease what I was about to do.

Ending it was something I would have done eventually even if Julianna wasn't part of my life. Despite the wonderful times we had together, I never felt for Jennifer the way I did for Krista. I had rationalized the lack of those feelings by thinking it was impossible to have them for anyone else other than Krista. But after being with Julianna I realized it was possible to love someone just as much as I loved Krista. The hard truth was that I had pursued a relationship with Jennifer because I was lonely. And when the opportunity presented itself to be loved again, I took it.

I listened to a couple of songs on the radio, putting off the inevitable. The music was happy and made me think of being with Julianna. Finally the music broke to a commercial. I turned off the radio and got out of the car. I unlocked the door to the house. In the dark, I took off my shoes and walked to the couch. I lay down and dialed Jennifer's number and waited. There were two seconds of silence before the lines connected. Jennifer answered the call on the third ring.

"I've been trying to call you all afternoon," Jennifer said. She sounded excited to finally talk with me.

"I know. I got your messages."

"Where were you?"

"That's what we need to talk about," I said.

# CHAPTER
## Thirteen

I was sitting in the backyard, thinking of Julianna and watching the sprinkler turn in a circle as it watered the grass I had planted in April. The grass was dark green and thick and had somehow survived the blistering Utah summer despite a lack of regular watering. My yard didn't have a sprinkler system, and any moisture the yard received came only when I had time to hook the sprinkler to the hose.

Since our afternoon on the mountain, Julianna had come over to my house for dinner after church on Sunday, but we parted that evening without making plans of when to see each other again. Julianna seemed reserved, and I was unsure how much she had enjoyed that evening with me.

Water from the sprinkler sprayed near my chair. I had a bowl of ten apricots my mom had given me on my lap. "The last ones from our tree," she said as she handed them to me in a brown paper sack. I decided after I had eaten the last of them that I would call Julianna and see if she wanted to go out again this week. Since I was worried about whether she'd agree to another date, I ate the apricots slowly, one half at a time, planning out what I would say to her. The apricots were dark orange and slightly overripe, just the way I liked them. Their flesh was juicy and sweet.

As I was biting into the fourth apricot, my cell phone rang. The caller ID showed Julianna's number. I answered it on the first ring.

"What are you doing Friday?" she said.

"Friday night? Not a thing," I said. My heart skipped a beat. Julianna was asking me out. She must have been happy with the way things were going.

"Actually I want to know what you are doing Friday morning," Julianna said. "About five AM."

"I'm usually running at that time."

"I thought, perhaps, you might like to run with me instead."

"I'd love to." I tried to keep excitement out of my voice. This was the moment I had anticipated since I learned she was a runner. Asking me to partake of something she loved to do most likely meant things were going even better than I thought. I told her I'd be at her apartment at five on Friday. After I hung up, I pumped my fists in the air, ecstatic at the invitation. The bowl of apricots skidded off my lap, but I didn't care. The apricots rolled onto the lawn, looking like small round balls against the green grass. As I picked the apricots from the grass, I noticed the evening light was the same color as the fruit. Never again would I describe a sunset as orange. Every sunset from then on would always be the color of apricots.

I woke up every hour Thursday night, afraid I had forgotten to set the alarm clock. I'd double check the settings and try to clear my mind and go back to sleep. By the time the alarm went off at quarter to five, it felt like I hadn't slept at all. When I knocked on Julianna's apartment door fifteen minutes later, I was still rubbing the sleep out of my eyes.

Julianna invited me in. She was dressed in a T-shirt adorned with a marathon logo and purple running shorts—the same shorts she wore when she ran the Ogden Marathon. She laced up her running shoes and we were out the door.

"It's an easy run today," she said. "Three miles, at just under eight minutes per mile. Can you handle it?"

"I'll be right next to you," I said. I wasn't worried. My morning runs averaged seven minutes and thirty seconds per mile. If this was how fast Julianna trained, maybe I could win a marathon too. If she had only told me the route we were running, I would have been far less confident, and all thoughts of even entering a marathon would have been scuttled.

The run started along Harrisville Road for about a third of a mile. At Five Points we turned left and started up Second Street.

"Where do we go after this?" I asked.

"Straight," she said.

This was when I became worried. I made sure my running courses were as flat as possible. The biggest incline I ever faced was running over the railroad tracks on my way into the business depot. Julianna was heading on Second Street where the road sloped steeply to the east benches of Ogden.

"How far up this road are we going to run?" I said. Inside I was screaming, *No way! I don't do inclines!*

Julianna looked at me for a second before returning her eyes to the road. "All the way to the top." I must have done something to indicate I was worried because she quickly added, "But we also run all the way down." Her voice sounded so sprightly. I began to really worry.

The first quarter mile of the hill wasn't bad. I kept up with Julianna without too much difficulty. Then my legs started burning as the muscles started to tighten. I dropped a few steps behind Julianna.

"Am I running too fast?" Julianna asked.

"You're fine," I said, though I had to strain to sound like I wasn't tired. I had been telling Julianna what a good runner I was and didn't want her to have the impression that a hill was going to give me problems.

By the time we reached the top of the street, I was four seconds behind Julianna. I caught up with her as we headed downhill. I told myself I could have kept up with her if she hadn't kept talking on the way up. I was used to running in silence, and every breath I took to answer a question was one less I used to help me reach the top of the road.

We finished side by side when we reached the apartment complex. Julianna stopped her watch as we ran across the entrance. "About 7:50 a mile," she said. "Good job."

"Just another morning run," I said. I tried to hide the fact that I was breathing harder than usual. I could feel my face burn, so I had to be as red as a strawberry.

"Would you like some water before you head back?"

I looked at my watch. To make it to work on time, I would have to leave her place in ten minutes and then drive back home and ready myself for the day.

"Water sounds great," I said. I was thrilled to just spend a few more minutes with her. I noticed she was barely breathing hard and had only a little sweat on her forehead. I wondered how I could mask the fact that I knew I looked much worse.

On Sunday Julianna and I sat together at church for the first time. It was on one of the side pews near the front where about everyone in the chapel could see us. Personally I would have preferred a seat more toward the back, out of the view of everyone, but this was the area Julianna usually sat. I agreed to sit next to her without any objections even though I knew the congregation would be abuzz about the two of us.

During the services I kept looking back at my family sitting on the back row to see how they were handling it. From where we were sitting, I couldn't gauge their reactions and only caught them looking our way a few times.

After church I made a dinner of taco casserole and fresh corn on the cob from my parents' garden. Then we went for a walk through the surrounding neighborhoods.

"If you want, we can walk one of my three-mile running routes," I said. "They're flat and not as exciting as yours."

Julianna laughed. "You've never really told me why you run," she said.

"To lose weight," I said. "When I started running two years ago, I weighed fifty more pounds than I do now."

"You're kidding."

I shook my head and patted my stomach. "I topped the scales at two hundred and thirty-five pounds. That's what sitting in front of a computer and drinking several sodas a day will do to you."

"What made you decide to give running a try?"

"I came home from work one day and looked in the mirror. I didn't like the way my body looked. Growing up, I had always been very thin. I wanted to be happy with my body again and feel like I was in control of it. I rummaged through the closet and found a pair of running shoes and drove to a nearby high school and started running around the track."

The memory of that first run was still fresh in my mind. I had barely made it around the track once before I felt like my legs were going to fall off and my lungs were going to explode. It was a hot summer evening and I was sweating profusely, but I was determined to stick with it. Every day after that I tried to run a little farther. After a month I was up to a mile a day. By the time fall arrived, I was easily running three. Within six months, I had shed fifty pounds.

"And you stuck with it?"

"I liked the way it made me feel. I slept better, felt better emotionally, and felt like I was back in control of my body."

"Did Krista run with you?"

It still surprised me how easily Krista would come into our conversations now. Though I always answered Julianna's questions, I was still hesitant to bring up subjects relating to Krista. I didn't want Julianna to think Krista was always on my mind.

"Krista ran with me for two months. But when the weather cooled down, she lost interest. I think she was surprised I stuck with it after I reached my target weight."

"Did she encourage you to keep running?"

"She always said she was happy with the way my body looked. That was all the encouragement I needed."

We walked past a home with a freshly cut lawn. There was a strong smell of grass clippings in the air and flecks of grass scattered on the sidewalk.

"What was it like to win the marathon?" I said.

"That was awesome," she said smiling. There was a happy glint in her eye. "It was one of the best experiences of my life."

"Tell me about it," I said.

"It didn't seem real. Even as I was approaching the end and they rolled the tape across the finish line, it felt like a dream. It wasn't until they called my name over the loudspeaker and announced me as the first woman to cross the line that I realized I had indeed won."

"Were you in the lead the whole time?"

Julianna shook her head. "A few miles into the race someone told me I was in third place. A few miles later I passed the woman in second place. It wasn't until I was running down Ogden Canyon that someone told me the woman in first was struggling. I passed her with about two miles to the finish line."

"When you started the race, did you think you had a chance to win it?"

"Winning a marathon isn't something you expect to do. It's not something you think will happen. There are too many things that can happen to slow you down. An injury, for example, or you could be unprepared mentally."

"Unprepared mentally?"

"Is it easy for you to go running in the winter when it's dark and cold outside?"

"No. That's the hardest time of year to run."

"What makes you leave the warmth of the bed and do it?"

"I tell myself it's something I need to do."

"That's the way it is when you run a marathon. Your mind has to be prepared to handle the distance. If you don't think you can run it, you won't. It doesn't matter what kind of shape you're in."

We were now walking through a new development of duplexes. Behind the structures, fields of wheat and alfalfa lay in colorful patches. Across the fields I could see the back of my parents' house and their large garden.

"Think you'll win another?" I said.

"I don't know," she said. "As long as I feel I ran and trained to my potential, I won't care if I win or not."

We walked through the subdivision and then headed back up Seventh Street. The sun was to our backs, and our shadows were elongated ahead of us. I looked at Julianna out of the corner of my eye. I wanted to put my arm around her waist and pull her close but decided against it. After my fast-paced relationship with Jennifer, I didn't want to rush into anything. I wanted to wait until the time was right.

"Do you want to run with me tomorrow morning?" Julianna said.

"I'll be there at five," I said. I was glad she asked. I was unsure if her running invitation the previous week was good only for one day.

"It's a long run," she said. "Nine miles. Pace."

"Pace?"

"Six minutes and fifty seconds per mile."

"That's fast."

"If it's too fast for you, I'm okay running it alone."

"I wouldn't miss running with you for anything," I said.

I had no illusions about matching Julianna stride for stride on her pace run. I did, however, expect to stay close to her. And for the first two miles, I stayed right with her until breathing became so difficult, I had to slow down. As the run continued, the distance between us slowly widened. I'd watch as she'd run by a parked car or a street light and then count the number of seconds it took me to reach the same spot. By the end of the third mile, her lead had widened to fifteen seconds.

So far the run had taken us down Washington Boulevard, a wide, four-lane thoroughfare connecting the cities of Ogden and North Ogden. This run was another example of how our running tastes differed. I preferred quiet neighborhood streets where at five in the morning, cars were the exception, not the rule. I was hesitant to run on main streets, even ones like Washington Boulevard that had wide ten-foot shoulders because the last thing I wanted was to be hit by a car. Julianna, however, didn't seem worried about the traffic. It wasn't until weeks later I learned part of the reason she liked the busy roads early in the morning was she felt there was less of a chance of being accosted by someone when lots of cars drove past.

Right before mile three and a half, Julianna turned right on 2600 North and disappeared around the corner. I started counting. When I counted to twenty-one, I turned the corner just in time to see her running through the orange circle of a streetlight and disappear into the darkness. I was running as hard as I could. I tried not to think about the pace or how many miles were left—mentally it would have been too difficult for me. I was beginning to understand what Julianna said about longer runs being more mental than physical.

The road sloped gradually uphill. With each step I could feel myself slowing down. Every step was a struggle. Julianna appeared every so often under a streetlight. Her lead was increasing rapidly, and I stopped counting the distance between us. It was too frustrating.

Just when I felt like I couldn't run any more, I saw Julianna running toward me. She must have reached the four-and-a-half mile mark and was starting the second half of the run. Unsure where the turn-around point was and not wanting to be left too far behind, I turned around, looking over my shoulder occasionally to make sure Julianna was still running behind me. It took her only three minutes to catch up with me.

"How are you doing?" she asked.

"Great," I gasped. I could barely force the words out. It took too much energy to speak—energy I couldn't spare. I hoped I wouldn't die before the run ended. It would have been too embarrassing. My thoughts were muddled; I was so exhausted.

Step by step, Julianna pulled ahead. And soon I started counting the seconds between us. I increased my pace, determined to keep up with her, but suddenly found myself coughing. I stopped running and kneeled in the gravel by the side of the road. I started dry heaving, and it took several minutes to catch my breath and feel like I could continue running. When I looked up, Julianna was gone.

During the first half of the run, Julianna looked over her shoulder every three or four minutes to see where I was. For some reason I expected her to notice I stopped running and turn around to find me. Instead the road was dark and empty. I ran to the corner and headed south on Washington Boulevard. I looked down the shoulder of the road, hoping to spot her in the glare of the oncoming headlights. I saw nothing.

I started to worry. What if during the time I was dry heaving by the side of the road, someone had assaulted her or she was hit by a car? I could see someone jumping from the dark side of the road and dragging her out of sight of the traffic. It would be my fault because I was unable to keep up with her. The fear that something had happened to Julianna gave me added adrenaline to keep up what felt like a very fast pace. I kept hoping to see her somewhere ahead, running under a streetlight or a silhouette illuminated by the headlights of oncoming traffic.

It wasn't until I turned down the street that led to her apartment complex that I saw her. By this time there was a gray glow in the east, and I could see all the way to the finish line. She was walking slowly up the sidewalk in my direction, hands resting on her hips. When I saw her, the worry dissipated and the anger became stronger. Why hadn't she waited for me? Would it have killed her to slow down or turn around when she noticed I was no longer behind her? She had turned around and looked for me, right? A seed of doubt crept into my mind as to whether I wanted to continue running every morning with her.

Julianna clapped her hands when she saw me turn the corner. When I was in shouting range, she encouraged me to finish the run with a burst of speed. I couldn't do it. I ran at the pace I had been maintaining for the last two miles. I stopped when I reached the entrance to the apartment complex. I felt like collapsing. I was exhausted, not only from running but from worry. I had never been so glad a run was over.

"You did great!" Julianna said. She looked at her watch "You were only four minutes behind."

Four minutes? It seemed like I was much slower than that. I walked to my car. There was no time to stay and talk to Julianna this morning. I had a full day of work ahead of me. And even if I left for home right now, the odds were I'd arrive at work later than usual. But at that moment, I didn't care. All I wanted was a nice shower and a cold glass of water.

"Time," I said after I had caught my breath and was leaning against the car. "What was your time?"

"A little over fifty-eight minutes," Julianna said. There was a hint of pride in her voice.

I was too tired to do the math. "What's that per mile?" I said.

"Six minutes and thirty seconds."

I stopped, trying to figure out my pace per mile. "If you ran that fast, then how fast—"

"A little over seven minutes a mile," Julianna said.

"Are you sure?" That couldn't be right. All summer I had struggled to break the seven-thirty minute per mile mark. This morning I had shattered it. I had Julianna recalculate my pace several times. The anger toward her was replaced with a feeling of pride in what I had managed to accomplish. The fatigue in my arms and legs dimmed too. Maybe I could keep running with her a while longer.

The last thing I told Julianna before driving away was that I would run with her the next morning.

Morning runs together became part of our daily routine. Depending on her training schedule, we ran between three and ten miles a day. We averaged about thirty miles a week. It was the most I had ever run. But I loved spending time with Julianna and wouldn't have given up those mornings together for anything.

Watching Julianna run was something I never tired of. She kept her arms low, hands loose. Her breathing was steady and relaxed. She took long strides. It was more than her technique that made her runs beautiful. She never cut runs short or said she wasn't up to running that morning. Like an artist at work on a masterpiece, Julianna put her heart and soul into each run. There was never an excuse to do less than she thought was possible.

One morning after a grueling seven-mile run, I was sitting on the floor of her kitchen, drinking some ice-cold Gatorade. My right knee had stiffened up during the last two miles, and I kept resting the glass on it in an attempt to make it feel better. Julianna sat beside me, resting her head against the wall.

"After work, would you like to have dinner?" Julianna asked.

The question took me by surprise. "Sure," I said. "Where do you want to go?"

"I was thinking we could have dinner here. I'll make you something."

"I'd like that," I said as calmly as I could. Inside I was bursting with excitement, which was something considering how far we'd run. I'd wanted to spend more evenings with her, but Julianna still seemed cautious about moving the relationship quickly. I had been waiting for her to feel more comfortable with me before I was going to suggest it. Instead Julianna had beat me to the punch.

Julianna made a simple but delicious meal: a green salad and pizza bagels. Between our large appetites from running, we ate everything she had prepared. After we cleaned up the kitchen, we wandered to the living room. I sat on the middle of the couch cushion to see how close Julianna would sit to me. She sat on the next cushion, leaving a good two feet of space between us. I had wanted to kiss Julianna for several weeks, but up to that point we hadn't even held hands. Because of her concerns about dating a widower, I had been content to let her take things at her own pace. But I was growing increasingly impatient. Each day as my love for her grew, so did the desire to kiss her and be close to her.

I shifted my weight and closed the space between us by twelve inches. Julianna turned so she was facing me. She looked into my eyes for a split second and then, as if reading my thoughts, looked away. I moved in to kiss her but pulled back before Julianna could see me. That moment of hesitation was all it took for Julianna to start talking and the moment to be gone.

"Was Krista a competitive person?"

I returned to a sitting position, frustrated.

"Sometimes."

"What was she competitive in?"

"Games, mostly. Board games, computer games, word association games, trivia games. It didn't matter. If you played any sort of game with her, she would never show you any mercy. Kind of like when I run with you. You never slow down."

"Do you wish I would slow down?"

"I did at first, but not anymore. My running has improved tremendously over the last few weeks because of you."

"So she wasn't competitive in physical things like running."

"No. The few times Krista and I ran together, she couldn't have cared less who won."

"I guess in that way, Krista and I are opposites," Julianna said. "I don't care if I win board games."

With that comment I realized what Julianna was doing: she was seeing how she stacked up to Krista.

"I don't compare the two of you," I said.

"Krista was part of your life for years. How can you not notice the things I do differently?"

"You're a different person," I said. "You have different interests and abilities. If I wanted someone like Krista, I'd date a crazy blonde English major who writes poetry."

"It's not that," Julianna said. "I know in some ways I could never measure up to her."

"Why do you want to know so much about her?" I said.

"I'd like to meet her." Julianna looked away, embarrassed. "I wish I could talk with her and know what kind of person she was."

I stood up and walked to the far side of the room in frustration. I leaned against the wall and looked at Julianna.

"Why do you want to know so much about Krista?" I said.

"She's always going to be part of our relationship. It's not that I can't live with that. I want to know more about her so I can understand you better."

I walked back to the couch and sat next to Julianna. She rested her head on my shoulder and put her arms around me.

"I know things are moving slower than you'd like," she said. "Just give me some time. In some ways this relationship is very hard for me."

I tried to kiss Julianna twice the next day, but each time Julianna looked away. When she looked up again, her eyes pleaded for patience. The kiss finally came the next Sunday after a dinner at my house. The meal I made hadn't turned out as planned. The casserole was burned on the edges and cold in the middle. The soup was watery and weak. The only thing that was edible was the salad, which wasn't enough to fill us up. In the end we heated up leftover pizza.

When we were done, Julianna brought the last of the dishes from the table and set them in the bubble-filled water. I put my arm around her waist and pulled her close. This time she didn't look away. She took a step toward me as I embraced her so her body was pressing against mine and we kissed.

The kiss wasn't perfect. We were both hesitant, and our lips didn't quite mesh at first. But to me that didn't matter. That spark I never thought I would feel again was present. It was the same feeling I had felt years ago when I kissed Krista for the first time. A warm feeling spread through my body as if to confirm the woman in my arms was the right one for me. It seemed like forever since I had felt this way toward someone.

When we finally pulled away from each other, Julianna leaned her head on my chest and put her arms around me. I kept one arm around her waist and rested my other hand on her head, holding her close. We stood like that for several minutes, feeling our bodies rise and fall with each breath.

"Are you sure you want to do this?" I said.

"Yes," Julianna said. "I want this to work."

# CHAPTER
# *Fourteen*

By late August, Julianna and I were spending every free moment with each other. From running early in the morning together to dinner after work, our lives slowly became one. Our conversations grew more comfortable and intimate, and soon we felt more comfortable talking about Krista, though I was still hesitant to voluntarily share information because I didn't want Julianna to think I was comparing them. One evening I took Julianna to an out-of-the-way Chinese restaurant Krista and I had frequented when we were in college.

"The food's really good," she said near the end of our meal. "How did you know about this place?"

My first impulse was to tell a half-truth, that it was a place I learned about in college, leaving out the fact that Krista and I had lived two blocks away. I worried if I told Julianna, she wouldn't want to return because it would be something associated with Krista. But I knew that being open and honest about Krista was important. So I told the truth.

"The first apartment Krista and I shared was just down the street," I said. "We found it when we were walking through the neighborhood one day."

Julianna seemed unfazed by it and twirled a bite of orange chicken with her fork. "So the two of you ate here often?"

I nodded.

"We'll have to come back," she said. "The orange chicken is fabulous."

I took a spoonful of the hot mustard and mixed it in with my food.

"Does it bother you that Krista and I used to come here?"

"Not really. Does it bother you?"

"No."

"Then why do you think it would bother me?"

"Because if the situation were reversed, I'd have a hard time with it."

Julianna put down her fork. "You and Krista spent most of your lives in Ogden," she said. "You've told me that there isn't part of this town that doesn't remind you of something the two of you did together. It's not easy for me to know that. But there's nothing I can do about it. Hopefully we can make some of our own memories."

"I think we already have some good ones," I said. "I seem to recall something that happened in a restaurant on our first date."

We both smiled, remembering how badly that date had gone. I was glad we had reached a point where we could smile about it.

"Maybe we should start making some good ones," Julianna said.

We laughed and returned to our food. Julianna finished her chicken a minute later and pushed her plate to the center of the table.

"Are you still angry at her?" Julianna asked.

I looked at the table and herded a snow pea to the other side of my plate with my fork before answering.

"It depends on the day," I said. "And how much I've been thinking about her."

Julianna leaned toward me. She did this when she wanted my full attention.

"Do you think about her often?"

"Every day," I said.

Julianna dropped her eyes to her plate.

"Did you think I was going to say something else?" I said.

"No," Julianna said. "It's the answer I expected. But it hurts to hear you say it. A girl likes to think she's the only person in a man's thoughts."

The waitress stopped and cleared Julianna's plate and refilled our glasses with water.

Julianna watched as the waitress walked back into the kitchen. She picked up the glass of water and sipped it slowly.

"The reason that I ask about the anger is that you seem to be handling everything so well," she said. "But there are times when I see flashes of rage in your eyes. I don't blame you for feeling that way. I only want to know if there's anything I can do to help."

"I wish there was something you could do," I said. "But that's something I have to work through on my own."

I was doing my best to make room for two in my heart. And for the most part, I thought I was succeeding. I could honestly say that I loved Julianna and could see myself spending the rest of my life with her. But my anger toward Krista was stopping me from making a permanent place in my heart for Julianna. Before there could be room for both of them, there were some issues I still had to resolve.

After I dropped Julianna off at her apartment, I drove home and sat in my car, thinking about forgiveness. Forgiveness was something my parents and religion had instilled in me from the time I was young. For the most part I never found it difficult to forgive anyone, but only because I had never been seriously hurt or offended before.

It would be so much easier to forgive Krista if I had an explanation for her actions. But the only person who could tell me what was going through her mind when she put the gun to her head was dead. I had no doubt that wherever Krista was, she was aware of the consequences of her actions and regretted what she had done. However, she wasn't in a position to explain why she had done it or to tell me how she was sorry for the pain and anguish she had inflicted upon me and others who loved her. It would be so much easier if she could just apologize.

I also wanted to say how much I regretted ignoring the three promptings that could have saved her life. I still felt guilty about my inaction and wondered how different life would have been had I only listened to those quiet warnings when I had the chance. I needed a way to share my feelings with Krista and know that she had forgiven me. It would be the first step to forgive her and myself. Somehow I would have to find a way to do it without an apology and knowing that there would always be some things that I would never know the answer to.

The next day I worked through lunch and left work an hour early. Instead of heading home, I drove to the cemetery. I knelt in front of the headstone and cleared away the dried grass that had accumulated in its corners. I traced Krista's and Hope's names with my finger. And for a while I was lost in good memories. It was easy to pretend my life with Krista was perfect and that she had never been pregnant or killed herself. Enough time had passed that, aside from her suicide, I had to struggle to think of fights or other bad moments we had together. I could almost understand why Julianna was so hesitant to become involved with a widower. It would indeed be difficult to be second in line to a person who, aside from the way she died, seemed so perfect.

Eventually my thoughts shifted to Hope. Nine months. That's how old she would be if she had she lived. I tried to think of what babies were like at that age. Is that when they started to crawl? I couldn't remember. Though usually I could picture my daughter growing up, that afternoon the only way I saw her was in the hospital, lying motionless in her bed bathed by the bright, warm light.

Thoughts of Hope being so vulnerable and untouchable made me cry, and I let the tears fall. I found myself wishing for other memories of her besides those days in the hospital. I would often tell myself that if it had been possible to take her home and have her live a normal life even for a few days, it would be less painful to think of her. But that was a lie. Hope would always be the daughter I never had a chance to raise, and thoughts of her would always leave a tight feeling in my throat.

I sat next to the headstone with my knees pulled to my chest. *Talk to me, Krista,* I thought. *Tell me why you did it.* I thought those words as if I expected her to somehow answer me. I sat like that for an hour, waiting. When it became apparent that no answer was coming, I stood to leave. But before I left, there was one thing I still had to do.

*There's something I need to tell you,* I thought. *Something about the day you died. You see, I had several chances to save your life that day and I didn't.* I bowed my head and told Krista about the mistakes I had made the day she died.

Labor Day brought with it an invitation to another family barbeque. This one was to be a more intimate gathering than the one on the Fourth of July. Only immediate family and a next-door neighbor had been invited. Though my family had met and spoken to Julianna at church, this was their first chance to really spend some time with her. I thought it best to prepare Julianna for the worst.

"I'm still not sure how open my family is to our dating," I said. I was sitting on the side of the bathtub, watching Julianna use the curling iron. Containers of mascara, blush, eyeliners, and lotion were spread out on the sink. I picked up the mascara and twirled it with my fingers.

"Do you think they might be mean to me?" Julianna asked. She looked at me via the mirror. Her eyebrows were knit in a way that indicated she was a little concerned about fitting in with my family.

"Like you or not, they'll be polite," I said. "I'm telling you this so that if for some reason there's a problem, you won't take it personally. It's not you they'll have a problem with per se. The bigger issue is them adjusting to seeing me with someone else."

"I don't want them to feel like they're being rushed to accept me," Julianna said. She unplugged the curling iron and set it on the countertop. She took the bottle of mascara from my fingers, pulled the cap off, and applied the mixture to her eyelashes.

"How do I look?" she said, blinking at me.

"Beautiful," I said. I stood and kissed her on the forehead.

"I can't be anyone else but myself, Abel. I hope your family doesn't expect anyone other than me to arrive."

"Cross your fingers that everything works out."

We arrived just as my dad was putting hamburger patties and hot dogs on the barbeque. The meat sizzled on the grill. He greeted Julianna warmly.

For the first hour Julianna didn't stray from my side. She seemed nervous as we talked to the dozen or so people in attendance. Gradually, she became more relaxed and opened up to them. By the time we were done eating, she sat next to my dad and told him about working in the crime lab and the different types of evidence she analyzed.

I was pleased and relieved that the family seemed to like her. Unlike Jennifer, everyone seemed happy to have her at the party. Still, inside, I remained uptight and watched my family all evening, looking for any sign that something was amiss.

It wasn't until after the barbeque that my dad said anything about her. We were both watching Julianna talk to Liam. They seemed to be having a good time together.

"She seems like a nice girl," he said.

"You like her then?" I said.

"She's very sweet," he said.

In my dad's language, that meant he approved.

For the first time that evening, the anxiety that had built up inside me was gone. Liam said something and Julianna laughed. My family had been more accepting of her than I thought possible. For the first time, I thought there was hope that they were slowly moving on too. I couldn't wait to tell Julianna the good news.

In the first month that we ran together, Julianna would soundly beat me on any run over five miles. It was discouraging to watch her body melt into the darkness as she widened the gap between us with her long, powerful legs. When I could no longer see her, I worried about her safety until I saw her waiting for me at the end of our run. But I was becoming faster and was slowly closing the time between our finishes. After Labor Day I had cut her margin of victory on a seven-mile run to under a minute. It wasn't until the last mile that Julianna pulled away from me. According to Julianna, all I had to do was convince myself that I could push my body a little bit faster every day. Even though I had mastered the mental part of rising early in the morning and running every day, telling myself that I could keep up with Julianna was something I couldn't do.

I blamed the hills.

Any run over five miles would, at some point, turn east toward the mountains and involve a series of hills. I was convinced it was impossible to run up them at a reasonable pace. Julianna, however, thrived on them, and that was where she would usually pull ahead. Often I would tell Julianna I could keep up with her better if only the courses we ran were flat. Julianna would shake her head and tell me that I had the power and the stamina to keep up with her. The only thing that was holding me back was my mind.

The most difficult of all the runs was a ten-mile loop. It started at her apartment complex and then headed up Second Street toward the mountains. Once we reached Harrison Boulevard, we headed north, running with the hilly road until we reached 2600 North. That road was, thankfully, all downhill until we reached Washington Boulevard. From Washington it was three and a half miles of flat running back to her apartment. On this run Julianna would pull ahead on the hills of Harrison Boulevard. By the time I reached 2600 North, Julianna was usually several minutes ahead of me. No matter how hard I ran, I was unable to close the distance between the two of us.

Julianna was planning on running the St. George Marathon at the beginning of October. Each morning she trained hard for it. Our runs had become faster, and I found myself tired most of the day. The week after the Labor Day barbeque, another ten-mile run came due. When I awoke that morning, it was the first time that I didn't want to run with her. Physically, I knew my body could handle it. Mentally, I didn't like the idea of doing five miles of running up and down hills and having Julianna pull far ahead of me by the second mile. Despite these thoughts, I kicked off the covers and prepared myself for another run. *It's the last one until her marathon in October*, I told myself. *Do this and it will be months before we'll run it again.*

When I arrived at her apartment, Julianna was excited. She relished the longer runs. If her training schedule called for it, I had no doubt she would run ten miles every morning. As we ran up Second Street toward the hills, Julianna kept looking up at the sky. Between breaths I managed to ask what she was looking at.

"The stars," she said. "They're very vibrant this morning."

I followed her gaze. It was one of those mornings where, despite the lights of the city, the stars looked bigger and brighter than normal. To the east, right above the mountain, I could make out the constellations of Orion and Taurus.

Even now I'm not sure exactly what I thought about during that first part of the run. Maybe the heavens served as a distraction. But the next thing I knew we turned left on Harrison Boulevard, and I was running right next to Julianna. The usual fatigue that set into my legs at that point was absent. For the first time, I thought it might be possible to keep up with her for the entire ten miles. If I could just make it all the way to 2600 North, I felt confident I could stay with her the rest of the way.

Harrison Boulevard rose and fell with the hills. Instead of counting down how many hills remained, I took them one at a time, telling myself each hill was the last. I fought back my body's urge to slow down when I neared the hill's peak and ignored the burning sensation in my lungs when I made it to the top of each one.

It worked beautifully. By the time we reached 2600 North, I was still at Julianna's side. Even Julianna seemed a little surprised I had kept up with her this long.

"You're running very well this morning," she said.

I acknowledged her comment with a grunt. I didn't want to say anything because it would require an extra breath.

I stayed next to her until the last mile when Julianna pulled a few steps ahead. At first I thought I had unconsciously slowed down. But as I increased my speed to catch up with her, I realized Julianna kept increasing her pace about every hundred yards.

"What's the hurry?" I said. I forced out the words quickly, in one breath.

"You know I usually finish with a sprint," Julianna said. She increased the pace again. "Come on! Catch me!"

The teasing way she said it was just the motivation I needed to stay with her. By the time the end of our run was in sight, I was only two steps behind her. Julianna put on a final burst of speed. Her lead widened to three steps, then four.

"You can do it!" Julianna said over her shoulder. "We're almost done!'

I tried to keep up, telling myself the end of the run was only one hundred yards away.

"You're doing great!" Julianna said.

Spurred on by Julianna's comments, I ran the final fifty yards as fast I could. My lungs burned in my chest, and my legs felt like they were going to fall off. Then, suddenly, the entrance to the apartment complex was upon us and I finished the run two seconds behind Julianna.

Julianna turned to hug me, but I flopped down on the strip of grass between the road and the sidewalk and gasped for breath. I felt like I was going to throw up. Julianna kneeled next to me. Several drops of sweat ran down the sides of her face and landed on my neck. "You stayed with me the entire way!" She put her arms around me. She had a big smile on her face and sounded proud.

I was still fighting for breath, unable to respond. I looked past Julianna to the sky. The stars that were so big and bright when we started the run were gone. Only a half dozen, the ones that were the biggest in the night sky, remained.

"How fast?" I said between breaths. "Our time. What was it?"

Julianna checked her watch. "We ran it in one hour and eight minutes," she said. "That's about six fifty a mile."

It didn't seem possible I had run that fast for ten miles. I grabbed Julianna's wrist and pulled it close so I could double check our time. The digital display read back 1:08:34.

I looked back up at the heavens. One by one the stars twinkled one last time and then were hidden by the rapidly bluing sky. The sick feeling slowly subsided, and I was finally able to sit up and give Julianna a hug.

"Thanks for not slowing down," I said. I knew I would never have a problem keeping up with Julianna again.

That evening after a dinner of spaghetti and garlic bread, we lay on the couch and watched TV. The morning run had left us both too tired to do anything else. Fifteen minutes into the movie we were watching, Julianna fell asleep. Her head rested on my shoulder, and her right arm lay across my chest.

I muted the television and put my arms around her. Julianna's breathing was slow and relaxed. I matched my breaths to hers until our chests rose and fell in unison. I closed my eyes and enjoyed the slow and steady movement of our breathing and enjoyed feeling like one with her.

It's hard to describe how wonderful it felt to have her resting in my arms. I wanted to hold Julianna forever and never let her go. I was learning how precious and fragile love can be. I regretted that I had taken Krista's love for granted. It was something I thought would always be there, something I never thought would be suddenly taken away. As I held Julianna in my arms, I told myself her love was something I would always treasure.

I rested my head on hers. Her hair had a faint smell of flowers that I found comforting and vaguely familiar. Krista might have had some lotion or perfume that smelled similar. I tried to recall an instance where Krista had smelled like that, but my tired mind was unable to tie the smell into a specific moment.

Soon I fell asleep. It was a light sleep, one where I would wake up every few minutes on my own or when Julianna stirred. But during those few minutes of sleep, I dreamed. The dreams were hard to remember. I'd awaken unable to recall the specific details about them. Only small fragments remained: umpiring a Minor League Baseball game or driving along a dirt road in Wyoming. The dreams left me feeling disoriented and confused.

This went on for about an hour. Then suddenly I dreamed about Krista. She was reading me a paper she had written for an upper-level

English class and wanted my feedback. It was something she used to do quite regularly when we were together. We were laughing over a pun she had used in the paper, and we were having a good time.

Julianna stirred, partially waking me from my dream. In my half-awake state, I thought it was Krista I held in my arms. Julianna raised herself on the couch and said something about it being late. Her words made it into the dream. I heard them, but they were Krista's words, not Julianna's.

"I don't want to go home, Krista," I said. "I want to stay here with you."

The dream faded. I opened my eyes, expecting to see Krista's blue eyes looking into mine. Instead Julianna was staring at me. She looked confused. In an instant all traces of sleep left my body. We stared at each other for several seconds. I was unable to tell whether or not she had heard what I said.

"You're right, *Julianna*," I said, making sure to emphasize her name. "It's late. I need to go home."

I walked to the door, slipped my shoes on, and looked back at Julianna. She still looked confused, almost hurt. Thinking a kiss would help the situation, I returned to the couch and kissed her forehead and left. I thought I had dodged a bullet and that my words had been too mumbled to understand or Julianna had been too tired to listen. But the look on Julianna's face the next morning let me know that my words had been heard.

Instead of heading out the door for a run, Julianna invited me inside. "We need to talk," she said. She motioned to the couch. I sat on the middle cushion. Julianna sat several feet to my left. Her arms were folded across her chest, and her legs were angled away from me.

"Last night you called me Krista," she said.

With those words, I felt all the progress we had made the last month was gone. Instead of being boyfriend and girlfriend, it was like we were on a first date, starting from square one. I tried to put my arm around Julianna. She moved her shoulders in such a way to tell me my touch was not wanted. I leaned back on the cushions.

"I wasn't sure you heard me say that last night. Why didn't you say anything?" I said.

"I was too stunned and hurt."

"It was an accident. When I realized what I had said, I panicked. I thought it best to leave before I slipped up again."

There was an uncomfortable silence between us. The ceiling creaked as someone walked across the living room upstairs.

"What were you thinking when you called me Krista?" Julianna finally said.

"I was dreaming," I said. "Krista was part of the dream. For some reason when I woke up I thought it was her and not you I was lying next to."

"Do you ever pretend that I'm Krista?"

"I've never once held you in my arms and thought I was holding Krista. What happened last night was a fluke. It's never happened before. It will never happen again."

"Why do you think you said it?"

"I don't know. It just came out."

The look on Julianna's face let me know she was accepting of my response but was still very hurt by what I had done.

"I've become extremely comfortable with you," I said.

The only thing I could think of was that I had reached a physical and emotional comfort level with Julianna that I had only felt before with Krista.

"Last night on the couch while you slept in my arms, I was thinking how nice it was to be that comfortable with someone again. I never thought I could feel that way about anyone again, but having you lying there, feeling us breathe together just made me feel how perfect we are for each other."

I moved closer to Julianna and pulled her close.

"I'm sorry it happened," I said. "But you have to believe me when I tell you it was an accident. It wasn't my intention to call you Krista."

"I know you think about her," Julianna said. "I never expect you to not think about her or Hope. But these last few weeks . . ." Her voice trailed off and she looked lost in thought. "These last few weeks have been wonderful. You've made me feel like the center of your universe, like I'm the only woman you've ever loved. There have been moments where I've almost forgotten you were married before."

I bent my head so my mouth was next to her ear. "Before you came into my life, I wondered if I would ever laugh or smile again. But now I do because I can share it with you. Before I fell in love with you, it was hard to wake up every morning. I had to force myself out of bed. Now you're my first thought in the morning, and I jump out of bed because

I have the honor of running with you. And at night instead of going home and being alone, I want to stay with you. You have made me love life again, Julianna. And because of that, I would do anything to make you happy."

Tears ran down my cheeks and landed on Julianna's shoulder. I could feel her body tremble as she tried to hold back the tears. Julianna put her arms around me. A hot tear fell from her cheek to mine.

"I love you," she said.

We held each other and cried for several minutes. When the tears stopped falling, I looked at Julianna and said, "You really want to go through with this? I can't promise there won't be hard moments like this in the future."

Julianna nodded her head and leaned her head on my chest. I ran my fingers through her hair. It felt good to have her head resting on my chest. It felt natural. It felt right.

Finally Julianna looked at me and said, "Do you still want to go running?"

"More than anything," I said.

Julianna laced up her running shoes, and we headed into the cool September morning for a three-mile run.

CHAPTER

*Fifteen*

T
wo weeks before the St. George Marathon, I ran with Julianna on her last long training run. It was the first time she had let me join her on a run over ten miles. To me it was proof that our relationship was growing stronger and that Julianna didn't view me as a hindrance to her training.

I mapped out a twelve-mile course that snaked through the business depot. The route took us past warehouses, abandoned trains, and old ammunition bunkers. The latter was left over from when the facility was owned and utilized by the U.S. Army. I thought the route would be a nice change from the busy, main roads we usually ran. Being Saturday, the streets of the depot would be empty.

The run started like any other. We maintained a constant seven-minute-and-thirty-second pace through the first six miles. Between breaths we talked about the upcoming marathon, how fast Julianna wanted to run it, and traveling with her family to see it. I was looking forward to the trip; it would be a good way to get to know Julianna's family better.

As we started the seventh mile of the run, I noticed Julianna's pace had slowed, and she seemed to have a slight limp in her right leg. With each step she grimaced ever so slightly, as if she was trying to hide how much pain she was in.

"Are you hurt?" I asked.

Julianna nodded. "My right leg."

"Is it a cramp?" To mask my worry, I tried to say it like it was no big deal. For the last week Julianna had been experiencing discomfort in her right leg during our regular morning runs and would down several ibuprofens and a glass of milk when we were done. I had asked her what was wrong, but she had dismissed my questions by saying it wasn't anything to worry about.

"I'm fine. Keep running," she said.

We ran for another mile. Up ahead was a major cross street. Turning right would cut the run short about four miles. Running straight would take us along the perimeter of the depot, down a long straight road with warehouses as big as football fields on our right, and a chain link fence with barbwire looping around the top to our left.

"Maybe we should head home," I said as we approached the intersection. "No point risking further injury."

"I can do this," Julianna said. "The pain isn't too bad."

As we ran through the intersection, I looked right. I could see up Second Street, all the way to my house. I longed to turn right and get Julianna off her leg as soon as possible. Julianna didn't look to the right or the left. She kept herself focused on the course.

By the time we started the eighth mile, Julianna's pace slowed to about eight and a half minutes per mile. Her limp became more noticeable. Her face was flush, as if running was pushing herself to the limits.

"I really think we should call it," I said. We were running slowly enough that I could talk in complete sentences.

"I can finish," Julianna said.

"Don't you want to run the marathon?"

Julianna didn't say anything.

"Then why not take it easy? Cutting this run short by a few miles isn't going to slow you down come race day. If we keep running, you risk further injury. You might not be able to run the marathon at all."

"I'll rest tomorrow," Julianna said. "Next week is short runs. I'll be fine."

I grabbed her hand and tried to slow her down. "You can rest while I run home. I can be back with the car in less than ten minutes."

Julianna shook my hand from her arm and continued running. She didn't stop until she reached my house. By that time she could barely walk and was doing her best to fight back the tears. She leaned on me, and I helped her slowly walk to the house. She sat down on the porch and leaned against the side of the house.

I went to the kitchen to retrieve a glass of water and ibuprofen. When I returned, Julianna was lying on her back, staring at the sky. She had a faraway look in her eyes, as if she was remembering something.

"You know what's wrong with your leg, don't you?" I said.

Julianna nodded. She sat up and swallowed the two pills and half the glass of water. Then she lay down on her side so she was facing the street. I sat by her head and ran my fingers through her hair.

"My second year at the University of Puget Sound, I fractured my right femur," she said. "The pain feels exactly the same."

"How long did it take to heal?"

"About nine months. The doctors wouldn't let me run during that time."

"Is a doctor going to look at your leg before the race?"

"I have an appointment next week," Julianna said.

"And if your leg's broken?"

"I've trained too hard not to run," she said.

We sat on the porch, watching the nimbus clouds blow in from the west and head over the mountains. I started massaging Julianna's shoulders and back. Slowly the tension in her muscles dissipated. She relaxed and leaned against my chest. We waited until Julianna said the pain in her leg had subsided enough that she could stand. Then I helped her to the car and drove her home.

Julianna saw the doctor Tuesday afternoon. She didn't ask me to go with her. I was a little hurt by her actions. I tried not to let it bother me even though I wanted nothing more than to be with her.

That evening I fixed dinner for myself. It was the first time in over a month I hadn't spent the evening with Julianna. It felt strange to eat alone. It was a sober reminder of what my life was like before Julianna became a regular part of it—when the loneliness of the house seemed to be my constant companion.

While dinner was warming in the microwave, I walked out to the mailbox. Mixed in with the junk mail and bills was a large manila envelope that had Primary Children's Hospital as its return address. It had been months since I received any mail from them, and I wondered what it contained. Back inside the house, I tore open the envelope and dumped the contents out on the kitchen counter. Two photographs of Hope floated to the counter and landed face up.

They were the last things I expected to see, and I was unprepared for the memories they unleashed: her lying in her incubator, trying to curl her hand around my finger, holding her in my arms as she died.

The tears came quickly. I leaned against the metal stove and slid to the floor. The microwave beeped, and there was a faint smell of warmed up tuna casserole. My body shook as I recalled Hope resting in my arms, gasping her final breaths.

When I finally composed myself, I picked up the photographs, trying to decide what to do with them. There was something strange about them. I looked closer. Hope's face had a yellow tint to it. The only time she had looked like that was when she died. I couldn't recall anyone with a camera in the room when Hope died, and I wondered when the photographs had been taken. I thought back to Hope's final moments: the doctor declaring her dead and me holding her briefly before handing her to the nurse and walking out the door. There seemed to be something I was missing, something I must have forgotten. I thought again, longer and harder, replaying the scene over and over again in my mind.

Then I remembered.

As I left the room, the nurse asked something about having photographs taken of my daughter. I must have said yes because as my dad and I were walking down the hall, I recall a nurse walking toward the room, pushing a cart with a camera attached to it. I put the photographs back in the envelope. I was grateful to have them. I only wished they hadn't caught me by surprise.

I took the envelope to the room where Krista's things were stored. In the spring, my mom had created a scrapbook full of photographs of Hope's brief life. I had only looked at the book once. The grief rose to the surface too quickly when I opened the scrapbook, so I had stored the book along with Krista's things.

The scrapbook was buried deep under three-ring binders filled with Krista's papers and journals. I put the envelope in the back of the scrapbook. I decided not to look through the rest of it. I had experienced enough memories for one day. As I was placing a notebook of Krista's writings back in the box, a group of loose papers slid from their bindings and fell to the floor. I briefly looked through the papers;

most of them were assignments she had written for her college English classes.

I read the first page of one essay, and with it came a memory of Krista writing it on our computer late at night. I read a second, then a third. Each personal essay or story critique came with its own special moment, a reminder how wonderful and creative Krista had been. Lost in good memories, I sat on the floor, amid the boxes, and read the first few pages of every paper. By the time I finished reading, I felt happy. It was nice to think of Krista and remember what she was like before the darkness had overtaken her.

Behind the last paper, stuffed in the back of the notebook in a mishmash fashion, were a few of Krista's poems. I always considered them the most personal of her writings, and I hadn't read any of them since she died. But I started sifting through the poetry. I read her poems out loud, one by one. I had always been envious of the way Krista was able to string words and images together. And as I sat there reading, I wondered how someone who was capable of writing such beauty could take her own life.

Then I read the last poem in the notebook. And everything stopped.

### Ten Toed Children of Eve
My parents were married
under the constellation of the aardvark
in the year of the swan.
I was conceived on Strawberry Hill—
which isn't a hill— but a two dollar wine.
Don't, however, make the mistake
of thinking maniacs cannot love deeply,
or underestimate the children of
their kind of frenzy.

It is true that Susan has since seen visions
and has mistaken the garage for
Eden on quite a few occasions (only
you can't smoke near the gasoline).
It rains rhinestones on the lawn for her;
Just put up your lithium umbrella

and dance along.
Todd can fix anything . . . broken.
He repairs trees in the garden
for Susan who has woven
spark plugs into her hair.
She sings "the tree of life is a tobacco plant"
but don't make the mistake of thinking
that life isn't found in strange paradises.
"I have born only good sons," she says.
And that is one up on the original Eve.

I read the poem again and again. Each time I pictured Krista's parents in my mind. I could see Susan raving about hidden cameras placed all over her house by the FBI or claiming the garage was indeed Eden. I remembered Todd chain smoking as he fixed their lawnmower for the umpteenth time that summer.

Then I thought of Krista and wondered what it was like for her growing up with Susan and Todd as parents. I could see why she was so hesitant to talk about them when we were first dating and even more cautious about having me meet them. As I read the poem a final time, I realized "Ten Toed Children of Eve" was about more than her parents' insanity. Krista was part of the poem too, a warning not to underestimate what she was capable of based on the genes she had received from her parents.

Since Krista had told me about her parents, openly and honestly, I had always thought that she was immune to the mental illnesses that afflicted them. In reality, I had misjudged how powerful genetics could be. Krista had been suffering from something, I didn't know what. But at that moment I knew taking her own life wasn't something Krista would have chosen if she had been in her right mind. Accompanying that thought, I was filled with a feeling of peace. I held onto that serenity as long as I could.

Julianna stopped by as I was getting ready for bed. The unhappy look in her eyes told me the news she received from the doctor wasn't good. It turned out the diagnosis was just what Julianna had feared. An X-ray had revealed a hairline fracture in her femur.

"What did he say about running the marathon?" I said.

"He said it would be better if I didn't run it," she said. The tone of her voice indicated that the doctor's words had devastated her. "If I decide to run, he suggested I not do any more training runs between now and race day." She put her arms around me and rested her head on my shoulder. "I was looking forward to this marathon. I've been running so fast. I thought it would be a great opportunity to improve my time."

"Maybe your leg will feel better if you stay off it until race day," I said.

Julianna shook her head. "Injuries like this don't heal overnight. I know that after a few miles my leg will be in pain again come race day."

"Are you still going to run?"

Julianna nodded. "I have to run no matter how much it hurts. I've trained too hard to simply give up."

Instead of running every morning, we went to the fitness center at her apartment complex and worked out. While I ran on the treadmill, Julianna rode the stationary bike—the only workout that wouldn't further injure her leg. Each morning she pedaled fast and furious for an hour. In the afternoons after work before I returned home, she rode the bike for another hour. It became part of the routine for me to come home and find her preparing dinner dressed in her workout clothes, sweat still lingering on her brow.

I had never seen anyone work so hard at something. If it was me with the broken leg, there was no doubt I would have stopped working out and wouldn't have even thought about running the marathon. But Julianna was determined to race, and there was nothing that she would use for an excuse to stop.

Julianna insisted on running at least one good run a week before the marathon. We ran it in Salt Lake near her parents' house. Her leg still hurt, but it wasn't as bad as it had been weeks ago. As we drove back to Ogden, I was going to tease Julianna about making up the whole broken leg thing just so she wouldn't have to run anymore. But Julianna had a faraway look in her eyes, and I could tell she hadn't been listening to me recap the run.

"What are you thinking about?" I said.

The words seemed to bring her out of her trance.

"You," she said.

"What about me?"

"How you're doing," she said.

I thought she meant how I was feeling after the run.

"I feel a little winded," I said, "but otherwise I feel great."

"That's not what I meant," Julianna said. "How are you doing as far as moving on? You know, with Krista."

I thought I was slowly coming to an inner peace with Krista's suicide, even though there were still many unanswered questions surrounding her death. I wasn't actively grieving anymore and talked about her openly with Julianna.

"All things considered, I think I'm doing rather well," I said. I briefly took my eyes off the road and looked at Julianna. "Why do you ask?"

"I think there's some work you need to do," Julianna said.

Her words stung. I tried to think of anything I might have done to give her the impression I was having a difficult time moving on. I thought about my house. I had moved photos of Krista and me from the living room and hallways back to my bedroom. The rooms that Julianna spent most of her time at my place—the living room and kitchen—were now Krista-free. I tried to treat Julianna like the number one woman in my life.

"What am I doing wrong?" I asked.

"I just don't think you're ready, that's all."

"Ready? Ready for what?"

Julianna shrugged her shoulders and looked back out the passenger window.

"You can't say I'm not ready and not tell me what it is," I said.

"All I'm saying is that I don't think you've moved on enough."

I gripped the steering wheel tightly and gritted my teeth.

"You're being unfair," I said.

"Please, Abel," Julianna said. "Trust me on this one."

I spent the next ten minutes trying to coax the information out of Julianna. After it became apparent Julianna wasn't going to give in, we drove the rest of the way home in silence. I dropped Julianna off at her apartment instead of taking her back to my place. I was frustrated enough that I didn't want to spend any more time with her that day.

Once home I walked through the house, double-checking everything to make sure there were no signs of Krista in the rooms Julianna frequented. Not finding anything that said I wasn't moving on, I pondered over the last few days and weeks in my mind. What hadn't I done right?

Frustrated and still sticky with sweat from my run, I decided to take a shower. I turned on the water and let it run while I undressed. Before stepping in the shower, I looked in the mirror. Around my neck was the necklace from which hung my wedding ring. The ring had been around my neck since January. It had become a part of me, and I often forgot it was there. I set the necklace on the sink while I showered, the whole time wondering if this was what Julianna was referring to. I didn't see how it could be. Though she knew about it, Julianna rarely, if ever, saw it. I never wore it running because I was afraid of losing it. The more I thought about it, however, I remembered how Julianna would occasionally rest her hand on my breastbone. Those times when she rested her hand there, I thought nothing of it, but now I seemed to remember her hand slowly moving over my chest as if to see if the ring was still there.

After the shower, I sat on my bed and held the ring. If it was indeed what she had been referring to, I could understand why it would make her think I wasn't moving on. But why hadn't Julianna told me about the ring and how it made her feel? I removed the ring from the necklace and put it on my finger. It felt heavy and foreign, like it didn't belong there. The gold sparkled in the sun that was now peeking through the clouds.

Part of starting a new life with Julianna was being able to put certain things from my first marriage away. My wedding ring was one of those objects. It was a symbol of the love and devotion Krista and I had for each other. If I was to be serious about starting a new life with Julianna, I couldn't let the symbol of my first marriage come between us.

In the back of my T-shirt drawer was Krista's jewelry box. It contained her wedding ring, a few necklaces, and other jewelry Krista wore. I placed my wedding ring next to Krista's. Wherever life took me, I knew the jewelry box would always be with me. But it would remain closed, packed away. My ring wasn't something I needed to remind me of Krista's sweet influence and love. She would always be part of me wherever I went.

I took one last look at the ring and closed the lid. I placed the box back in the drawer and covered it with socks. I never opened the jewelry box again.

I didn't see Julianna until I picked her up for church the next morning. Neither of us mentioned the conversation from the day before. For the most part, our relationship seemed back to normal. She held my hand during the services and occasionally ran her fingers up and down my back.

After church we ended up at my house, lying on the couch side by side, talking. The couch was narrow, and to stay on it we had to press our bodies close together. I thought it would be the perfect opportunity for Julianna to touch my chest. She never did. Occasionally she would touch my face or arm or grab my hand, but her hand never came close to my breastbone. I began to wonder if I had been right about the ring. Maybe Julianna had been referring to something else. My curiosity was driving me crazy. I couldn't live without knowing if the ring was what she had been referring to. If that wasn't what she had been talking about, I planned on pressing her for an answer.

"Last night I spent a lot of time thinking about what you said on the way back from Salt Lake," I said.

Those words brought a serious air to the conversation, which to that point had been light, flirtatious banter. Julianna sat up partway on the couch so she could look down on my face.

"I couldn't figure out what you were talking about. I walked around the house, seeing if I had left some pictures or other things of Krista up. It wasn't until I decided to take a shower that I saw the wedding ring around my neck."

Julianna made a move toward my chest. I grabbed her hand before she could reach it and moved it slowly back down to her side. I didn't need any other proof. It was the ring Julianna was talking about. Julianna's eyes darted from my neck to my chest, trying to see if it was still around my neck.

"I took it off," I said. "So you know, I didn't do it just so you'd think I was moving on. I did it because it was something I wanted to do." I brought Julianna's hand to my chest and pressed her palm to my breastbone where the ring usually lay.

Julianna's hand slowly moved over my chest. Then she started to cry. I kissed her forehead as the tears fell.

"Why didn't you tell me it was the ring?" I said after her tears had stopped falling.

"I didn't want you to take it off for me. It needed to be something you were ready to do and wanted to do," Julianna said.

"I was ready to take that step," I said. "I don't want anything to come between the two of us."

We drove to St. George on a Friday, following Julianna's parents' white minivan. They and Julianna's four sisters who were still living at home were all going to cheer her on. Though I hadn't spent much time with Julianna's family, I liked what I had seen. They were supportive of Julianna's running and attended all of her races. Even from those brief interactions with them, they were everything I had always wanted in in-laws, something I had always wanted Krista's family to be. They weren't perfect, but they were good people who had worked hard to raise a family of seven girls. I hoped this trip would serve as a good chance to get to know them better.

It was late when we arrived in St. George. We checked in to our hotel and ate dinner. Soon after, Julianna went to bed, though there was little chance she would sleep anytime soon. Instead, she would spend the next few hours relaxing her body and mentally preparing for the race. I spent the rest of that night with her family. I enjoyed our time together as we talked and joked. And when everyone finally retired for the evening, I knew that if things worked out with Julianna, I would have no problem spending time with her family.

At five in the morning, her father, Steve, and I drove Julianna to the bus that would take the runners to the starting line approximately twenty-five miles out in the desert. Julianna was quiet, her mind focused on the run ahead. I gave her a kiss as she exited the van and told her I would see her soon.

We went back to the hotel and waited. The plan was to wait a few hours. Then I would start walking the marathon course until I found Julianna and run the final three or four miles of the race with her, giving her whatever support she needed to make it to the end.

I tried to stay awake, thinking of Julianna as she ran, but I fell asleep.

The next thing I knew, Steve woke me up, telling me it was time to go. We parked the van near the course as it came into St. George. There were people lined up and down the street, sitting in lawn chairs or on the curb, waiting to watch the runners. The lead runner with a police escort in tow ran past the finish line, and a cheer went up from the crowd. Another cheer went up thirty seconds later as the second place runner followed.

I started up the course. Every thirty seconds or so a runner ran by on his way to the finish line. By the time I had walked a mile up, the lead female runner came into view. She was followed by a pack of six other women, all vying for the lead. I scanned their faces to see if one of them was Julianna. She wasn't among them.

The number of runners heading toward the finish line gradually increased. I kept my eyes open for Julianna and her turquoise running singlet with no success. Finally at mile marker twenty-two, I spotted her approaching the aid station. She grabbed two cups of water from a volunteer's outstretched hands. She drank one quickly and poured the second one over her head. She looked tired and worn out. The grimace on her face told me she was running through a lot of pain.

"How's the leg?" I said.

"Not good," Julianna said.

We didn't talk much until the next aid station. I offered occasional words of encouragement, hoping they would help somewhat. After a mile and a half, the road crested and the city of St. George and the next aid station were visible.

"It's all downhill from here," I said.

Julianna stopped at the aid station. She drank some water and rested her hands on her knees. Her breathing was hard and labored.

"I hurt," she said.

I rested my hand on her back. Her body was trembling. I thought back to the ten-mile run that had pushed my body to the limit. I thought of the words of encouragement she had given me and how much they had helped me finish.

"You are running an amazing race," I said. "Let's keep going."

Julianna continued resting, her hands on her knees.

"Come on," I said. "Less than two miles to the finish line. You're almost done."

Julianna crumpled the paper cup in her hands and tossed it to the side of the road. She started running slowly at first but then picked up speed. After a quarter mile, she began passing other runners.

The faster she ran, the more words of encouragement I offered. We ran into town and down the broad streets that made up St. George. Finally we turned a corner and the finish line was in sight. The sight of the finish line gave Julianna some hope. She put on an extra burst of speed and crossed the finish line.

Behind the finish line was a fenced off area where runners could eat, cool down, and relax. I waited with Julianna's family near the exit. Julianna made her way out of the area ten minutes later with a banana in her hand. Her face was flushed, and she walked with a noticeable limp.

We returned to the hotel. Julianna showered and then sat in the hotel's hot tub. The hot water seemed to put her in better spirits, and soon she joined the rest of us in the pool. As the day wore on, her attitude improved. She seemed glad to have finished, even though her official time of three hours and thirty-eight minutes was a much slower time than her goal.

Julianna seemed anxious to put St. George behind her. We left early the next morning before her family was ready to go.

"Thanks for coming and supporting me," Julianna said. "It meant a lot to have you run those last miles with me."

"It was an honor to run them with you," I said. "You and your broken leg."

For the first time since the race, Julianna smiled. "I like running with you," she said.

The freeway rose up through the mountains. Occasionally bits of the desert were tinged with the reds and yellows of fall. It added some color to what was, for the most part, a brown and bleak drive. When the road finally crested, the town of Cedar City came into view.

"If Krista hadn't killed herself, do you think we'd be together?" Julianna said.

"If Krista wasn't dead, I'd still be married to her," I said. I flashed a smile in Julianna's direction, so she'd know I was being facetious.

"You know what I mean," Julianna said. "If you had never married Krista, do you think we would have ended up together?"

A hawk circled a field by the side of the road, floating on the wind. I put the car on cruise control and stretched out in the seat.

"I doubt it," I said.

I waited for Julianna to say something, but she just stared at the road ahead.

"Krista's death sobered me up," I said when it became apparent Julianna wasn't going to say anything. "I feel like I've emotionally aged twenty years since she died. I'm nowhere near the person I was before she killed herself. I was so different back then. I had a temper and was quick to anger. I doubt things would have worked out between us. I don't think I would have been mature enough for you."

Julianna looked out the passenger window. She seemed far away and distant, lost in thought. "I've seen flashes of the old Abel," Julianna said. "I've seen you become very frustrated once or twice, and I see the old you come out for a second or two. But it's gone a moment later, and the Abel I know and love is back."

"There's always a chance the old Abel will rear his head again."

"Do you think you're capable of being the person you were before Krista died?" Julianna said.

"I don't know," I said. "I would hope all I've experienced the last year would serve as a constant reminder of why I don't want to be that person again."

I took the car off cruise control and merged into the fast lane to pass a semitruck with the word *Wal-Mart* emblazoned in big blue letters on the side.

"Do you think Krista's death happened for a reason?" Julianna asked.

"The one thing I've come to believe is everything happens for a reason." I pushed down on the gas pedal and we sped up a bit.

Julianna's next question came out quietly, like a whisper. "Why do you think you had to experience what you did?"

I looked out past the sagebrush and scrub oak that seemed so prominent in this part of the state. In seconds I relived the entire day Krista killed herself. I could smell the bitter stench of spent gunpowder.

"Just because everything happens for a reason doesn't mean we'll always know why it happened."

Julianna looked back out the window. "I ask because I have mixed feelings when I think about what you went through. If Krista hadn't died, we never would have met or fallen in love. That sounds awful and selfish, but it's something I think about occasionally."

I held Julianna's hand. "If someone told me eleven months ago that I'd be in love and happy less than a year after Krista died, I wouldn't have believed them. Just because I don't fully comprehend why things happened the way they did, doesn't mean I'm not grateful to have you in my life."

Julianna moved slowly in her seat, as if she were uncomfortable.

"Is your leg giving you problems?"

"My whole body hurts. Every muscle aches."

The town of Cedar City became a distant speck in the rearview mirror.

I looked down and found myself rubbing my chest where the ring had rested for months. It still felt odd not to have it there.

Julianna leaned her seat back to a reclining position. She took my hand and held it to her stomach.

"I love you," she said as she closed her eyes. In a few minutes she was asleep, and I felt relief and a quiet happiness that she had a smile on her face.

As I drove through the empty stretches of central Utah, I thought of how much I'd been blessed in the last few months. Life had always been worth living, though I hadn't recognized how much sweeter it was when I had someone I loved to enjoy it with.

I gave Julianna's hand a squeeze as we barreled down the highway. I was not only looking forward to taking the journey with someone, I was glad it was Julianna, a woman so brave that she ran a marathon on a broken leg.

# CHAPTER
# *Sixteen*

The morning of November 10, 2002, I awoke to a pitch-black room. The sound of the wind blowing leaves across the driveway reminded me of running water. I didn't bother looking at the clock. I instinctively knew it was much earlier than my usual five AM wakeup.

I pulled the covers to my chin and tried to fall back asleep. It was pointless. The leaves continued to make scratching sounds as they were carried from the driveway to the street. Then the furnace kicked on with its customary clatter. Usually I would have found such noises comforting. But that morning my mind was too active and alert for them to be anything but unwelcome.

After what seemed like an eternity of lying in the dark, my alarm clock buzzed at five AM. I silenced it and lay there, letting the thoughts of the day weigh heavily on my mind. Throughout the day I would think back to what I was doing one year ago and relive every moment, every mistake, exactly like it happened.

My eyes became accustomed to the dark, and I could just make out the lines where the ceiling met the walls. I wanted to sleep the day away or at least as many hours of it as I could. But I knew that wasn't going to happen. My body was already filled with anxious anticipation. For the last year I had counted the days, weeks, and months since Krista died. After today, I would start counting years.

When I was ten my mom told me about a book she had read about a man who survived a battle with cancer. This was during the early 1980s when surviving cancer was rare. My mom had tried to explain to me how the man found his battle with cancer to be a spiritual experience.

At the time I didn't understand how going through something so horrible could be spiritual. The year before, when I was nine, I watched as a great uncle lost his battle with bone cancer. The memories of him lying naked in bed, grimacing from the pain, were still fresh in my mind, and I wondered if my great uncle had found a spiritual aspect in his suffering before his death.

What my mom was trying to explain to me was something I didn't understand until that morning: personal and spiritual development doesn't come when life is good and unchallenging. It's the hard times—the ones when we are forced to wake up every day and put one foot in front of the other—where the real growth occurs. I was learning that difficult times helped me appreciate the sweet ones. And if I let them, these trying moments would teach me what was truly important.

What the last year had taught me was the incredible value of the people I love. It was my parents, siblings, friends, and loved ones who made my life worth living. And though I always knew this to be true, it took the death of the two most important people in my life to realize how precious the time we shared together really was.

The darkness gave way to a cold, gray dawn. As I watched the shadows recede from the room, I realized the light was similar to the morning in which I had seen Krista alive, lying in bed with the covers wrapped tightly around her body, her arms wrapped around her protruding belly that contained our daughter, Hope. The memory floated through my mind for a minute before I dismissed it. I felt dark and empty as I got out of bed.

I took a long shower. The hot water had a cleansing feel as it cascaded from my head to my feet. I fought off memories of Krista's death. One thing I had learned over the last months was moving on isn't forgetting about the past but knowing when to remember it. I needed to do my best to let those who were with me know how much I loved them instead of dwelling on the past. I focused my thoughts on Julianna: the first time I saw her walking up the aisle of the chapel, the first time we held hands, our first kiss.

I dressed for church and made breakfast—eggs and toast. To my surprise I wasn't hungry. I ate only a few bites before I pushed the plate away and looked outside at some magpies jumping among the branches of a box elder tree. I had hoped the weather today would be different than what it had been a year before. I wanted gray skies and rain. Outside everything seemed exactly the same: blue sky with a touch of haze and the same sickly yellow light that seems to accompany even the brightest winter days.

As I threw away my uneaten breakfast, I glanced at the clock. Eight fifteen. I realized at this time last year I was just starting to run my errands. And for a moment I saw myself back in the car, driving toward the intersection and deciding whether or not to drive straight or turn left. Usually when I thought about this moment, I would curse myself for not listening to the subtle prompting telling me to drive to the apartment. Today was different. Instead of beating myself up emotionally, I thought about how one seemingly insignificant choice had changed my entire life.

My thoughts drifted over different choices I had made in the last year. For some reason my mind kept coming back to my decision to buy the house. I remembered sitting amid the dead bugs and feeling that I should buy it even though it was the last thing I wanted to do. There were times I still regretted buying the house. It meant living in a city I didn't want to be part of anymore and a long commute to work, which meant less time with Julianna. Then it hit me. Julianna was the reason I bought the house. Never before had a thought come to my mind with such force and clarity. If I hadn't bought the house and if I had moved closer to work, I never would have met Julianna.

I tried to think of what my life would be like without her. I doubted the happiness and contentment I now felt every day would still be there. Julianna was such a wonderful blessing to me. I couldn't see my life without her.

Smiling through the tears that were running down my face, I got to my knees and thanked God for second chances.

Julianna greeted me with a kiss when I picked her up for church. The kiss, along with the look in her eyes, told me she was willing to help me in whatever way she could today—even if that meant doing nothing more than being with me. She invited me inside and went to the bedroom to put on her shoes and coat. Earlier in the week we discussed that this day might be particularly difficult. We had both agreed to be patient with each other and hope the day would turn out better than we thought.

As I waited, I looked over at the textbooks on her bookshelf. Organic Chemistry. Physics. Calculus. Those books provoked thoughts of one of my favorite college professors, Dr. Shigley, who taught Renaissance literature and courses on Elizabeth Bishop. She was married to an engineer and would sometimes share stories about being with someone who approached problems so differently than she did. I had always thought it odd that two people whose interests were so diverse could be so happily married. This was probably because when it came to our interests, Krista and I were very similar. I remember thinking at the time how fortunate I was to have someone who had the same tastes in literature, poetry, and art.

It never occurred to me that I could love anyone who had such a scientific mind. Julianna had proven my assumptions wrong. Even though she was very different from Krista as far as her interests and view of the world were concerned, they weren't as important as the things I admired about her. Julianna was active in church, had a positive outlook on life, was patient with me, and had a kind heart. She had introduced me to a new self within because she was not only so different from Krista but also from myself.

There was a melancholy air on the drive to church, as if we both wanted this day to be over. Julianna took my hand and held it, as if to let me know she understood that day was difficult. It was comforting to know I wasn't the only one who felt that way. At church I couldn't concentrate on the services. Instead I was either replaying parts of that sad day in my mind or counting down the hours and minutes until Krista killed herself, which happened at ten minutes to two. The last prayer of the service was said, and Julianna and I headed home.

My mom was knocking on my door when we pulled in the driveway. There was a sad countenance about her, and for a minute I thought she had bad news. My heart sunk, thinking I didn't want to hear about anything else that was sad. I should have realized my mother would be as depressed as I was, for the same reason I was.

"We're going up to the cemetery to visit Krista," she said. "I wondered if you wanted to go up with us."

"Thanks, but we're going up later."

My mom seemed a little surprised by this but seemed okay with it. "If you change your mind, we'll be leaving in about fifteen minutes."

The wind had picked up, and we hustled into the house, hoping for warmth. Inside we prepared lunch. Julianna fixed sandwiches while I made a salad.

"It seems like your family wants to spend time with you today," Julianna said. "Yet you seem to feel the opposite."

I put down the tomato I was dicing and stared out the kitchen window at the empty lot next to my house. The chain link fence had leaves piled against it. They looked brown, wilted, and sad.

"The month after Krista died, I had a lot of support from friends and family," I said. "If it wasn't for their love, I don't know what would have become of me. I love my family, but they haven't made the same progress I have. Today that makes it hard to be with them. I feel that being with them would take me back instead of forward."

The decision to move on with my life, no matter how bleak each day seemed, was something I had to do by myself. Friends and family had been there to support me, but in the end I was the one who had to make those decisions.

"And that's why you don't want to go to the cemetery with them?" Julianna asked.

"That's part of it. It's really something I want to do alone."

By the silence in the kitchen, I could tell that Julianna had stopped making sandwiches. I realized we hadn't discussed whether or not Julianna would go with me to the cemetery later. I turned and saw confusion in her eyes.

"If you feel comfortable coming," I said, "I would like you to join me."

"Are you sure? If you want to be alone, I understand."

"You're the only person I would like to be with me," I said.

Julianna nodded and added thin slices of turkey and Monterey Jack cheese to the bread.

"Thanks," she said. "For wanting me there, for letting me be part of this."

I pulled her close and kissed the top of her head. "Thanks for wanting to be part of it."

We were spooning on the couch at ten to two. I could just see over Julianna's head to the clock on the VCR. The light streaming through the window had the same pale, dreary look to it that it had a year ago as I had climbed the stairs to our apartment complex. I closed my eyes and let the memory flow. There was no point trying to stop it. This was something I had to relive one last time.

Everything was just as I remembered it: the matted, miserable-looking grass, the dark windows of our apartment, and the feeling inside that something wasn't right. I took the stairs to the door and unlocked it. At that point there was a part of me that wanted to stop. I had gone far enough. There was no need to go farther. Proceeding wasn't going to change anything.

Instead I called out for Krista. And a second later, I heard the crack of a gunshot exploding from the bedroom. I ran back and there was Krista. Every horrible detail from the color draining from her face to the sound of blood gushing from the hole in the back of her head was real and vivid.

Only this time one thing was different. Instead of the panic I felt upon discovering Krista's body, I felt calm. Where shock and fear had ruled my emotions, I was strangely composed. I kneeled next to Krista's body. The blue in her eyes was fading to gray. She didn't have long.

"Oh, my love!" I said. And I reached for her and held her in my arms until she died.

Back on the couch, tears were streaming down my cheeks and falling into Julianna's hair. "Abel, what's wrong?" Julianna said. She tried to turn and comfort me, but I held her so she couldn't move.

"I'm fine," I said as the tears fell faster.

"What can I do to help you?" Julianna said.

"There's nothing you can do," I said

"Then let me comfort you," Julianna said. Her voice had a pleading quality to it. I relaxed my grip, and Julianna turned and wiped the tears as they fell. When the tears finally stopped, I pulled her close and held her in my arms.

As we lay on the couch together, I realized there was something different. It took me a minute to realize what it was. Usually after remembering Krista's suicide I was filled with anger, grief, or a strange mixture of the two. None of those emotions were present this time. Instead there was serenity and peace. Somehow over the last weeks or months, I had found the ability to forgive Krista for what she had done. No longer when I thought about her death would I feel bitter toward her. There would always be questions, but the rage that had filled a part of my body for so long would never rise inside me again.

I opened my eyes. Julianna was looking up at me. Her eyes looked sad and her brow was wrinkled in worry.

"I'm fine," I said.

We waited until four o'clock to visit the cemetery. I thought it would be late enough that Julianna and I would be alone. To my surprise, a dark red Ford Taurus was parked on the gravel road near Krista's gravesite. There were two occupants sitting in the front seat who appeared to look back through the rearview window as we parked. For a second I thought that it was Krista's parents. I hadn't seen them since Hope's funeral, and they were the last people I wanted to see at the moment.

"What's wrong?" Julianna said.

"I was hoping it would just be the two of us," I said.

The wind had picked up a little and buffeted the car. Then the person in the driver's seat opened the door. I sighed with relief when I recognized the familiar face.

"Do you know who's in the car?" Julianna said.

"It's James and Grace," I said.

"Do you want to wait until they're gone?"

I shook my head, opened the door, and walked toward Krista's headstone. Julianna followed close behind. James and Grace joined us a minute later. We exchanged hellos and then stood in silence for a few minutes, staring at the tombstone.

The sound of gravel popping under tires made everyone look up. Another car parked next to mine. Maria, the director of the college writing center, emerged. After another round of hellos were exchanged, I introduced Julianna to Maria. Then the silence and the standing in the gray weather returned.

"I can't believe it's been a year," Grace said several minutes later.

James nodded in agreement.

Maria wiped tears from her eyes. "I still can't believe she's gone," she said.

I felt that I should be crying or saying something profound. But my mind was blank, my eyes dry. I had already shed my tears and said my good-byes to Krista earlier in the day. Standing by her headstone was a mere formality.

Julianna stood with her arm around me. I moved a strand of hair the wind had blown into her eyes behind her ear. Then I returned my attention to the headstone. I realized how happy Krista would be if she knew her friends and old boss had come to pay their respects. James, Grace, and Maria were some of her favorite people. And I felt glad that I was able to share this moment with them.

Soon Maria gave me a hug and returned to her car and left. A few minutes later, James and Grace did the same. Julianna and I watched their car drive down the gravel road. We stood at the headstone a few more minutes. Julianna leaned her head on my shoulder. Our shadows grew longer, and the cold seeped through my jeans.

"Let's go," I said. "We've been here long enough."

We got in the car, and I turned the heater so it blew on our faces and feet. I looked back at the cemetery, unsure if I would ever return.

As if reading my thoughts, Julianna said, "You can come back whenever you like."

"I know," I said. I squeezed her hand and then put the car in drive.

I stopped the car for a moment before exiting the cemetery and took one last look back. One last look at Krista and Hope.

In my mind I started to piece together what I planned on telling Julianna later in the day on why I would never return to the cemetery. I wasn't worried about Julianna being supportive. I knew she would let me visit as often as I wanted. But that wasn't why I didn't want to return. Krista and Hope would always be a part of me. Memories of them would forever linger somewhere in the back of my mind. But if I wanted this relationship with Julianna to work, I needed to look forward to the future without regrets or memories of the past holding me back. All of my energy needed to be directed toward making a new life and new memories with Julianna. She needed to feel like she was the center of my universe.

As we drove down the main road, I looked over at Julianna and squeezed her hand.

"I love you," I said.

"I love you too," she said. Her green eyes shone with unshed tears. "Thanks for coming. I know that wasn't easy for you."

"I don't think it was easy for anyone."

I gave Julianna's hand another squeeze. She leaned her head on my shoulder. I looked in the rearview mirror. The tops of the trees from the cemetery were all I could see. Then as the road sloped downhill, they disappeared completely.

We held hands all the way home.

# ABOUT THE *Author*

PHOTO BY TREVOR HOWARD

Abel is a columnist and editor of FreeCapitalist.com and host of the radio talk show *The Abel Hour*. He has been a website programmer and technical writer. Aside from writing, Abel enjoys running and lifting weights. He has a bachelor's degree from Weber State University. He and his wife, Julianna, are the parents of two boys and a girl. His website is www.abelkeogh.com.